bôàt peõplê

Also by Mary Gardner

Milkweed

Keeping Warm

bôàt peõplê

MARY GARDNER

A Novel

W. W. Norton & Company

New York / London

First Edition
All rights reserved
Printed in the United States of America

The text of this book is composed in Bodoni Book
with the display set in Bodoni Bold
Composition and manufacturing by the Haddon Craftsmen, Inc.
Book design by Jaye Zimet

Library of Congress Cataloging-in-Publication Data

Gardner, Mary.
    Boat people : a novel / Mary Gardner.
        p.   cm.
    1. Vietnamese Americans—Texas—Galveston—Fiction.   2.
Refugees, Political—Texas—Galveston—Fiction.   3. Galveston
(Tex.)—Race relations—Fiction.   I. Title.
    PS3557.A7142B63   1995
    813'.54—dc20   94-27505

ISBN 0-393-03738-X

W. W. Norton & Company, Inc., 500 Fifth Avenue, New York, N.Y.
10110
W. W. Norton & Company Ltd., 10 Coptic Street, London WC1A 1PU

1 2 3 4 5 6 7 8 9 0

This book is the winner of the Associated
Writing Programs Award for the Novel,
1993. AWP is a national nonprofit organiza-
tion dedicated to serving American letters,
writers and programs of writing. AWP's
headquarters are at George Mason University, Fairfax, Virginia.

This book is a gift to and from An, Andy, Anh, Anthony, Cannithy, Chanh, Cindy, Chuong, Cong, Cu, Cuong, Cut, Danny, Dau, Di, Doi, Dung, Duong, Duyen, Elizabeth, Emily, Gai, Gary, Hai, Hanh, Hao, Harry, Hen, Hieu, Hoa, Hoang, Hong, Hue, John, Johnson, Kham, Khanh, Khoa, Kieu, Kim, Lach, Lan, Lang, Linh, Long, Melissa, Michael, Minh, Muon, My, Nga, Ngoi, Phuoc, Phuong, Que, Qui, Quoc, Quy, Quyen, Sang, Son, Sophie, Suong, Sy, Thai, Thanh, Thao, Thu, Thuan, Thuy, Tiet, Trang, Tri, Trung, Tuan, Tuy, Van, Vanessa, Vien, Vinh, Xan, Xao, Xuan, Xung.

bôàt peõplê

1 Hai Truong had been in the hospital before. If something hurt her, she went there.
Her husband took her, only he did not
seem like her husband. When the cloud
came inside her head, she would have to
go to the hospital again. They would ask her what hurt her.
How could she tell them, even in her own language?
Clouds and ghosts had no sharp edges. They were not
hurtful in a way an American doctor could understand.

Timidly, Hai Truong put one hand at the corner of the
wall over her kitchen table in the little Beach Terrace
housing project apartment and began to walk, dragging
her arm behind her, her fingers always touching where it
was solid. She was safe in her house, even though the
house wasn't hers. The city gave it to them because they
had no money. This was her table, though, and her chair.
The door, the cabinet, the sink, the stove—they were not
hers. She could not always tell what was hers and what
was not.

Outside, the black children were shouting motherfuck
motherfuck. They were bad words. Her husband, Phuong
Nguyen, said they were bad words. Only he did not seem
like her husband. Her real husband was the cloud who

[11]

lived inside her and made her head hurt. He was a ghost. He wanted her to be sad, but he didn't want her to die. If she died, then he would be a drifting spirit in Hong Dieu. He would have no home. No one would give him oranges or burn incense. His hand was in her throat, but he would let her swallow a little rice, a little tea.

Her children were not home. They were at the market—Linh and Harry and Gary. Harry and Gary were American names. Her new husband said it was good for American children to have American names. Maybe it was. But they did not seem like her children anyway. Her children blew in the wind from Hong Dieu. They rested on the tree in the backyard. Her ghost husband combed their hair with fish bones.

Forehead against the floor, Hai rocked herself back and forth. Where was her mother?

"Ma oi, cuu con voi!" She heard her own voice call, but her mother didn't answer.

"Ma!"

Her mother had told her she would grow fat in America. In America there was so much rice that men came to your house and filled baskets with it. There were chickens that grew big in a week, and they cost only a little piece of money. On New Year's, there were so many dumplings that the dogs ate them, and there would be noodles and broth for everyone.

But she was thin, thin. Even when Trang Luu brought her pancakes she had cooked in her aunt's house, they did not make her fat. The food would not go down. Her ghost husband had his hand in her throat. And her mother might be dead with no one to put oranges on her grave. The Communists had chased the people from her village. There was no medicine if you were sick. Her brother had never come home. Trees grew in the family graveyard. Her mother was hungry.

Even though her knees hurt, Hai squatted against the wall by the stove. Around the kitchen, her fingers had worn a line in the paint. The line tied her to the floor like a boat to the dock. If the line was broken, she would float away. The sharks would eat her. There would be no oranges on her grave.

"Ma oi, cuu con voi!"

They were coming. The children who were not hers were coming. The other husband was coming.

If she got low, they couldn't find her. She got down low. She pushed herself under the table. The table's legs were like trees, but she got through them. She hid against the wall. The wall smelled of oranges.

"Ma!"

"Mother!"

"She don't eat. That what she say." Phuong Nguyen moved his mouth carefully around the English syllables.

"She's saying *what?*"

"She say she don't eat."

"Mrs. Reeves, where's the outpatient chart on this woman? She's been in the ER before."

"She put rice in mouth, but it don't go down." The small Vietnamese man rubbed his temples. "Throat no good," he said.

"Mrs. Reeves, who *is* this man?"

"Her husband, Dr. Adams. His name is Phuong Nguyen. Her name is Hai Truong. They've been waiting since noon. He found her hiding under the table at home."

"Why don't they have the same name?"

[13]

"Vietnamese women keep their maiden names."

Gently, the Vietnamese man tapped the doctor on the shoulder, then tapped his own forehead. "She say her head hurt all time," he said.

"She's got headaches?"

"It hurt all night. She no sleep."

"Did she try Tylenol? Mrs. Reeves, there's no medication history in this chart."

"Yes, Tylenol. No sleep."

"Here's the history, Dr. Adams. In the back."

"Who put her medical history together? I can't make head or tail out of this."

"Dr. Zachovic, when he saw her last month in the clinic."

"Did he have somebody translate for him?"

"The Vietnamese lab tech on 2-South. You can understand her English, just. Shall I phone her?"

"It's Saturday. She works a regular schedule. Isn't there a Vietnamese resident floating around?"

"Dr. Lang Nguyen. He's off duty now."

"Shit. Is he related to her husband?"

"Many Vietnamese are named Nguyen." Mrs. Reeves looked as if she had made this speech before. "They have only a few different last names in their country."

The Vietnamese man took a Kleenex from his jeans pocket and spread it over the palm of his hand like a napkin. Then he wiped the drool from his wife's chin with it. "Throat no good," he said, smiling.

"How are you supposed to say her name?"

"H-a-i T-r-u-o-n-g. H-a-i. Like 'Hi.' That's her first name."

"How do you know all this, Mrs. Reeves?"

The nurse shook her head. "I'm the one who has to ex-

[14]

plain things when they don't speak English. We're on an island, remember? Galveston Island, Texas. We get a little of everything in the ER."

"Okay." Bryce Adams mouthed the name. "Hai. Hi. Hi, Hai. God." He turned to the husband, raising his voice. "Okay. Tell me. She take sleeping pills?" Each sound dropped like a pellet.

"She no sleep."

"Great. Mrs. Reeves, check her chart to see what Zachovic prescribed last time."

"Elavil."

Bryce Adams turned to the Vietnamese man. "Ask her if she takes her Elavil," he said.

The Vietnamese man bent to his wife and clattered out a few words. In a whisper, she answered.

"What's she saying?"

"She ask red or green?"

"Red or *green?* Are we decorating for next Christmas?"

"Red pill or green pill." The Vietnamese man patted the edge of the chair where the doctor was sitting. "She take white pill too. American pill very good."

"Jesus."

"Maybe blue pill?" said the Vietnamese man.

Bryce Adams, sighing, wrenched an Admissions form from the stack on the back of the desk. "Call Psychiatry, Mrs. Reeves," he said. "I'm expanding their cultural horizons tonight until some brilliant Asian Freud can evaluate this on his own terms."

"You're going to have to call in someone who has some knowledge of the language," Dr. Smith-Fragon said. "And

[15]

I think you should have been aware of that earlier. The lab tech? She's certainly Vietnamese."

"They used her yesterday." Bryce Adams gritted his teeth. Tuesday-morning rounds were always difficult, even when there were no problems of ethnicity. After the weekend, Dr. Smith-Fragon had an erratic interest in the smallest ward details, but it took him all day Monday to build up sufficient hostility to torment residents about them.

"And what were the results?"

"Not very good." The lab tech, her garnet-encrusted glasses glittering, had spoken to Hai Truong's hairline, snapping out Vietnamese before the nurse had even finished the statements to be explained. As for her competence as a translator back into English, there was no way of knowing. Hai Truong had said nothing.

Dr. Smith-Fragon heaved a deep and heavily controlled sigh. "Could we perhaps have a brief case history?" he asked. "A slight sign that someone somewhere is aware of the details involved in this case."

Bryce Adams was ready for that. He had read the chart and made the proper notes. He had seen the patient huddled in her room. He had even admitted her.

"The patient was brought to the hospital by her husband around noon on Saturday, February twenty-third. I was the junior psychiatric resident on duty. No one in the ER spoke Vietnamese, and she speaks no English. Fortunately, the lab tech was in first thing on Monday, so we got some information straightened out."

"Let us have no editorial comment, Dr. Adams. I am already aware of the lab tech's role in this matter." Dr. Smith-Fragon looked at his watch.

"Her husband did tell us that there was something wrong with her throat. And her head."

"Family history?"

Bryce Adams pushed back his resentment at being interrupted. "Three children, a girl of ten or thereabouts and two little boys. They weren't with her. They live in the projects," he added.

Dr. Smith-Fragon gave no response.

"When I attempted to talk to the patient, she refused to respond. Her husband's English was inadequate. I did figure out that she was on some medication from previous hospital visits. We decided to admit her until her case could be clarified."

"And who is this 'we'?"

Bryce Adams coughed, then bent his head. "I am," he said.

"I would suggest that you unravel your pronouns in English before you attack another language."

"Yes, thank you." Bryce tried to keep the sarcasm out of his voice. "Her name is Hai Truong," he said, realizing that the name should have come first. "Her husband is Phuong Nguyen. Same last name as the Vietnamese first-year resident here," he added. "She had six prior visits to the ER within the year, one of which resulted in an admission to ENT for diagnosis of her throat problem. At that time, she left against doctor's advice after twenty-four hours."

Dr. Smith-Fragon sighed, checked his watch, looked at his thumbnails. Racquetball at two. He'd skip lunch. "Symptoms?" he asked.

"She talks and gestures when no one is present. She refuses to eat hospital meals, though she will eat small quantities of food which her husband brings. He says her daughter can cook. She walks slowly and only when guided. Otherwise, she sits on her bed.

"What medication?"

"Seven milligrams of Haldol."

"That was your recommendation?"

Bryce knew he was on shaky ground. "For now," he said. "She certainly seemed psychotic."

Dr. Smith-Fragon hoisted his shoulders away from the chair back and stood up. "Check her blood level," he said. "We'll discuss it on rounds tomorrow. Contact her daughter for information. She probably knows more English than the husband. And see if you can locate the other Nguyen, so we can get some kind of assessment of what he feels her condition to be."

"The girl doesn't visit. And Dr. Lang Nguyen isn't on duty in the clinic until Thursday."

Dr. Smith-Fragon turned around. "Have you ever used a telephone, Dr. Adams? Even Vietnamese project families have them. As for Dr. Nguyen, *call him at home.*" The elevator doors closed behind his tightly erect figure before Bryce had properly caught his breath.

2 Linh Nguyen, Hai Truong's daughter, put down the phone. Outside, the shadows in the project had all merged, and the gray mist of the evening was clustering around the twisted bushes near the street. The voice on the phone had been like a mist too, despite the clear English words the doctor spoke. "What?" "When?" "How long?" She had answered what she could, but with growing discomfort. It was not right to explain her mother's feelings. And the doctor had her mother in the hospital where he could find out those feelings for himself! She was afraid to think of what might be in her mother's head.

"Who was that calling?" On the chair across the kitchen sat Trang Luu, who lived across the street and down the block. Trang's house was not in the projects, but the city of Galveston paid the rent for it anyway. Trang lived with her aunt and uncle and all their children. She had to work hard for them because she had no mother in America.

"It was the doctor."

"Why'd he call you?"

"He asked about my mother."

[19]

The steam from the pots on the stove had begun to cloud the windows, covering the smudged glass with a damp blur. Trang made a trail with one finger down the pane, then a second trail next to it. She held her wet hands up to the light in the ceiling and danced them around each other. The steam thickened.

"It rains in this house," she said. "*I* make it rain."

On her side of the kitchen, Linh began scrubbing the paint on the wall above the table. At ten, she was big for her age, and she hardly needed to stretch. Behind her, a damp line extended horizontally along the kitchen wall about three feet above the floor. Before her, the same line continued, but marked with a dark shadow instead of dampness.

"Why you wiping that off?" Trang asked.

"I make it clean." The line was more than dirt, and it seemed worn into the wall. Linh scrubbed harder.

"Your mother never cleans house."

Silent, Linh pushed her rag against the wall as if she were buttering the plaster. All the fishermen and their wives were talking about her mother in the hospital. It was all right to get hit by a car, or catch your arm in a fishing winch, or cough until the Chinese doctor in Houston rubbed your forehead to let out the bad winds. But if you had a ghost in you, that was not all right. In America, they put you in the hospital and made you stay in a room with no other Vietnamese to talk to. They made you sign papers. They gave you lumps to eat that tasted like dishcloths.

Trang stood up so she could reach the damp window better. With her forefinger, she drew a man, his arms outstretched. Next to him, she drew a small figure with long hair. The moisture on the glass loosened and ran them together. "Where'd your father go?" she asked, sucking her finger.

"He is working on the boat."

"Too cold to work on the boat."

"He must fix it." Since Linh's mother had gone to the hospital, her father had stayed away from home even more than the other fishermen. When he came back, he smelled of beer. Sometimes he did things that fathers were not supposed to do. Trang had no father, so Linh could not ask her what was right. Trang did not like questions anyway.

Leaning back against the chair, Trang began to roll up the sleeve that covered her left arm. Her dark hair under the light did not look as black as Linh's. It had a funny brown shine to it.

Trang thrust her arm out at Linh. "Look," she said.

Linh put down her rag. "Look at what?"

"Where my aunt pinch me."

On Trang's arm was a pattern of blue marks dug deep into the flesh. Around the darkest one was a border of yellow. Hesitantly, Linh touched them. "What you do?" she asked. When her father or mother hit her, it was always because she had made a mistake. Trang was fifteen, too big to make most mistakes.

"I don't cook supper."

"But you cook good!"

"I go to the library."

Linh nodded. She liked the library too. She went there almost every weekend. But Trang's aunt and uncle were strict with her all the time. They made her take care of their babies. Even their bigger son, Tri, who was Linh's age, got to go out more than Trang did. But she was not their real child, and her mother was still in Vietnam. She had no father to pay for her food. So perhaps it was all right to hurt her.

Pulling down her sleeve, Trang stood up. Even though she was almost five years older than Linh, she was hardly any taller. Edging past her to the stove, Linh dug her shoulders together and bent her knees toward each other. She was too tall for her age. She ate too much American food at school. When she grew up, nobody Vietnamese would want to marry her. She would have to find an American, and then her family would never speak to her again.

"Maybe I go to church school next year." Trang's voice was sharp.

"You go to *church* school?"

"That counsel man in the principal's office said they wanted to buy Vietnamese girl."

"What?" Linh could not help the question.

"He tell me last week. They are tired of all white children, and I am smart." Trang stood back from the window until her face appeared in it, blurred at the edges. "I will talk to them, but I won't go," she snapped.

Puzzled, Linh shook her head. Americans bought many things, but surely not children. And Trang was in Galveston Central High School already. She was too big to buy! She would be very expensive!

The face in the window suddenly stretched out. Trang had wedged her fingers in the corners of her mouth, pulling it wider. Her teeth lined up across the top under her thin lip. She did not look Vietnamese anymore.

"Don't do that." Linh held her voice steady.

Trang let her mouth pop back. "I am ugly," she said. "I make myself *more* ugly."

Without arguing, Linh opened the lid on the big pot. She scooped out a curved mountain of *bop chuoi* and small shrimp into the bowl her mother had always used. "You eat?" she asked, but it was not really a question. As if she were the owner of the house, she placed the bowl in front of her guest.

"My aunt will beat me if I eat here." Trang's voice did not sound frightened, but she did not pick up the chopsticks.

"Then take this with you." Linh swung a section of tinfoil over the top of the bowl and pressed it into Trang's hands. Even if Trang's aunt took it away from her and ate it herself, there would surely be some left over.

Holding the food absentmindedly, Trang moved to the door. "This is a cold place," she said. Across the street from the worn brown grass of Beach Terrace, a row of shabby houses leaned against each other, their windows blank, their sides gray. One toward the end had been refinished with yellow siding, and a neat porch was attached. Then the gray began again. A block down the street, the Section Eight welfare home of Trang's aunt and uncle huddled on the corner, and Trang knew that no sunshine color would ever lift it up off the earth into the sky.

"Vietnam is the warmest country," said Linh as if she were reciting a geography lesson. "My mother is from Hong Dieu. It is the most warm place there." Trang was already stalking erect on the path past the broken project swing set, the bowl held high in front of her.

Now it was time for Linh's father to come home. Once again, she moved toward the stove and began to chop the fresh *bop chuoi* very tiny, as her mother did. She had to stretch a little in order to angle her chopping hand correctly, but she was almost tall enough.

Her mother always had the oil steaming. Was that what the American doctor had wanted to know? Her mother had been gone only a few days, and yet already the oil bottle was almost empty. The boys were so naughty too. Yesterday, Harry had taken one of Linh's school papers from the table and drawn a picture of a woman with no clothes on. "Mama!" he'd said, grinning. He didn't know anything. Gary had already broken two dishes, but not the best ones.

It seemed like a long time since she had seen her mother. Her mother had been hiding in the corner of the kitchen under the table. Her father had pulled her out. Then he had pushed her out the door to the hospital. Her mother had screamed. Was she screaming now in words the American doctor could not understand?

Linh dumped the *bop chuoi* into the oil, then a handful of tiny shrimp. The shrimp shells would fry crunchy, like crackers. The hot air above the pan wavered. Linh threw in the green onion. If the oil got too hot, it set off the smoke alarm. Then the lady in the project office got angry, especially if the firemen had to come. Harry and Gary liked having the firemen come, though, and sometimes when her mother wasn't home, they lit candles. She would have to watch them more than ever now that her mother was in the hospital.

Harry and Gary were sleeping. They had crawled upstairs before Trang came. And she had done all her homework hours ago. But she had already missed three days of school, so maybe it wasn't the right homework. When she went back to her class, she would have to give a note to the black lady in the office. This time she would spell the words right.

The steaming oil hissed. Linh wrapped her hand in a dish towel and flipped the contents of the pan into the big bowl. Then she set it on the counter for her father. Maybe it wouldn't be enough. Her mother always made enough.

Tired now, Linh moved across the kitchen into the living room, where their altar stood next to the sofa. She had put new oranges on it and asked her ancestors to bring her mother home from the hospital. But their spirits would have to come a long way from Vietnam to do it.

Then she heard the neighbor's dog barking. It was against the law to own a dog in the projects, but the neighbor sold drugs and needed protection. The black children said that. It was a big skinny dog.

"Daughter!"

Linh jumped up.

"Daughter!" Her father called through the screened door the way she had heard bad men might do. But this time it was all right to open the door, and she did, rubbing her eyes. Outside, the air was steaming with moisture, and the lemon grass by the door was thick with silver drops. She had forgotten to add the lemon grass! Her mother never forgot!

With a lopsided grin, her father came inside. He smelled of beer. As fast as she could, Linh took the bowl of food and set it on the kitchen table. She put down the good chopsticks that they'd bought at the Houston market, took rice from the cooker. Already the grains were drying to the sides.

It must be very late. The clock was in the living room, but she was afraid to go look at it.

"Get me my *nuoc mam!* I want my fish sauce!" Her father stirred the heaping bowl with his chopsticks. As Linh set the bottle on the table, her hand trembled, but her father was not really angry. "You are like your mother," he said, with his crooked smile pushing into the prickles in his cheeks. "When the doctors tell her to come home, I'll sell her and keep you instead."

He had had too much beer. Linh knew that. She stood by the stove and watched him eat. She was not old enough to be her mother. She had forgotten the lemon grass.

"You know, I see Quoc Luu today. His boat has engine trouble, so he is at the store to get parts. He says his niece Trang is a big girl now. She works very hard. When Quoc Luu's wife is sick, Trang is like a wife to him."

Linh knew that Trang only worked hard sometimes. But she did not contradict her father.

"It is good when a girl works hard."

Linh nodded. She knew that was a compliment for her. When her father's bowl was empty, she carried it to the sink with both hands.

Her father got up from the table. "I go to bed," he said, unbuttoning his shirt. "Tomorrow you cook for Mama. Make the beef noodle. I bring it to her."

Linh nodded. He was standing very near her. It was hard to raise her head.

"You are a big girl now." Her father put his hands on her shoulders. She felt his fingers through the cloth of her blouse. Her shoulders were tight in his hands.

Upstairs, Gary let out a scream. *"Ma!"* he said. Then he screamed again.

Her father removed his hands. "Go up," he said to Linh. "Tell Gary to go to sleep. Stay with him if he wants." He rubbed his mouth with his fist. "It is late for all of us."

3 "Dr. Lang Nguyen?" The nurse rose to acknowledge his entry. Since Lang had received the phone call from Bryce Adams about the Vietnamese patient, he had been overwhelmed with clinic patients of his own, full of every possible ailment. Some of them had had difficulty with his English, but he set that aside. In Galveston, not everyone was educated to understand properly.

"Yes, I am Dr. Nguyen." Bryce must have written about the phone consultation in Hai Truong's chart.

"I think Mrs. Truong is sleeping now, but we can go over the chart together." The nurse was exactly his height, which meant that she was small for an American woman. Her hair was yellow as the sun, bouncing in handfuls of tiny curls around her face. Lang knew that her name was Shirley and that she often worked the evening shift on Psychiatry. Sometimes she was on 4-South and sometimes she was on 3-West, as tonight.

"She's been here a week now."

Lang took the chart, his hands clasping the corners. He noticed that Shirley wore no gold on her hands, and none around her neck either. Her blouse was open at the

[27]

top. The medical center encouraged psychiatry nurses to dress as if they were not medically affiliated. They were supposed to look like other women so they didn't frighten the patients. Doctors were supposed to frighten the patients, but only a little.

Paging through the chart, Lang checked Hai Truong's medical history. It gave her family background: husband a fisherman, three children, throat problems. She had been a faithful visitor to the ER. This last time her behavior had been so bizarre that she had been hospitalized. She did not eat the hospital food, and her husband brought her food from home, along with chopsticks. She at least tasted that food. The chart notes indicated that she had been willing to get on the scale only if the nurse allowed her to squat on the platform.

"Tea?"

Lang looked up. Shirley was holding out a hospital cup. Steam rose from it and from the second cup on the counter next to the little plug-in water heater.

"Thank you."

"It's not like Chinese tea, I know."

"I am Vietnamese." He closed the chart and took the cup with his free hand.

"I guess I knew that." A blush began to color Shirley's cheeks. She lifted her own teacup suddenly as Lang pushed the chart onto the counter, and the cardboard cover jolted her arm. The tea rose out of her cup, looping into the air, then splashing down the lapel of his lab coat in a brown flood. He grasped his cup with both hands to prevent disaster, but hers spun to the floor. The sound of breaking china rang out louder than the whine of the fluorescent lights.

Down the hall, a voice called out, not in English. As if in response, the elevator light blinked, and the door began to slide back. Lang and Shirley looked at each other, she covering her mouth with her hand.

"My God, people, what is going on in this place?" A sturdy black woman pushing a book cart moved toward them from the elevator, her eyes on the china shards in which they were both standing. In her free hand, she held a monumental purse, raised as if to attack. It was red leather, gold trimmed, with double straps hanging down toward the floor like embroidered snakes.

"Nothing," Lang said. "We drop cup."

The black woman suddenly smiled. "I work all day in a grade school," she said. "You wouldn't think any little mess in my volunteer time would shake me up."

"Ma!" came the voice down the hall.

"What's that?" The woman lowered her purse.

"Our Vietnamese patient," said Shirley, the red on her face retreating until only the bones of her cheeks bore its imprint.

"The little lady who wouldn't stand herself on the scale last Saturday?"

"Yes, that one."

The black woman shook her head. "My mama would have called that the Chinee squat," she said. "Not that my mama was any Oriental expert. But she read her books and thought her thoughts." Flashing a smile spotted with gold, the woman ground the book cart toward the other hallway and moved after it.

Shirley's eyes moved down to Lang's lab coat. "That'll stain," she said.

"They wash it in the laundry."

"I should hang on to things better."

The Vietnamese voice rose again. *"Ma!"* Both of them hesitated.

"Shouldn't you go check?"

"She just does that." Shirley bent down, began to pick up the china fragments. "Does that mean 'mother' in your language?" she asked.

"Yes."

"They didn't mention her mother in the chart. Do you think she lives in Galveston?"

"Not many mothers come on the boats." A whole kingdom of elders had been left behind. Lang didn't know a single Vietnamese woman over forty in Galveston, and hardly a one in Houston either. Duc Minh had brought his father with him, but his mother had been killed by the first of the bombing, so there had been no one to care for the old father if he had been left behind.

"It must be hard," Shirley said. She started to stand, both hands around the broken bits of the cup.

"It is not the way life should be." Lang caught a glimpse of the part in her hair as she rose. So white! "Who is the lady with the cart?" he asked. He knew Shirley could not read his mind, but he did not feel it seemly to be thinking about her skin in this way.

"Her name is Azelita Simpson. Her mother died here last spring, and she's been working as a volunteer since then. She said she was very close to her mother. They lived together."

The black people were like the Vietnamese in this regard, Lang knew. Even Claude, his dissecting partner four years ago, had visited his mother in Texas City twice a week and planned to have her with him once he was settled into his practice. His own mother and father lived

[30]

near his sister Thuy and her new husband. It was not as if he had abandoned them.

"Do you want to see Hai Truong?"

Lang nodded. "Is the Haldol working?" he asked. He was skimming through the chart as he spoke.

"Her blood levels stay low." Shirley paused. "Dr. Smith-Fragon is going to try shock in another week if they can't get them up to an effective level."

"Perhaps she don't swallow the medicine." Lang caught himself. "Doesn't swallow." He glanced quickly at Shirley, but no smile flickered across her face.

"I've thought of that."

"Someone should watch her to see if she spits it out later."

"We try to do that."

Lang rubbed his cheek. "I think different people respond different ways to meds," he said.

"That's not what Dr. Smith-Fragon thinks, but I believe that too."

Together they walked down the hall to Hai's room, where the door was slightly ajar. "She hasn't been eating," said Shirley.

"Maybe she don't . . . doesn't . . . like the food."

"You're probably right. I guess scrambled eggs and french fries aren't popular in Vietnam. But her husband sometimes brings her things that her daughter cooks."

"Does she eat them?" Lang knew the answer from the chart.

"Not much. He finishes it when she won't hold the chopsticks anymore."

Lang tapped the door with his knuckles. No sound. Shirley reached around him and pushed the door farther open. "Hai?" she asked.

For a moment, looking at the thin figure squatting on the bed, Lang forgot that she was Vietnamese. She seemed more like a child, any child. But her eyes had the same slant as his did, and her hair stuck out from her head in a black mop. Unaware, she hunched in the middle of the mattress, her arms around her legs, knees under her chin. Occasionally she reached up with her right hand cupped in the air and snatched at an insect, though there were no insects in her room. She was wearing a polyester pink blouse, with the top and bottom buttons missing, and black slacks, also polyester, with an elastic waistband that hung loose. Her feet were bare, her cheap plastic shoes on the floor by her bed.

"Did she have breakfast this morning?" Somehow he was unable to speak directly to Hai in Vietnamese. But she paid no attention to him anyway.

"She wouldn't eat any."

"What is her weight?"

"She won't get on the scale now. Two days ago it was ninety-two pounds." Shirley bit her lip. "Do you think we should start an IV?" she asked.

"Vietnamese women are naturally thin." But he was not thinking of Hai Truong. In his mind he saw his mother, her body frail as a wand. He saw the shoulder bones of his sister Thuy.

"I don't think she's a typical schizophrenic."

"No."

Hai Truong raised her left hand as well as her right and began snatching at the air with both of them. Her bare toes clung to the hospital coverlet. *"Co nhieu,"* she said. Tears gathered in her eyes. *"Co nhieu."* She folded her arms across her breasts, barely noticeable under the worn blouse, and began to rock from side to side.

[32]

Quietly, Shirley shut the door. "Maybe she'll talk to you tomorrow," she said.

"Maybe."

The book cart was crunching back in their direction. Lang and Shirley turned to look as the black woman elbowed it into place by the elevator. She glanced back cheerfully as she buttoned up her sweater, her fingers moving industriously over the solid phalanx of her bosom. "We all suffer in this world," she said, "but we keep on working. *Both* my mama and my sister said that. Maybe if I'd listened to them, I'd have moved faster and further on whatever it is the good Lord's got set up for me."

The elevator door opened, and she shoved the cart through, balancing herself on her high heels. "Night, chilluns," she said as the door slid shut, though she was not old enough to be their mother even if she had hurried about it.

Back in her room, Hai Truong was still rocking from side to side. It was no good to sit quiet. Even if she huddled in the corners, she could not hold still. Her shoulders and her hips ached with the waves' battering. She held baby Linh on her belly, then between her breasts, then wrapped in her arms, the black shock of birth hair tight under the curve of her chin. The waves moved back and forth, back and forth, and the bottom of the boat rolled as if wheels were turning it. Overhead the sky was covered in gray puffs. When they drew away, her mouth dried and burned. The boat rolled and rolled. She held herself against it, but it didn't help. She braced her feet on the wood, but her husband, the one who wasn't real, pulled them away.

"Hai," he said, *"Anh dung lam nhu the."* He told her not to do it. He told her again and again.

Finally she had begun to rock too. That was better. She was her own boat. She could rock herself to sleep.

"Ma! Ma oi, cuu con voi!"

4. Outside the hospital, the air parted for a moist moment, then wrapped Lang like a blanket as he hurried down the sidewalk. His car, a blue Renault with edges already browned by Gulf Coast rust, was parked two blocks away. Now, in the early March heat that was abnormal even for Galveston, he would have liked not walking so far. But that was childishness. He was becoming lazy with the easy living of a doctor, even one only in the first year of residency. Sometimes they still called it "internship," and he was not entirely sure which was right. But he was a real doctor. Shirley had respected his authority even in her American way.

His car was waiting where he had parked it next to two overgrown oleanders. It was too humble for anyone to steal. He opened its door, slid the ignition key from under the floor mat and sat down behind the wheel, adjusting his feet on the pedals. Other Vietnamese in America sent their parents pictures of their cars. He had never done that.

Once on Broadway, Lang entered a stream of evening traffic. At the light of Fifty-first, the line of cars at a standstill, he lifted a large envelope from the seat beside him.

[35]

Like a golden kite, it seemed to contain the possibilities of flight. Even the clot of garish stamps at the upper corner was obliterated, no longer a message of place or a stirrer of memories.

At the next light, Lang slid out the photograph inside. He could still recognize his parents, though the stroke had twisted his father's mouth down into the line of his cheek. His mother, except for the white hair, was unchanged. Even when he had left, she had had a wing of it across her forehead, so he had nothing for which to blame himself.

His sister Thuy had not been included, but she was married now, to a man he had never met. So perhaps she had not even been there when the picture was taken. It would have been different if she had married Thanh, his friend since childhood. She had been promised to Thanh, but he had gone off to the army. "Little brother-in-law," Thanh had said to him before it was time for the soldiers to leave. After that, one letter came. Then there was no more news.

Dead? So many were.

There was only one more light before the turnoff into Sand Dollar Estates, his apartment complex. Lang replaced the picture carefully in the envelope. There had been no letter. Since the stroke, it had been harder for his father to write, and his mother had gone to school for so short a time that she was ashamed of her handwriting. When she had written him of his father's illness, she had put the words on paper with the unsteady lines of a child.

Lang parked his car in his assigned place. Karl Mike Rehberg, his roommate, was not there yet. The oil gleamed in a puddle under where the hood of his car would have been. He was careless with machinery, Karl Mike was, and he was a terrible tease. Of course, he tried not to laugh at Lang's accent, but he sometimes forgot. Americans were very free with their laughter, however. And Karl Mike always pronounced Lang's last name, Nguyen, correctly, as if it were the word "win." Americans hardly ever got that right.

Upstairs, Lang unlocked the door, then locked it carefully behind him. The living room of the apartment was strewn with Karl Mike's belongings. Hai Truong's project house probably looked no worse. At first, when Karl Mike had answered his ad for a roommate on the medical school bulletin board, Lang had thought that the big curly-headed American would be more subdued and organized. He had had his money ready, and he had moved in with only two suitcases and a trunk. But in the year they had lived together, Karl Mike had more or less exploded.

In his own room, every item neatly arranged, Lang slid the brown envelope into his desk drawer. If he had had an altar, he would have offered up the joss sticks to his parents' well-being. But an altar would have looked very strange in this white-walled plaster-boarded American apartment. Only the fishermen would be superstitious enough to have one.

"Winner!" The roar permeated his room. *"Winner!"*

As Lang rose, he could hear their front door shaking in its frame, and as he went into the living room, he saw the doorknob wobbling. Karl Mike must have forgotten his keys again.

"Winner, for Christ's sake. Stop praying to Buddha and let me in, goddamnit."

Lang unlocked the door and stepped to one side. Karl Mike burst in, tossing his jacket on the already overburdened sofa. "Where were you?" he rumbled.

[37]

"Here."

"I could have figured that out for myself. Deeply engrossed in your medical library, no doubt. In which case, you can lend me your pathology text, so when I report next Tuesday, I don't have to make up the stats." His one-sided grin softened the edges of the demand.

"Why you need pathology? You rotate on Psychiatry." Karl Mike was a fourth-year medical student, a whole year behind Lang. It was pleasurable to be superior to someone.

"Dear Dr. Smith-Fragon, the Bouncing Brit, has an obsession with deviant cells. He is even postponing his various sports club activities to listen to me tell him what he already knows. I am so honored that I feel the obligation to get it right."

Lang moved to one side, not able to hold back a smile. "I sell old pathology," he said. "Remember, *you* are medical student yet. I am full doctor. Passed national boards. Next year, when I am true resident and not intern, I buy brand-new one. Lots of money!"

"You Vietnamese. Sell your souls. We Americans ruined you before you ever got on the boat."

Lang turned away. He knew Karl Mike was teasing, but an image of Hai Truong rocking side to side on her bed had come before his eyes. She had indeed been ruined, whoever had done it. And even Shirley's sympathy would probably not make her well again.

"I hurt your feelings? Or is it English failure?" Karl Mike was pouring milk into a bowl of Frosted Flakes on the kitchen counter.

"No." In Lang's mind, Shirley's and Hai Truong's faces flashed next to each other, as if in a photograph. "I am thinking about women," he said.

[38]

"What? Are you saying that the Vietnamese have a sex drive along with their other virtues? I thought the Communists took that too."

"Karl Mike, stop it." For a moment, Lang considered sweeping the cereal bowl onto the floor, but one broken dish a day was enough. And Karl Mike meant no harm. He simply could not shut his mouth once he got started.

"I thought you weren't interested in women."

Lang turned back toward his own room. "I am waiting," he said.

"For what?"

"For the woman to be my wife." He stopped at his doorway and looked back. "Vietnamese are not like Americans," he concluded.

Karl Mike swallowed a spoonful of cereal, leaving a milky patch on his upper lip. "Right," he said. "They're smaller. Their skin is yellow. They have black hair. They leave out verbs. They eat those white noodles that are four feet long. But as far as I know, Winner, they don't have their kids by spontaneous combustion. Or did I miss something in my last clinical rotation?"

"You talk too much, Karl Mike."

Karl Mike nodded. "Right," he said, "I sure do." He lifted his cereal bowl and drank down the last drops. "You ever get lonely, Winner?" he asked.

"No."

"How many Vietnamese *are* there in Galveston?"

"Some." Lang paused. "Eleven medical students," he said. "Many in pharmacy and med tech."

"And in the projects too. I keep seeing those little fisherfolk every time we do drop-in clinic. They bring their kids for every runny nose." Karl Mike put his cereal bowl in the sink, an all-time first. "And believe me, Lang,

[39]

whatever your feelings on the subject, fertility is *not* a problem."

What could he say? The project Vietnamese, Hai Truong among them, were a whole different world. Even their accents were alien. But to Karl Mike, there was no distinction. In his most perceptive moods, all the little yellow people still looked alike.

5 "You're a very intelligent young woman, you know." The nun looked down at Trang. "And when you perfect your English, you'll be eligible for any number of college acceptance lists at graduation. Do you think you'd like to go to school here with us? We are arranging scholarships for some of the minority children, and you were recommended by the Central High School counselor."

Trang looked around her. The chandelier of the Queen of the Sea High School entry hung so high above her head that anyone standing under it would seem tiny. She said nothing.

"I know that your family is not Catholic, but we thought Queen of the Sea might be useful to you in acclimating, and we have been given additional fellowships this year. You'll be able to go home on weekends since you live in Galveston. The other girls here are very helpful and kind. One of them is from Laos. You'll get along with her."

"Lao pig," said Trang.

The nun turned her head until it slid halfway inside her white hat. "You don't mean that," she said.

"Lao dirty pig," said Trang, her voice dark.

"Your father wouldn't like you to talk like that."

"I don't find my father."

"What?"

"I live with my uncle."

"Not your parents?"

"Not father. Not mother."

"Where is your mother, then?"

Trang looked up at the chandelier, as bright and far away as the moon. She tried to move her mother's face into her mind. It wouldn't come. "Got no mother," she said.

The nun turned aside. Trang looked down at her green plaid slacks and pink blouse, at the plastic slippers on her broad feet. She didn't look like the other high school students, and she knew that. She didn't look like anyone but herself.

"How old are you, Trang?"

Trang stopped to think. "My paper say I born in 1972," she muttered.

"What paper?"

"The paper they give me in the camp."

"But is that your real age?"

"I born a long time ago," Trang said.

"But are you older than fifteen?"

"Maybe I old enough to marry."

The nun bent down, her habit folding around her. "Trang, *would* you like to go to school with us?" she asked.

Trang was looking at the chandelier.

"What *would* you like?"

"I take care of my uncle's house."

"Surely there is someone else who could do that."

"My aunt is sick many times."

[42]

"Aren't there any other children who could help?"

Trang kept her eyes directed upward, but she was listening. "Tri don't know how to cook," she said.

"And can *you* cook?"

Now the eyes came down, and Trang put her hands in front of her as if she were supporting a dish. "I make pancakes with shrimp," she said. "I give them to Hai Truong, Phuong Nguyen's wife, when she is sick. I make the orange sauce. I put the carrots in *nuoc mam.* I make *cha gis.*" She looked up with a smile that revealed a baby tooth to the side of her mouth, a white zigzag in the upper row. "My uncle like what I cook." She stopped. "He like*s*," she said, hitting the "s." "He like*s* what I cook. He say*s* I cook better than my aunt. He say*s.*"

"Trang, do you like school?"

"My school?"

"Yes. Central High."

"I know." Trang bent her head. "Sometimes the children there talk too much," she said. "But I talk when the teacher asks me."

"So you'd like to continue going there?"

Trang didn't answer the question directly. "I walk with my cousin Tri," she said. "He goes to Lafitte School near the Central." She stood up straighter, brushing the front of her plaid slacks down over her flat stomach. "Thank you, teacher," she said. "I very busy. Maybe when I am bigger, I go to your school."

Without argument, the nun let her outside. The heavy cypress door moved slowly on its wrought-iron hinges. Then when the door had shut safely behind her, a Vietnamese boy appeared at the edge of the sidewalk. "You go?" he asked Trang. "You go with the sisters?"

"No." Trang started down the sidewalk, her hands at

her sides. The boy walked a pace behind her, but she stayed clearly centered in his vision as they headed for the corner.

"They are not good people?"

"No, they are good."

"My father says you do what you want."

"I know."

At the corner, as if they had already decided, they turned up Twenty-fourth Street and headed south. Several blocks farther on, the street simply ended, the buildings on each side cut off. Down behind them came the blue sky like a backdrop. This was the seawall, the peak of the island, built, they said in school, to protect everyone from the ocean if a big storm came. Once you got there, you looked down the high wall to the beach and then to the water. If you walked down the steps, you could go through the hard damp sand, gray as cement, and out to where the waves came in. People visited Galveston to sit on the sand and watch the water, renting red umbrellas against the sun instead of the rain. But now it was only March, and the people were asleep in their houses far away from the sea.

Tri reached into his pocket and lifted out three peppermint candies wrapped in cellophane. He gave two of them to Trang. "I'm not hungry," he said.

Trang took one of the candies and unwrapped it, putting the crumpled cellophane in her pocket. The teachers said don't litter. She wanted to be a good American. Some things she couldn't do because she had been born in the wrong place to be an American. She did the things she could do.

They reached Seawall, the street at the top. When the light turned green, they crossed. Beach Terrace and their ramshackle Section Eight house were fifteen blocks away in the other direction. Trang's uncle and aunt, Tri's parents, were off with their little children cleaning the boat and wouldn't miss them. Trang's aunt liked her new baby best of all. She never let him down on the ground outside, and even in the house he rode her hip. She talked to Tri as if he were grown up already, but he was the oldest son now, and Vietnamese mothers did that.

For Trang it was different. She had to sleep on a pile of blankets underneath the table in the kitchen, and she got yelled at all the time. But late at night when the grown-ups were asleep, Trang could sneak into Tri's room and lie on the floor next to his bed. They talked in the night, but very quietly. They talked in Vietnamese, but with some English words for the things that happened only in English, like progress report, and shutyourmouth, and achievement. Sometimes when they were both sleepy, Tri let his arm slide down, and Trang would put her hand around his fingers.

Today was a day when the spring haze of Galveston hung in the sky even over the ocean. Trang and Tri stood facing outward, out toward the horizon where three oil rigs stood, two relatively near, one so far that it was only a gray peak cresting out of the water. The waves broke on the sandbar fifty yards out, then churned in rows toward the beach where they broke again, this time with a succession of splashes, gray foam, gallons of water that turned from blue to green to brown and finally merged with the pale sand. In the summer the big storms would come. Then the water could kill you. Now it was safe if you were careful.

Tri looked out at the ocean. "It's big," he said.

Trang let her toe touch the foam.

Head bent, Tri touched the foam too. "I know how to swim," he said. "You just move your arms and your legs and hold your head up. The water carries you like an elephant."

Trang moved her foot back. A wave had reached for it.

"When I get in high school and buy a car, I'll go swimming in the summer," Tri said. "I'll buy a kite and fly it on the beach. I'll pick up shells and make you a necklace, Trang. I'll dance in the waves. Like this!" Tri started down the beach, leaping on one foot and then the other, his hands in the air, his fingertips touching. He had all his clothes on, but when he had gone a certain distance, it was impossible to tell.

He came back. "That's what I'll do, Trang," he said. "Americans swim all the time." He pushed his hair down on his head, though Trang knew it would be prickly in a moment no matter what he did with it. Then he bent down to the damp sand and wrote his name with his fingers. "T-R-I L-U-U," he said, and then the water came up and made canals in all the letters.

"You like it, Trang?"

"What?"

"You like the ocean?"

Trang looked out, out at the oil rigs, the two that were easy to see and the one that was almost beyond seeing. It was like a person gone from sight. Just beyond her feet, the roiled sand churned in the waves as they broke. The smell was sharp, but there was a rotting edge to it. The waves never stopped breaking on the shore.

"I want to go home now, Tri."

"Okay." He looked up at her. "Are you sad?" he asked. Her eyes stayed on the water and she didn't smile, even though the light on her face was turning golden.

"I am thinking."

"When I grow up, you go swimming with me."

"I can't swim. You know that."

6 Once they'd put the new siding on the house, it had been as if she'd moved into another country, Azelita thought. First the choices: wood, aluminum, vinyl. Then the colors: blue, tan, yellow, white, a whole collection with names like "Sunshine" and "Earthtone." The contractor: either a friend who would do it for a discount price and probably staple the siding on, fodder for the next hurricane, or someone regular from the white side of town who'd park his truck two blocks away, around the corner, safe on Broadway where the police patrols ran every half hour. The money: a loan from the credit union for public school employees at 11 percent but no trouble to get, or cash from Uncle Washington, with no interest but the understood obligation of weekly visits and payments in stationery store envelopes, tucked down between the cushions of his worn brown sofa but always where he could retrieve them. "You is not a forgetting woman, Azelita," he'd say.

Vinyl. Sunshine. Roger Rosenblum, the same contractor the doctors used for their remodeling, and Jewish as well. Uncle Washington, because 11 percent was a lot of extra cash on the salary of an office aide at Carver School.

Azelita sat in the porch swing, her Amoco glass of lemonade in her hand. She pushed with one leg against the porch boards, arcing the swing back toward the railing. The lemonade rose on one side of the glass as she put her mouth to it, tickling her tongue. The swing moved forward; the lemonade slid in the other direction. Fragments of pulp touched the crease on her upper lip. She licked it off. Her mother had brought the glass juicer over from Credence Parish when she'd first decided to trust her life to Texas instead of Louisiana. Her mother had been a practical woman.

Across the street, where the Beach Terrace housing project began, three black men, darker even than Azelita, dug into the innards of an old car. One of them held a crowbar balanced between his two hands as if it were a scale and he were weighing his actions. Their hair was shaved down smooth, with zigzags cut through to the bare scalp. Grease was out, cornrows were out, Afros had gone out once no white man dared say "nigger" anymore. Azelita sighed, ran her fingers through the tight black knobs clustered on her scalp. She *owned* that hair. It was altogether native to her head. Nobody *touch* that hair without her having a good word first.

"Hey, man!"

"You know from nuthin', man!"

"Time she runnin', we be the oldest niggers on this island, man."

Beach Terrace covered 19 blocks. It held 382 separate apartments of two, three and four bedrooms. Azelita knew all the figures. Tenants paid according to income, documented with W-2 forms, letters from employers, photocopies of food stamp allotments from welfare. Some old ladies, like Mrs. Jefferson Smith, lived as free as birds.

Her son paid for her cable TV, the Medicare paid for her clinic visits, the food stamps paid for her chitlings. Chitlings! Azelita took a strong mouthful of lemonade. Germans had veal cutlets for their Wiener schnitzel, the French had bread so hard and crispy it crumbled all the way down to your tits. Leave it to the niggers to eat pig guts.

In the last of the sun, her siding looked like top cream. Azelita floated in it, rocked and bottled. She finished the lemonade, let it slide all the way down and tuck into her belly. Lose a pound today, lose one tomorrow. Skinny as Oprah in a month, even if it didn't last. Find yourself a big black chitling, one who wouldn't buy if he couldn't get his hands around it.

Across the street, the men were leaning against the open hood of the car. The shortest one had a bottle that he was passing around. They were waiting for the beginning of something. Their eyes ticked over the porch like clock hands, ticked over Azelita and her swing.

"Little black pussy over there."

"She no little pussy. That one, she got more parts than pussy. She got the green, man. She sit there green as grass."

"She swing you around, that one. She take you up, put you down. That one no half-ass nigger, man. She bad mama, that one."

Azelita looked at her vinyl siding, its ripples made to imitate wood grain gleaming as the sun tucked itself behind the Beach Terrace roofs and marked the front of her house under its eaves. She could have had the porch railing vinyled too, built in solid with plywood and then covered over. She could have had the porch glassed in tight and set herself there after work like the eye behind the camera. It would have cost her an extra two thousand dollars and an extra year from Uncle Washington. She could have bought those bamboo shades that rolled up to the window tops and then came all the way down to the sill. But she hadn't. "You ain't got nuthin' to hide, girl," her mama had always said. Her mama had weighed 250 pounds, and the Beach Terrace niggers had taken their hats off when she walked up the block to the Shop 'n' Save.

The men across the street had turned back to whatever they were doing with the car. Two spotted puppies, slung close to the dirty grass, were yapping at a collection of project children. One little boy wearing jive-green pants was throwing something at them, white rectangles that floated through the air like cotton. The nearest dog grabbed one and started to tear it up, growling ferociously while the men watched. Another flew through the air and landed on the dog's back. He leaped up after it.

Pads. Kotex. Lord, Lord.

The phone rang. Azelita heaved herself upright. At thirty-two, she had a touch of rheumatism, as her mother had always called it. And she needed to lose forty pounds, which had all settled around her waist like an old afghan. If the world got colder, which it didn't look like it was going to, she could stew herself in her own fat, chitlings and collard greens.

It was her sister, calling from her two-story Dutch colonial in Baton Rouge. She'd married white and had two little boys, kinky brown hair and noses straight as hat pins. Her husband taught at the university, collected rocks from highway diggings, thought Azelita should go back to school and be a teacher instead of picking up after them and shuffling their forms in a grade school office. He'd made Labella get her four-year degree in accounting when the woman couldn't even keep track of her own checkbook, and he'd given her her own little Pontiac when she'd graduated.

"You, woman. What you doin'?"

"I sittin' on my porch listening to three fool niggers running their mouths across the street."

"Nobody in her right mind live across the street from that Beach Terrace project."

"Labella, we grew up in that project, and Mama planted her tea roses there. You know that."

"I know it, and you know it. But you got no need to keep it in your eye, sister. You niggerfy yourself any chance you get."

"I got all my siding on. I intend to drink my lemonade and swallow that siding right down with it."

Labella laughed. "You know, woman, there be easier ways."

"I go my *own* way."

"You the one of us most like Mama. Lord knows that woman knew only one way to do it, and it always grew out of her own head."

Azelita leaned against the phone table, rocking it dangerously. "Remember when she chase your boyfriend flat out of the bathroom?"

"You make that up, woman."

"No *suh*. You so young, your tits like little marbles. Mama thought he had you in there too, sticking it in. She saw he by hisself, she still so mad she sent him *running*. Broom at his behind."

"And then I go and marry white. Mama push that little nigger so far I gotta go lookin' for another color."

"You know Mama love Richard like her own son. And your two boys, they like kings in her eye."

[52]

On the other end of the line, Labella breathed so deeply that Azelita could hear the air push out. She knew what was coming.

"Azelita, you go look at your own self sometime. Richard never stop talking about how you should be *teaching* in that school, not cleaning up after those white teachers ain't half so smart as you. Time you got *over* Mama and did what you put on earth to do."

"Labella, you leave me be in my life! Time you remember *I* the big sister here. You boss your men around, *I* boss *me.*"

"Mama be proud if you go back to college," said Labella, but before Azelita could big-sister her another sentence, the conversation moved on to the boys' schoolwork, Richard's fossil rocks on the dining-room table, then finally the recipe for baking powder biscuits that soaked up honey like spring rain. Azelita pushed out her good-bye with the taste of flour and cream of tartar in her mouth. Nobody went back to school like some puny chicken when she already had a good enough job. Nobody with any sense let her little sister tell her what to do.

"Slavery days ain't died out yet," Azelita muttered as she opened the house door and went back onto the porch. The sun had gone low enough to blanket the Beach Terrace roofs with its gold. She'd had her Beach Terrace years, and Mama too, and yes, Labella, though she was such a big-time lady now in Baton Rouge that you'd have thought she'd forgotten. But she hadn't forgotten. Nobody'd forget the children banging rocks off your house, and the worn linoleum, and the inspections from the welfare to make sure you had just the amount of beds you were signed up for and just the right people in them. Nobody'd forget, not ever, the lady at the rent counter in the project center with her pink powder like sand in her wrinkles and her tight little rings with the fat white flesh pouching out on each side when she took your dollars without reaching too near and counted them like they'd been hers from the beginning. In the summer the dust and the dirt and the broken bottles and the dealers with their big cars and their big shoulders, and in the winter the layers of fog that knew what to hide and came down so thick around the project houses that the damp ate your insides when you went out into it.

She remembered. She'd had no intention of sticking it out one month longer than necessary. She'd started working full time as soon as she graduated from high school, with Labella already thinking Louisiana and Mama getting fatter and fatter as the water built up around her heart and the clinic gave up on getting her to take her medicine. Azelita had saved every penny she could and lied about what she was earning to the pink lady and her rings. It had taken her ten years, but she'd finally had enough savings, all news to the welfare people, to make a downpayment on the house with its porch right across the street from where they'd all started. Even Mama had settled in without too much yelling, and when she'd finally passed on, every no-good nigger across the street had lined up to watch the funeral man take her away. Azelita had let Labella spend some good Baton Rouge money on the coffin just to prove she was still part of the family.

And now she was supposed to go back to school like some little kinky-headed gal? Nobody was ever going to own *this* black lady again!

Across the street, the three men were sitting on the curb, passing the bottle back and forth in a brown paper bag. From this distance, the crinkled paper looked like the skin of a small animal. They were quietly laughing among themselves. Next to them, the hood of the car was still open. The engine was not running.

Azelita leaned heavily on the palms of her hands pressed against the railing. She felt herself growing bigger like one of those balloons in the Thanksgiving parade. She shuffled the men together into the center of her vision and put her own mark on them. The porch walls expanded away from her with her breath. Nobody and no thing was about to say no to her in her own house.

Behind the men, in the first project building, a door opened and a girl walked out. Her skin was brownish and her hair black, but she wasn't any Beach Terrace nigger. She was young too, really a child. In her hands were several books with colored covers, thin children's books, which she held in front of her as if they were a shield.

The library was four blocks away, Azelita knew, built before the neighborhood had sprung up into projects. The three intersections all had stoplights. The girl could get there safely.

Azelita lowered her head, giving the girl her space. When she looked up again, the girl was standing on the first curb. She peered down the street as if it were a river, the ocean itself, her toes gripping the front margins of her thongs. She looked both ways, although the light was green. The pile of books was up against her chest, which, Azelita noted, was not completely flat against the faded fabric of her dress. Somehow she looked familiar, Azelita thought. One of the students from Carver School? She wasn't sure.

Then the girl crossed over.

7 He wasn't Mexican, that boy. Even though his hair was black and his skin was brown. He didn't look like Juan in her school, or Manuel.

From behind a stack of books that she had piled at the end of the row in the children's fiction section, Linh moved her head so her eyes could watch him. If he looked back, he'd only see the books, heaped up and teetering. He was busy anyway. He wouldn't see her.

On the new red library rug with the checkerboard woven right into it, two little black girls were playing. They were pretending to be playing checkers like they were supposed to, but Linh knew better. Both of them had their hair in lots of little braids with those clamps holding the ends together. They looked like their heads were exploding.

"Is this what you wanted?"

Linh jumped. She'd forgotten that she'd asked the librarian for a book about whales. Besides, she hadn't pronounced the word quite right, and the librarian hadn't figured out what Linh had wanted until Linh had told her it was a big fish. Then the librarian had printed out "whale" in huge letters and asked her if that was right.

Printing was for babies! She could write script! She was ten years old!

"Is this what you want?"

The librarian had funny brown hair that went up and down on her head. She ate off her lipstick. Why did American ladies wear lipstick if they ate it off?

"Thank you," said Linh, reaching her hand out just a little ways. But the librarian didn't give the book to her.

"There's a filmstrip on whales in the media section. Maybe you'd like to watch that. Then you could look at the book."

Linh knew the librarian didn't want her to have the book. To see if it would help, she reached in her pocket for her library card and held it out. Maybe this time they'd know that she'd signed her father's name for him, that it wasn't his own writing. Her mother couldn't write at all, and she was afraid to ask her father.

The librarian said something else so fast that Linh couldn't understand, but she didn't even look at the card. Then she touched Linh on the shoulder, hardly feeling her at all, as if the skin under her dress were not good skin, as if she were dirty.

"I . . . will . . . help . . . you," said the librarian, every word dropping by itself.

Linh just wanted the book. But the librarian had set it on one of those little tables next to the rug with the checkerboard. It wouldn't be polite to pick it up when the librarian hadn't wanted to give it to her. Looking down at her feet, Linh made herself small. She curled her toes as tight as she could into the rubber soles of her thongs and pretended she was somewhere else. After a while, the librarian went away, but she left the book behind.

At first, Linh was still afraid to pick it up. She went back to the shelf and pretended she was straightening the books there. When she peeked over the pile at the end, she couldn't see the boy who wasn't Mexican anymore. The black girls had stopped making noise, so maybe they were gone too.

The librarian must think she was stupid! Linh pushed her fingernails into the fat parts of her hands. She could read like everyone else in fourth grade. Americans talked so fast! And when they talked slow, they did it because they thought you were stupid like a baby. They even talked slow to Trang Luu, and she was almost a woman. She was almost big enough to be her uncle's wife!

"In Vietnam, I saw whales every day." At first Linh thought she had said it herself, even though that wasn't true because the words had come in the old language. Then she knew she wasn't the one who had said it. She turned to the table, where the black-haired boy, his head bent over her whale book, was whispering the words in Vietnamese.

"I kung-fu whales if they come to *my* house," he said, this time with his head turned toward her. The label on his shirt collar was sticking up into his neck. His mother hadn't checked him when he got dressed. He was stupid like Harry and Gary.

Linh didn't say anything back to him, but she knew he was listening.

"I swim so fast that even the sharks don't get me." This time he swung around in his chair and looked right at her. With one hand he reached back and shut the book with a bang.

Linh smiled a very little smile. A shark would eat every piece of him and make shrimp roll filling out of it.

[58]

"You see the big ball of the world they got upstairs? The globe?"

She shook her head.

"You ever go look at Vietnam on the globe? You can light up everything from inside. If you push the button, it all lights up like the sun. It's better than a map."

Linh knew she would be afraid to push the button.

"I show you," he said, and got up from the table. He reached out, but he didn't touch her like the librarian had. In Vietnam you didn't touch each other until you got engaged to be married. Even then you did it only when you were alone.

"When did you get here?" he asked.

She knew he didn't mean the library. "Eight years ago," she said.

"But you still can't understand English!"

"I can! That lady talks too fast! People talk funny in Texas too!"

The boy picked up the whale book. "I just got to Galveston," he said. "Last month. We lived in Wichita for a little while before. That's where my father met us. My father hits my mother all the time. He hits me too." With one hand, he rubbed his stomach, smiling with half his mouth. "He don't give me rice," he said. "Just a little bit."

Linh didn't know what to say. Maybe all big Vietnamese children got hit and pinched a lot. The blue spots on Trang's arm floated before her eyes. But Trang was surely never hungry.

Smiling a little more, the boy handed her the book. "You can take this home," he said. "If you got a card."

"No talking in the library!" said the librarian from over at her desk.

"She say shaddup," said the boy. "I know that word.

[59]

Shaddup, shaddup, shaddup. My teacher says that every day."

"Where do you go to school?" He was almost big enough to go to Central High with Trang. Linh put the whale book under her arm. If she took it home, Harry and Gary might tear it up because it had big fish in it. But she could carry it to the room with the chairs on the second floor of the library and look at it there.

"Carver School."

"Me too! But I don't see you there."

The boy lowered his head. "I am in the baby class," he said. It sounded funny in Vietnamese.

The librarian rose from her desk, scraping her chair on the floor as she started toward them. The boy made a very small kung-fu kick with his foot. He had sneakers on, but they were awfully big. Maybe they belonged to his father.

"Old bitch!" he said. First he said it in Vietnamese, then in English.

Linh started to laugh, but with her hand over her mouth. That was so naughty! And it was dangerous to be naughty when the librarian was around. Even Trang would have to be polite or get thrown out.

Gauging the librarian's progress, the boy lowered his voice. "I am Xan Tuan My Van," he said. "My father is An Thanh Van. My mother is Xung Thi Ngo. I come from Ha Tien Province." He lowered his voice even further and tilted his head so his slab of black hair slid down, splitting his face. "What's your name?" he asked, even though polite Vietnamese children never did that.

Linh thought for a moment, the whale book under her arm. Her father was at home. Her mother was in the hospital. Harry and Gary were probably sleeping.

"My name is Linh," she said.

"Jesus, you know what?"

"Tell us, Bryce. In fifteen seconds. Because by then the Brit in Breeches will be back to skin us all." The blond junior resident stroked his beard with two fingers, sliding them together on the point of his chin. He was transferring out of Psychiatry at the end of the year and going into Radiation Oncology. The world of the psyche bore little interest for him anymore.

"Remember the Chinese lady on 3-West?"

"Vietnamese." Lang raised his head. He was usually quiet when the more senior residents talked; he recognized the humility required of an intern. Even Karl Mike would have to shape up after he graduated. But Hai Truong was not Chinese. Despite her backwardness, she was one of his own people.

Bryce Adams corrected himself. It was Friday, and his girl was coming down from Houston. "Right on. Vietnamese. I know the difference. The little country hanging off Asia like an appendix. Not the big belly above it."

"Right." Lang lowered his head again. He knew that in America it didn't really matter.

"Anyway." Bryce flung himself back in the plastic

chair. One hand dangled over the charts in the nurses' station. "They did the final Haldol read-out last night. Should have been a five. Guess what?"

"Tell us." The blond resident was separating the hairs of his beard into clusters.

"A straight zero. Like she'd never swallowed a pill."

"Palmed them."

"Not likely. The nurse was watching. The little lady put them right on her tongue and swallowed them down. Nurse still watching. No way for any trickery."

"Bryce, one of the things you need to learn on the psych ward is that anything is possible." Behind the heavy fringe of his mustache, the mouth of the blond resident opened and closed in almost total secrecy.

"The mysteries of Asia, huh?" Bryce creaked back and forth in his chair. "Only now what am I supposed to do?"

"Could it be lab artifact?"

"I ran the final test myself. Same thing. This little lady does not absorb the best the American pharmacopoeia has to offer."

"So?"

"So I lie, right? Tell old Snot-Fart that we've been observing her closely and have our doubts about the schizophrenia. She isn't eating, isn't talking to her husband or to the kids. Looks more like classic depression. Hard to tell with the third worlders. Let him draw the conclusions."

"Antidepressants?"

"Not with her medication record. Probably shock, as we chatted about on rounds. The man likes those electrodes, believe you me."

Lang had started to leave the room but turned at the door. "She is not clinically depressed," he said, enunciating as clearly as possible so his accent would not blur his message.

Bryce and the blond resident looked at him. Lang knew that they did not regard him as truly one of the third world. He had been accepted into medical school, as they had, had passed his boards, graduated, had been placed on this rotation. They regarded it as an accident that he was so short and that his skin had tanned into gold rather than brown. That was how they surely all thought.

"So what's your diagnosis?" Bryce was standing up, rotating his shoulders forward, then backward. He was into exercise, that strange world. When they did rounds and he was in the rear, he practiced abdominal breathing. On Bryce's big American body, it was not the same as Zen.

Lang hesitated. In the visits he had made to Hai Truong, she had said a few things. Her husband had talked to him too. "She does not belong to herself," he said, hardly knowing how to arrange the words.

"What?"

"She belongs to a spirit."

There was a long silence.

"In Vietnam, in my village, there were several women who had this problem." Lang hesitated again, but plunged on. "We called it a ghost husband. There was nothing you could do about it."

The silence continued.

"But ghost husbands are almost always kind." Lang felt as if he were sinking into a well that had no bottom. "And they don't kill. They will go away. They are just lonely. When they aren't lonely anymore, they leave. Then the wives will become like before."

"And this is what you're going to tell Smith-Fragon in

grand rounds?" Bryce went over to Lang and put his arm around him, forcing the black head down against his ribs. "What language are you going to use to convince the Bouncing Brit of this? Do you have a tribal dance?"

Lang knew Bryce wasn't angry. He was like Karl Mike. This was just the way young doctors talked. Bryce thought it was all a joke. There were no ghost husbands. It was all peasant superstition. Medicine was a science. If a diagnosis was correct, then the treatment could begin in the right way. So many milligrams. So many teaspoons. Sometimes patients didn't swallow their pills. Sometimes the ghost husband sang at night. The reaction could vary. Things were different. Sometimes.

"Will you need an interpreter?" The blond resident was buttoning his lab coat.

"What?"

"To explain about the shock treatments to the family. To get permission for them."

"Oh God, I suppose so. And our expert doctor here will be busy." Bryce released Lang and turned away. "I can get that lady in the lab. About two feet tall and most of it those garnet glasses. She'll have to explain it to the husband so he'll sign. Phuong Nguyen. That's his name."

"I thought the little lady was named Hai Truong."

"She is." Lang raised his voice. "But in Vietnam, women keep their old names for always. Also when they are married."

"Quite a liberated appendix on the rump of Asia." Smiling, Bryce slapped Lang's shoulder. "Welcome to America, Dr. Nguyen," he said. "Our ghosts get two hours on Halloween, and that's it."

■   ■   ■

"First they give her a shot."

"Yes. Shot."

"Then they take her to the ECT room. She'll be sleepy."

"Yes. Sleepy."

"They put her on a table there. They put the electrodes on her head. They fasten wires to them. Then the doctor pushes a button and turns on the current. The electricity goes through the wires into her brain, but she doesn't feel it because she's sleeping. When she wakes up, she'll be better."

"My wife sick. I understand."

"Some people get a headache afterward. If your wife has a headache, the nurse will see that she gets aspirin. You know what aspirin is, right?"

"Yes. Aspirin. Tylenol. Very good."

"She may forget a few things. There's often some memory loss. But after a few weeks, most people start remembering everything again."

"My wife not swallow. Sometimes she don't eat."

"They'll continue the ECT for two weeks. Six treatments altogether. She'll be in good shape then, and you can probably take her home."

"Yes."

"You understand what I'm saying? You want me to get the lady to translate?"

"I understand. They put something on her head. She better."

"So please sign this paper."

"This paper?"

"Yes."

"Where I sign?"

"Here."

"Okay, I sign here. No money?"

"What?"

"I pay money?"

"No! Just sign it."

"Okay, I sign. Please."

"What?"

"Please tell all doctors thank you. They fix my wife. She be happy in America. Very good, America!"

9 Whenever the reference librarian looked at Trang, Trang looked right back. She widened her eyes so that she appeared more like an American and pushed back her hair from her cheeks the way the American girls did. Over the open books on the table in front of her, she laid her hands in a casual dance as if her fingers had more interest in the words than her eyes had. It was important to look as if what she were doing did not really matter.

In Galveston, the library was an old building, but they kept making it new inside. Today a black man had been washing the checkerboard rug with a machine that spread bubbles in circles and then ate them up again. Last week, two men, their skins halfway between black and white, had been putting up shelves downstairs where the children had their books. They had filled a whole empty wall with shelves, fastening each board with long pieces of metal that looked as if they could stab all the way through the wall. Today, when Trang had passed by the shelf, it had held one stripe of books on top of another. They were books about animals and trees. They had no men's names in them.

But these books did.

On the table in front of Trang lay *Who's Who in America*. It was open to the *D*s. There was also the *Dictionary of American Biography*, but some of those names were dead. Her English teacher had taught her that. There was a book of American generals, and when Trang had first seen that, her heart had risen. But once she thought about it, she knew her father could not have been a general. Generals earned much money and they owned their own airplanes. If he had been a general, he would have taken her and her mother back to America with him. They would have flown above the clouds like royalty.

Then there was the Galveston city directory. Trang did not think he was in Galveston, or he would have found her already, but it was certainly possible. Many people lived here. When she was older, if she had not found him yet, she would go to Houston and look for him in the directory there.

The reference librarian was staring at her again. Trang stared back, her hands wide on the spread pages of the books, the pads on the ends of her fingers touching the words. Her eyes straight ahead, she moved her hands gently down the crisp paper, slow enough so she would feel it if the right name came against her skin. Blood called to blood. Because he had never held her, his blood stayed deep inside her body. But when his name came against her fingers, the blood would move outward, and she would feel its warmth.

In one book at the far corner of the table were the pictures of Washington, D.C. The wall was in the middle section, where the book opened naturally. Many people were touching it in the first picture. Trang could feel the smooth stone through the paper, but she did not think his name was on it. Her mother had said that he was a very smart man, even though she did not remember his whole name. Smart men shot other people; they did not get shot themselves. He had come back home to America, she was sure of it. Now she needed only to find him.

The librarian was glaring at her. At home, her aunt would be glaring at her too. In Vietnam, her mother had forgotten her, or remembered only a little girl who had never learned to swim even though she lived by the ocean, a little girl who played with her cousins and cooked *cha gis* for New Year's even when she was still so small she had to stand on a stool. Whatever she did, she had to do by herself.

Shutting the books one after the other, Trang stood up. She began to put them back on their shelves, carrying the heavy pile wrapped in her arms against her chest. The books were so strong that they dug into her flesh. She liked how they felt.

"You bad girl Trang! Why you stand there like that? Why you not work like real Vietnamese girl? Why you let Xao cry? Why you not change his diaper, give him milk? Why you go ask your uncle for school money? Why you not ask me? Why you not let the nuns take you in their school? Why you sit and look out window? Why you read that book? Books are for boys—you work in house, you take care of children, you cook, you clean, you sew dress, you help me, you do what I say to you.

"I think you have mother in your head. I tell you one thing, bad Trang. Your mother crazy lady. She my sister, but she crazy. She steal money from me. Your mother go to my house, go in my bed, dig and dig and dig and find my money. Three thousand piastres! She take it all! Your mother have sex with Americans! They give her money for *lam tinh*. She go out in night, she find many men. She have big cunt, your mother. Want more, more!

"Your father, he American devil, he no want you. My husband and I, we help your mother when she have you. We never forget family.

"When your mother say she want you to come to America, I say 'All right. We take her. We feed her, we help her, we be good to her.' I good woman, I not say no. We take you on boat. You eat so much! You were little girl, but you eat so much! You eat all my food, all my sons' food. Tuan and Tri cry because they have nothing to eat. Your belly so big with everyone's rice!

"I not American, no, no. I live here, my husband Quoc has boat here. Tri learn English, my babies learn English, but I Vietnamese. Vietnamese, they don't cheat, they don't take money, they don't sit and read book. They are good people. Vietnamese ladies don't wear shorts! They pray to the dead grandfathers. They hold to family.

"You break my family! You make the bad waves come! You tear our family!

"Where my Tuan? Where my Tuan? Why you not dead instead of him?"

10 "My God!" Down the hall by the ungraded classroom, Azelita could hear a series of thumps interspersed with screams. She rose from her desk as if injected with adrenaline, banging her leg against the edge of her chair. Her hair raised itself slightly on her head, then resettled. She moved down the hall as fast as she could without breaking into a run. The principal's door opened as she passed.

"What is it, Azelita?"

"Lord knows." Azelita plunged onward.

The principal's door closed. Ms. Hopkins, as an administrator, encouraged Azelita to do a part of the Carver School discipline, a role that went considerably beyond her job description. On the other hand, Ms. Hopkins, her thin arms fluttering, relished all manner of paperwork. Justice was done, one way or another.

The thumping continued, along with waves of sound. Then silence. "Stand still!" said a gritty voice, female. Mrs. Fillmore, College of the Mainland graduate with all the special ed certifications. Her classroom was the civilizing conduit for immigrants and incorrigibles. Results, however, were not immediately guaranteed.

When Azelita pushed into the room, the Vietnamese boy was squatting on the floor, right where she could look down at the whorled black hair on the crown of his head. In the gaps between his belt holders, his jeans sagged out in semicircles against his brown skin. Didn't look like he had any underwear on him. No socks either, just the dirty ankles going down like bony branches into the dirty sneakers. Which were twice the size he needed, and knotted with green laces besides. The worst the Goodwill had to offer. Or were they his father's?

"Xan." Azelita remembered when he'd enrolled a month ago. A strange one, joining up with his father. She prided herself on her memory.

He hunched down farther.

"Xan!" Azelita squared her shoulders.

Nothing.

"Xan, stand up." He squatted like a rock.

"He was doing that kung fu again." Mrs. Fillmore wiped her forehead. Inside her room, a varied collection of faces was peering toward them—black, caucasian, Hispanic—but no other recognizable Vietnamese.

"Did he hurt anybody?" Azelita swept her eyes over the boy. The knuckles on both his hands were scabbed. Impetigo? Wrong place. His wrists were dirtier than his ankles.

"No. Jimmy got away. Then he did it to the wall."

"Whatever got him started?"

"I have absolutely no idea. We were talking about nutrition. I was showing pictures of vegetables and fruits that are high in vitamin content. Jimmy was passing them around. Xan jumped up from his desk and tried to kick Jimmy."

Azelita sighed. "Does he do this often?"

"Almost every day." Mrs. Fillmore turned back to her class. "Write a list of red fruits!" she said, enunciating each word. "First one to get five fruits wins an M & M." Mrs. Fillmore believed mildly in behavior modification and positive reinforcement.

"You can leave him to me now," Azelita said. She knelt down next to the boy, looming over him. "Get up, hon," she whispered.

"Better call him by his real name."

Azelita shrugged. "Maybe I don't pronounce it right."

Mrs. Fillmore lowered her voice too. "We all have to learn. Two more of them enrolled last week, but they aren't here today. The whole country of Vietnam is moving to America, and Galveston in particular. Must be the climate or the welfare. Half of them are fishermen."

Bracing herself, Azelita bent over even farther. "Come on, hon," she said, guiding her arm around the bent shoulders. "You know you can't kung fu people just like that."

"I don't think he understands that much English."

"Shouldn't he be in the primary then?"

"Look at him. He's at least twelve years old. Better he be here in ungraded, whether he can read yet or not."

Suddenly Xan shifted and stood up. He might have been twelve, Azelita supposed, but he was squat and short, ribs curved inward, shoulders like coat hangers. Azelita looked at the square brown face, the scabbed knuckles. His shoes were flopping on his feet. How could he kung fu anyone if he couldn't keep his shoes on?

"Come on, hon," she said again. "You have to go to the principal." She reached toward him.

His hands came up, jerking in front of his face. "Shaddup," he said, clear enough so anyone could understand it. Then he dug into his jeans pocket and pulled out

[73]

a crumpled picture. Glaring at Azelita, he handed it over, unfolding it as he did so.

"Xan, what's that?"

"Tao," he said. Then, slowly, "Ap-pel."

"What?"

"Appp-elll." He lowered his head.

Azelita took the picture. Must have been one that Mrs. Fillmore was handing out. Illustrations of all those vitamins. Why would Xan have taken it? What meaning could all those vitamins have to him when he could hardly say ten words of English?

Xan looked at her defiantly. She moved her hand gently to him, and he shrank back. She looked at the picture more closely. There were teeth marks on it.

"I hongry," Xan said.

"All we know is that he came here to join his father." Mrs. Fillmore, sitting in the after-school calm of the principal's office, held Xan's file in her hand.

"From where?" The principal held herself upright in the swivel chair.

"Vietnam, of course. But he'd been somewhere else after that. I believe his mother came with him too. Let me think. Hong Kong, that's it."

"But there is a gap, isn't there?" The principal indicated the file. "Four years. Too long for one of those camps."

"It's impossible to figure out. We'll never know. By the time they learn English, they've forgotten what happened."

"As long as they don't drive their teachers to distraction."

"This is an exception. Something is wrong with this boy. Usually the Orientals are saints. Work done, smiles, eager to help. Even if they don't know what's going on, they do it anyway."

The principal put on a look of sympathy. "Hard to know what he's been through," she said.

"But we can't have kung fu in the classroom. Background experience is no excuse."

"I'll check with the social worker. She has some connection with the medical school. They must have a Vietnamese student or intern or someone to interpret. Perhaps they can provide us assistance."

"I could manage him better if I knew what was going on."

"Where is he now?"

"Azelita sent him to the cafeteria. He's with Mrs. Moggle. She's cleaning up."

"What's he doing?"

"From what she says, eating everything in sight."

11 Lang Nguyen's running trail started from the Sand Dollar Estates, where he and Karl Mike lived, a block off the seawall at Seventy-ninth Street, and continued down to the ornate refreshment stand rising above the sand like an opened umbrella, green with red trim, sculpted hot dogs festooning its upper deck under the roof, puffy sodas with straws jigsawed out of the wood around the bottom windows. In the summer, it sold food and rented towels until 10 P.M., but in the spring of the year, the refreshment stand closed at 8:00, even 7:00, when the workers began snapping the blinds shut in the faces of the droppers-by who came after work for a snack.

At Fifty-ninth Street, Lang's breath began to come hard. He slowed down. The beach had narrowed until it was just a strip of dirty sand, hard as a floor, pressed up against the cement ridge of the seawall. Even at low tide, he ran in its shadow. A dead sheepshead, buck teeth glinting in the last of the sun, lay to one side of the line of washed-up seaweed. Inattentive, Lang almost stepped on it. Bad luck if he had. Sorry, fish. Sorry, little lord of the sea.

Across the street and high above his head was the San

Georgio Hotel, built up for ten floors with rows of sliding patio doors layered on top of each other until they blocked the sky. Palm trees clustered in the terraced garden around the swimming pool. The hotel owners dumped sand on the beach every three years, trying to extend it. No use. The little lords of the sea ate it up with gleeful vengeance.

Lang ran on. Even though he had been running for a year now, it still seemed an enormous waste of effort, an artificial attempt to mold the body that should have been developed through planting rice, through digging, through meaningful work. But if he didn't run, all his muscles slept. He did his rotations, wrote his charts, worked up patients and all the while his flesh whitened and softened until the skin of his chest began to slide downward and he could grip it with the fingers of both hands as it edged over his belt. Not even healthy fat, solid and nurturing, a sign of wealth, much rice, honor and pride. Karl Mike had a gut too, but he laughed about it, said it was his right as a fat-ass doctor, or almost-doctor. But he had never walked with the water buffalo, never cultivated the new rice, slender and green.

At Twenty-fifth Street, Lang slowed down into what the Americans called a jog. From the side of the sea, no one was watching him. It was too early for swimmers. Above him, above the seawall built to hold back the ocean when the hurricanes came and ate the island with wind and rain, two squad cars with lights flashing on and off charged to a stop almost over his head. Lang bent to catch his breath, his hands on his knees. Although he was resting, his heart hit his chest wall over and over. Surely it was not the police. He carried his hospital ID card in the pocket of his running shorts just in case. Even here, even

[77]

in this strange island city off the southern coast of the United States, a doctor was often immune. No bribery. That he had left behind. But as a doctor, he had the right to cut patients and to sew them up again. Even the police knew that and were careful.

A siren came on, whined for a moment, then stopped. Lang felt his heart slow, stay in rhythm but diminish, soften against his chest, retreat. He breathed little breaths. Up above him on the seawall, the two policemen had a man leaning against a palm tree planted in a sidewalk container. One was running his hands down the man's legs, a quick sinister movement. The other was talking on a little radio too small for Lang to see in detail.

Lang rose. As he did so, he turned toward the ocean. To his astonishment, he saw a girl standing in the surf about forty feet from him as if she had sprung up from the sand at the bottom of the sea. The water, as the waves crested inward, washed up to her knees. She ignored it. When the waves retreated, Lang saw that she wasn't even barefoot but was wearing rubber thongs. She paid no attention to her wet feet but looked straight out to sea.

No one else was on the beach. The evening air was chilly. The girl stood so still that she seemed part of the sky. Her hair was long and dark.

The next wave reached her thighs. When it receded, her slacks were plastered to her thin legs. She stood perfectly quiet, then began to follow the retreating wave into the ocean. She walked slowly but without hesitation. A second wave sent foam up to her waist, and for a moment she waved with it. Her hands moved sideways for balance. She kept on.

Lang stood transfixed. What action would possibly be appropriate? He hurried down the beach to her, the toes of his Reeboks gripping the damp sand. In some strange way, he felt that if he kept his heels off the ground, he could prevent her from going any farther. If he relinquished that part of his hold on the earth, it would send a message to her that she didn't need to relinquish hers. Madness. She didn't even know he was there.

The next wave was a big one. She staggered under its impact but didn't fall. One drifting hand came up to her hair and lifted it from her neck in a heavy coil. For a moment, Lang thought she would stop walking, but she didn't.

"Miss!" Like an alien, he sent out the strange English word with its hissing conclusion. Though he was coming up close behind her, there was no sign that she had heard.

"Miss!" The water was high over his Reeboks. Looking down, he could see them from the tops, strange little submerged houses with laced roofs under the trunks of his legs.

He raised his head. She was gone.

Lang dove. He slid through the oncoming wave, his hands directing his passage. Below him, on the bottom, the clouds of aroused Gulf sand blurred and settled. A small shell, perfect in its isolation, rocked in the swirling grains. Next to it was her arm, and he seized it as it floated by him. It looked like a white fish, moving sinuously through its element, and even as the thought passed through his mind, the arm slid through his fingers. Over him, the water pressed and crashed. He wrenched himself to the surface, choking, hardly able to keep his feet. To one side of him, a square of white cloth moved in the swell. He grabbed for it.

"Don't do it!" Legs wide apart for balance, he pulled the cloth toward him. It was unbelievably heavy. Her face broke the surface and he swiveled her upright. She stum-

[79]

bled back. They both began to cough.

"You mustn't." Her hair covered her face, and he couldn't tell if she had heard him or not. Water poured down her, gluing her shirt to her body. She was thin but not quite a child.

The next wave hit them hard, but Lang had anchored his heels in the sandy bottom. A plastic bottle suddenly bobbed by, smacking against the water that was bringing it inland. The sky was graying, and against the offshore horizon, the lights of three oil rigs glittered like Christmas trees. Fireworks. New Year's. Tet. Only the evening star had opened in the natural sky, and there was so much water in his eyes that even that little star flashed with the power of the sun.

The girl pulled her hair back and looked at him. She was not an American.

"Chi tinh lam gi vay?" He knew what she was doing without asking.

"Toi tinh roi khoi cho nay." She lowered her head.

His language. "You mustn't do that," he said.

She didn't reply.

Lang felt foolish. "You need to dry off," he said, realizing he was making what had happened sound like a casual swim. He touched her arm to guide her to the beach, the ocean pushing on them both. Holding her hands to her sides, she turned toward the seawall where the police cars were pulling away from the curb, their lights still flashing. They began to walk in.

"Is that west?" she asked in English. Her voice was as matter-of-fact as a list for market.

"No, it's south."

"I wanted to go back," she said. She was wringing out the hem of her shirt.

"Back where?"

She didn't answer. As they stepped onto the sand out of the line of the tide, her hands transferred themselves from her shirt and began to wring each other. Her face showed no emotion at all.

"But there's nothing out there but water."

Still no answer or argument. Her hands worked savagely at each other. Beyond her, a line of bicycles passed by on the seawall, each one with a helmeted rider bent low over the handlebars. Lang thought they looked as if someone had cut them out against the sky and then pulled them from one side of his vision to the other.

"Are you all right?"

Her teeth were chattering. Lang took her hands and tried to separate them, but they ground themselves into each other and provided no access. Her eyes were strangely wide as she looked at him.

"You are Vietnamese? What is your name?"

Her eyes held his. "Trang," she said. "I am *bui doi.* My mother is Vietnamese. My father is American."

He should have known. "How did you come here?" he asked, for she seemed to be waiting for the next question and would wait forever if it was not asked.

"With my aunt and her family." She pulled the damp rope of her hair over to one side of her head and began to wring it out with her small hard hands.

"When?"

"Five years ago."

Lang knew how it was in his country. The *bui doi* children, the dust of life, were scorned by everyone. If a girl was sent by her mother to live with an aunt and uncle, she would be treated like a servant. If both things came together, and with this strange break in life that the journey

[81]

to America represented, then who was to know what each day held?

"Do they treat little sister well?" It was not polite to say "you," not polite to ask even with the proper terms, not Vietnamese, not the way one should conduct oneself. But he was a physician after all, and although her face was still lifted with what looked almost like a small smile moving across it, her hands were wringing each other again.

She knelt at his feet before he had a chance to stop her. "I can't find him," she said. "I can't find my father."

Lang reached out his hand and pulled her to her feet. "Come with me," he said. At first he wasn't sure where he intended to take her, but then he knew. They would go across Seawall Boulevard to the restaurant with the clam shell on its sign, and they would sit in a booth there until she had calmed down. He would buy her whatever food she wanted as any uncle should.

Already she was walking erect beside him. Her fists were clenched, but her arms hung at her side. At the top of the seawall, she allowed him to take her elbow and guide her across, then down the sidewalk to the restaurant door. For a moment, her eyes gleamed as they stepped inside, and she tossed her wet hair back on her head. "Nice," she said.

They dripped brown footprints across the tan carpet as the waitress led them to a booth as far back as it was possible to place a customer. The girl walked behind Lang now, but so close behind him that when he slowed momentarily to edge his way around a misplaced chair, her chin nudged into his shirt, a tiny touch along the upper regions of his spine. When they were seated, each holding a flamboyant plasticized menu with vivid plates of meat and vegetables printed on it, she kept her eyes down, but when the waitress came to take their order, standing farther back than she needed to from the booth, the girl looked up and said "hamburger" with almost no accent. Yes, french fries too. No, no salad. "Yes, Coke," she said, this time with a little twist of misplaced sound.

Lang ordered the same thing, only with iced tea. He actually felt like hot tea, or even coffee, because the air-conditioning unit was blasting at him from the ventilator over the next booth, and his drying skin was covered with goose bumps. But iced tea was more appropriate in Texas. He felt it was extremely important to be appropriate.

"Are you all right?"

Her eyes circled the restaurant. "I never been here," she said in English.

"The medical students and doctors come here all the time."

Her eyes brightened. "You a doctor?" she asked as she began to fold her napkin into a series of overlapping triangles.

"Yes." Lang tried to make it sound authoritative, but his rear end was squishing on the plastic seat, undermining his dignity. "Only since last year," he said.

"I think I might like to be a nurse," she said, slipping back into Vietnamese. She spoke with a northern accent and a certain crudity that meant village rather than city.

"That's a good thing to be."

"I like to help fix hurt people." Then a wave of feeling crossed her face. "High school is very hard," she said. "The teachers talk too fast, and I can't always understand." She rubbed her thumbs together hard.

"You're in high school?" Across the room, Lang could see the waitress approaching, hamburgers held high. His stomach lurched. Even his iced tea in its tall glass had a threatening tint.

"First year." She kept her hands spread out on the place mat so when the waitress lowered her plate of food, she had to angle it in between. The girl seemed to be interested in the procedure, as if she were watching a ship come into port. When her plate finally came to rest, her index fingers caressed the undersides of the heavy china.

Lang found himself feeling like a village elder, something that did not attract him. "I think it is always hard for the Vietnamese when they come here," he said, trying to turn his so-called wisdom to profit. Tentatively, he lifted the corner of his bun. Underneath, the meat was slathered with mayonnaise and ketchup. Onions lay in a heap next to the french fries. He had eaten the same sort of thing ever since coming to America, but now it all looked exceptionally unappealing. Even the french fries piled to one side reminded him of limp tongue depressors.

Bent over his plate, he looked quickly at the girl. She stared back at him. "Where are the chopsticks?" she asked.

"But this is American food."

"I don't eat this way," she said. One finger hovered over the plate. "I should pick it *up?*" she asked.

"Yes."

Obedient, she put her hands on the top of the bun and lifted. Halfway to her mouth, the top came free, spilling the bun's contents. She looked down, holding the curved roof of bun in front of her little breasts. "Mess!" she said, and for the first time a real smile crossed her face.

"Don't you eat in the cafeteria at your high school?"

The girl's face was serious again. "I have the tickets," she said. "Because my aunt's family doesn't have money,

America gives us the tickets. But I don't like to go in the line. What if I take too much? What if the tickets are no good?" She sniffed a french fry, then licked the salt off with the tip of her tongue. "I hold my stomach in so it makes no noise. When I go home, I eat rice." Her face became stern. "My aunt says, 'Trang, you eat too much rice." Her chin lifted. "I *like* rice."

Suddenly Lang was embarrassed. In Vietnam, he would never have been in a situation like this. He would never even have talked to this Trang! She was from a low-class family; her every word marked her in that way. She had no Vietnamese father! When you came to a new country, it was important to do things the way people did them in that country. He had arrived knowing only refugee camp English and had started college two months later, taking care of the yard for his biology teacher in exchange for a room in the basement. Now he had become a doctor, a physician, and his diploma was framed in gilded wood over the sofa in his apartment. He had sent his parents a copy! It was true that he owed America many thousands of dollars, but they were going to trust him as he paid it back little by little. He had learned how to cure people no matter where they came from. He had been from a good family in Vietnam, and he had upheld them.

He looked at the girl. She was tying what was left of the hamburger into the bottom of her damp shirt.

Of course she saw him looking. "I take it to my cousin Tri," she said with perfect matter-of-factness. "He will be nice to me if I do it. I can watch him eat it."

Lang was flabbergasted. "Your name is Trang?" he found himself asking her senselessly, although he knew that perfectly well. Absolutely nothing else had come to his mind.

"Yes, Trang." She smiled again, but behind the smile was something flat and gray. "Trang Thi Luu. I have my mother's name."

"Do you know who your father is?"

"My mother said he was a smart man." Her voice rose. "You want me to come to your house and cook for you?" she asked.

Lang had a wild image of Trang and Karl Mike, noodles hanging from their chopsticks, rising from the unpolished kitchen table and beginning a dance together. "No," he said, choking. "But if you live near here, I can bring you home safely. And I will give you my address if you need me to help you." He spoke slowly, in English. What he was doing was not a Vietnamese thing at all.

Trang did not seem to listen. Instead, she rose from the booth, the hamburger bulging in its fabric cradle across her stomach. "I go," she said, speaking English as he had. "I help my aunt with my little cousins. My aunt is angry at me all times. She think I make the boat wreck and Tuan die. She make me help her very much." With deliberation, she flung her hair back and raised her chin. "My aunt not like it if you come to my house," she said. "She say I *bui doi* whore."

By the time Lang had retranslated the words from her accented English into Vietnamese, she had already reached the front of the restaurant and was opening the door to the sidewalk. There was nothing left for him to do except ask the waitress for the check, an action made more difficult when he found that his hospital ID card was the only thing in the pocket of his damp running shorts.

12 "Come on, Lang. You couldn't leave her to drown herself, for God's sake. You couldn't just take her up on the seawall and flag down a policeman. You had to at least give her a chance to dry out." Karl Mike pulled his T-shirt over his head and tossed it into the corner, where it joined a toppling pile of dirty clothes. "Why beat yourself about it? She'll go home to her aunt and make out okay. *You're* the one who's always telling me how tough the little yellow men from Vietnam are. I assume the little yellow women are just as tough."

Lang gripped Karl Mike's door frame and leaned forward. "She was from a small village," he said. "She was ignorant."

"So?"

"So perhaps I should help her."

"Like how? Give her five hundred dollars? Marry her? Commit statutory rape? You bought her a hamburger and fries, which I had to bail you out for. That's enough in the old U.S. of A."

"She *peasant,*" Lang said, his voice tearing out with such force that the proper English trimming flew away with it.

"Jesus Christ!" Karl Mike picked up his barbells and began to hoist them, one in each hand. "This is not a class-conscious country, fella. No peasants here. Those drunks with leg ulcers you treat on night rotation, they may be one day out of jail, living in boxes on the beach, but they're not *peasants.*"

Lang turned away. "You don't understand," he said, which was true enough, but even as he said it, he realized that *he* didn't understand either, not the little *bui doi* Trang, not his own contradictory impulses both to save her and abandon her, not the brave assumption that had led him to borrow eighty thousand dollars of good American money so he could put himself through medical school, not even his career, won with such pain. And not his family either, not his sister or his parents, the color of their faces fading into the blurred gray of an old photograph, their voices gone from his ears.

He was already down the hall when he heard Karl Mike calling. "Where do you think you're going?"

"To the hospital."

"Jesus, it's midnight."

"Hospital still there." The smart rejoinder. Karl Mike had taught him how to do it.

With a determined stride, Lang hurried down the stairs, then outside where the damp air wrapped itself around him. Walk? It was three miles, and after the evening's events, his legs were wobbling. Decision made, Lang trotted to the parking lot and opened the door of his little Renault, an error since the day he had purchased it. Already sweating, he slid into the driver's seat and started up the engine.

Because he was thinking of other things—wet cloth,

long hair, all the ways in which his birth language could be spoken—he was almost all the way down Seawall Boulevard before he thought to look at the speedometer. It stood at fifteen miles an hour over the limit, and it already was too late. The patrol car turned in behind him from the parking area across the street, with its dome light snapping on and off. If the policeman had had the siren on, Lang hadn't heard it, but he pulled over as fast as he could, edging his curbside tires up until the hubcaps rubbed on the cement. "Damn it," he said to himself. *"Me Kiep!"* Sixty dollars and three points against him, something he knew because Karl Mike had had the same thing happen earlier that year.

Lang set his mouth in resignation and waited. In his back pocket was his wallet with his hospital ID card reinserted. But he was so near the hospital that the police would be accustomed to doctors' errors and probably not inclined toward mercy.

"License?" The policeman's face bent across his window.

Lang had it ready.

"Registration? Insurance?"

Lang had those too. He had lived in America long enough to be completely familiar with the words. He didn't argue either; he knew his accent might be off-putting, and he truly had been speeding.

"Other identification?" The officer's voice had dropped as he balanced his tablet on the edge of Lang's rolled-down window.

Lang gave him his hospital ID card. Hadn't his license been enough? But it was late. The policeman was just doing his duty.

"Another gook doctor, right?"

For a moment, Lang thought the policeman was talking to someone else.

"You guys, you come to our country and we put you through school, feed you, give you a good life you'd never have in that Vit-nahm." The policeman's voice was dreamy, soft, as if he were reciting a legend to children. "Buy your cars, drive down our streets, send our good money back to all your gook family in that Vit-nahm. You can take this here ticket to the judge and buy him off, you got plenty of cash to do it. You think you run this place, don't you?" He tore off the ticket, his fingers holding it carefully at one corner.

A motorcycle roared by, cutting so close that the officer had to press his belly against the side of the car. For a moment, in the lee of the motorcycle's intrusion, Lang thought that the policeman was going to open the door and climb on top of him. He braced himself.

The officer was saying something. All Lang could make out was the vowel sound, the "eeee" that would have been a shriek if it hadn't been spoken in such a soft voice.

"What?"

"Eeeeee." A hand reached toward the ignition.

"What?"

The hand fastened on the key, pulled it out. The other hand folded the ticket and tucked it into Lang's shirt pocket. The first hand lifted the ignition key out through the window and tossed it into the gutter.

"Dig, gook," the policeman said as he walked back to his own car. "Get your gook doctor clothes dirty for once." Lang's ears had come open as if a bubble had burst, and his own pulse banged with the whine of Seawall Boulevard traffic as the officer pulled away.

■ ■ ■

"I can't believe he'd say that."

"I not believe it either." Lang felt his English going out of control. He leaned against the counter at the nurses' station, holding his eyes down.

Shirley shook her head, her curls, edged in gilt, springing up under the fluorescent light. "You could report him. He deserves it."

"I not take his number."

"Dr. Adams says the Galveston police are pretty corrupt."

"Yes." There was a smear of dirt across his right knuckles from reaching under his car for the key. Lang felt a wash of raw humiliation.

"Dr. Nguyen, are you all right?"

He couldn't find the correct words to answer.

Shirley slammed shut the chart she had been going through and came out from behind the desk. Lang knew she wanted to comfort him in that awful American way. They were always making everything right with understanding words. No one here knew the dignity of silence.

"Dr. Nguyen?" She was holding a wad of Kleenex. "Let me wipe it off."

Dumbly, he extended his hand.

"I know Vietnamese are always clean," she said. "Hai Truong takes two showers every day. Even if she won't talk, she tries to keep herself nice."

Lang wrenched his hand back. "What's wrong?" Shirley asked.

She was just like every other dumb American. "Nothing," he mumbled.

[91]

"Are you angry?"

"I am not *just* Vietnamese."

"Are you part Chinese too?"

How could anyone with hair like the angels lack all perception? But he knew he shouldn't say anything in response. He was her superior, he a doctor and she a nurse. Karl Mike said anyone with blond hair and freckles was a good lay. What did that mean? What did all those terrible pieces of English mean?

Lang realized he was holding his hand up by his shoulder, palm open. Shirley's eyebrows were lifted and her face averted. Clearly she had been expecting him to slap her.

"I'm sorry." It was impossible for him to do the right thing or even to know what it was.

Her lips tightened. He realized she was older than he had thought. "It's my break," she said. "The cafeteria's still open. Would you like coffee?" She hesitated. "Sorry, I mean tea."

"I drink coffee too."

Without answering, she walked to the elevator and pushed the down button. Lang looked at her back, arched so tightly within her dress that the curve of her spine made a little hollow from which the outside fabric hung loose. He felt like touching it, seeing how far the material would fold inward before it moved against her flesh.

"Hai Truong is still not gaining any weight," she said, as if she knew he was coming up beside her.

"Is she better in her mind?"

"*I* think she's worse, but the doctors have had a hard time evaluating her. They may let her go if the shock treatments don't show any further results."

"Perhaps they should."

The bell for the elevator rang. Lang realized he had never given a proper answer to her invitation. "I come with you?" he asked, embarrassed because he was already halfway through the sliding doors of the elevator.

Shirley turned to him. "Of course," she said.

13 It had begun to seem like Vietnamese week at Carver School, and Azelita felt ready for a little holiday. She knew that arrangements had been made for the Vietnamese medical intern to talk to Xan next week, so perhaps the kung fu would disappear if everyone was lucky. But what about the Vietnamese girl who had materialized at the office counter that morning, absolutely silent? She was vaguely familiar, a fourth grader if Azelita remembered right, who lived in the projects. Hadn't been to school for three weeks, not a call, not a note, not a word.

Linh Nguyen. That was her name. And today she had returned to school, checked in at the office. "Good to see you," Azelita had said absentmindedly, thinking *weekend.*

"I am here."

"Were you sick?"

"No."

"Do you have a note from your mother?"

"My mother not write a note."

"Well, why don't you go to your class and we'll deal with it later. Come back after lunch."

Thinking Vietnamese now, Azelita opened the gate

around the office desks, stepped inside, locked the little lock behind her. Lunch hour was officially over. One down, that was Xan. Linh would be number two.

Azelita sighed. Coming up that night was the party at her African-American Methodist Dance Club. Against her best intentions, she'd given in to hair straightening and a perm for preparation, and now one front wave was poking out from her forehead. Since she'd been a teenager, she'd let her hair have its own mind, a real shock to her Beach Terrace friends. Now Afros were old-fashioned. Now all those niggers worked on their hair, drew pictures on their heads with razors, plowed and furrowed their scalps like Georgia plantations. She was going to let hers go back to natural as quick as she could. Prettifying it had been an error.

"Busy day, Azelita?" Ms. Hopkins moved one white hand along the countertop as she passed by from the cafeteria, stepping on to her own office. "You've got it all to yourself today." Ms. Hopkins, always weighted with responsibility, lifted her hand so smoothly that it would have been hard to notice that the counter had ended at exactly that point. She opened her office door with a practiced twist. "If there are any problems, you can contact me, Azelita," she said. "I need to finish this grant application for the teachers' aides." The door shut behind her.

Azelita nodded. She opened the top drawer of her desk and lined up the free lunch sign-up papers. She pried her sweaty thighs apart and rose to adjust the thermostat for the air conditioning. She checked the hours the librarian would be present, although they were the same as in the fall, and she knew them perfectly. The afternoon was going to drag, she could tell. She looked at the calendar centered on her desk under the leather frame of the blotter. Easter coming. The weather was hot already, at least today. Anybody who came back from the dead in Galveston had to bring his swim suit. Then the Spring Festival program for all the parents, with the children dancing and singing and making general fools of themselves and everyone else. Then summer, when she came in half days. Not even a decent vacation like the teachers.

As if a cloud had risen, a black line appeared over the edge of the office counter. Then a brown face. As the figure straightened, her neck encircled by a white turtleneck sweater despite the heat, Azelita realized that Linh was not just a little girl. Her figure was beginning to curve outward. Puberty must be affected by diet, thought Azelita, as she pushed herself back from her desk. And Linh was not all that short either, especially for a fourth grader.

"Linh, thank you for being on time."

Not a word.

"I just want to find out about your absences."

Still not a word. Linh's chin tilted down, then reversed its motion and came up again. Around her waist where the white turtleneck was tucked into her jeans, she had a bright red belt with a sequined buckle. There weren't enough holes, and she'd wedged the metal piece around the belt's edge and then back through again.

"Is something wrong at home?"

Silence. The girl looked almost Greek—foreign, definitely, but not Charlie Chan. And certainly not black.

Another tack. "Are you hungry? Would you like some M and Ms?" Azelita got the packet in the top drawer of her desk.

"No."

"No candy?"

"No." Then, in profile, "I go to my class."

"Not yet, hon. I need to write down a reason for your absences."

"Principal don't care."

Right on, little lady, Azelita thought. It wasn't in her to reprimand. She stood up. "Linh, wait," she said, reaching out for the brown arm in the white sleeve. Linh shrank back.

"No!"

"What?"

"Don't touch me!"

"Hey, hey, young lady. What *is* this?" Azelita swung out of her chair, past her desk, out through the little gate. She caught Linh by both shoulders, her palms flat. It was like touching a two-by-four.

"Linh, what's wrong?"

"Not wrong!"

"Are you sick?"

"Not sick!"

"Then why were you out of school for so long?"

Linh stood so still that her chest appeared not to go in and out. She had clamped her lips shut.

Azelita looked around. No imminent crises. She caught the ring of keys from the counter, tucked it into her pocket and turned Linh around. "Let's go for a walk, sugar," she said.

For a moment Linh stood solid, her face angled toward the door, her feet still heading in the other direction. It was as if a swivel had come into play around her hips. She could go either way, thought Azelita. But then Linh followed her face around and stalked out, leading Azelita with such firmness that the choice seemed to have been made by both of them. The first-grade teacher, returning from the washroom, passed them as they headed for the outside door. "Marching on Saigon?" she asked.

"No way," said Azelita, and then they were outside. Linh turned right on the sidewalk and continued marching. Azelita lengthened her pace and came up next to the girl.

"Sugar, what's up?" But that was an idiom Linh might not know. "Tell me what's wrong," she corrected, and waited. "You got trouble at home?" Was that a slight hesitation? "Something you can't get your mom to write a note about?"

"My mom don't write."

First step. "Could you just talk to me a little about things?" They had reached the corner of the block, where Linh turned, and they passed a cluster of oleander bushes, already rampant with blossom. The pink flowers spilled to the pavement, turning against each other in the breeze. Their clusters looked like corsages.

"I am a bad girl." Linh's head went down.

"You're what?"

"I am a bad girl."

"No, you're not."

They were at the next corner. Forward or back? Instead of doing either, Linh spun around and glared at Azelita. Then her face crumpled. "I burn rice!" she shouted, and then, in a whisper, "I clean and clean, but it not good. My mother say, 'Work, work,' but I don't work right. I don't do what my father says." Her voice cracked. "And now my mother will come home from the hospital and she will be angry with me. Maybe she have to go back!"

Azelita reached out, caught the stiff shoulders. Behind them, on the other side of the block, there must have been an early school recess—faint shouts in the air, boy and girl shouts, and the shuffle of feet. Her perm rose in the breeze, but she had no regrets. The Dance Club could just shut their eyes.

"Your mom's been sick, hasn't she?"

Linh nodded.

"Do you know what's wrong?"

Linh turned her head as if she were speaking to someone behind her. "She crazy," she said.

"She's what?"

"She crazy. The doctor says. She crazy in her head."

"The psychiatrist?" Probably the word was strange.

"They keep her there, in the hospital. They put things on her head for medicine. She go sleep, she wake up. She don't know my father." Her face was smooth as soap, the black hairline, brown forehead, brows, cheeks. "And now she will come home," she said, a wail in her voice but only serenity on her face.

"Sugar, it'll be all right." But that was no comfort. "Sugar, listen. It's not your fault. *You* didn't do it." Suddenly Azelita knew the right words, understood the problem, the *real* problem. "You're a good girl. Your mom loves you. Something's wrong in her head. She doesn't see you the way you are. *All* children, when their mothers get sick, think it's their fault. They blame themselves. But it *isn't* their fault. Not at all. They're just fine. You're just fine, sugar. You're fine."

A single tear moved down Linh's cheek, ruler straight. She didn't sob, snuffle, wipe. Her shoulders relented. That was all.

"We go back," she said. She moved over on the sidewalk, not much, just enough so Azelita could fit beside her. If she didn't start any dance steps too soon. If she held herself as firmly together as a two-by-four.

[99]

■　　■　　■

"What you doing, woman, sitting in that corner like some old panda bear?"

Azelita tilted her head away from the blare of the music so she could hear what the tall man was saying. "I waiting for all these niggers to clean up and go home," she said. "So I can lock up this place and get me some rest."

"You the key lady, am I right?"

"For tonight, I the key lady." Azelita stretched her legs, shiny in their nylon stockings, and wiggled her toes until her pumps teetered on their tips and dropped neatly to the floor. "Reverend McCauley figure he need somebody he can *trust*. I be on the top of the trust list. Carver School. Uncle Washington. African-American Methodist Dance Club. Wonder Galveston ain't made me mayor, I be so easy to trust."

"Maybe they vote you in when the next hurricane come." The man squatted beside her. "They elect you mayor, you make me chief of police. World be better off if niggers be in charge of everything."

One of his hands was moving toward her ankle, Azelita noted. "You got a name, man?" she asked, swinging around in her chair. "I ain't appointing Mr. No-Name to run *my* police department."

"Name's Wilson Freeman."

"Suppose you already know mine."

"That's right, woman. You be number one on the dance club program. Knowed who you were from the minute I walked myself inside."

"You be one smart nigger."

"That's why I so rich and pretty." His hand had stopped at one of her pumps. One finger moved up along its leather tip. Azelita felt a twinge where her nylons were stretched tight along her own toes.

"I don't got no liking for pretty boys."

"You the one to say." He had picked up her pump and was holding it gently in both his hands.

"What you doing with my shoe?"

"Thinking that for a big lady you got mighty little feet."

"Little feet and no brain or I'd be doing something better with my life than sitting in a school office all day and talking to you all night."

"Woman, I like a little hot sauce with my meat." He rose to his feet, holding her shoe out on his palm. "You got yourself two choices now, you know that? I can pour some punch into this shoe, and we can drink it down together. Commit ourselves to something right up front. Or I can slip it on your pretty little foot neat as the shoeman himself. Save you the trouble. You get to know me, I be good at saving you trouble."

"You be trouble without any saving." But Azelita held her foot out, not even trying very hard to hide the smile on her face. Wilson Freeman smiled back at her and dropped to his knees, the shoe still safe in his hand.

14

"I can't believe the diagnosis committee is going to have our ass on one series of ECT with a goddamn Vietnamese fisherman's wife!"

"Not necessarily your ass, Dr. Adams. Maybe just a finger or two. This place used to be known as the shock center of the southern coast. The reputation was just simmering down, but nobody forgot. All the administrators were just waiting."

"We ran it by the book. Notification. Signature. Proper medication. Unsuccessful series of by-mouth meds beforehand. They're just out to make trouble."

"Right." Shirley Nelson riffled through her charts, checking meds, checking dates. She pulled Hai Truong's chart, began to page through it. It had many blank spaces. Hard to make complete histories for a woman who never said an English word. Hard to know if shock was the right thing or not.

"Why doesn't the hospital support its own people?" Bryce Adams drummed his fingers on the counter of the nurses' station.

"They do," Shirley said. "In their own way. They're the most accountable for their patients."

"I should have dragged that Dr. Nguyen in to interpret."

"Maybe so," Shirley pushed the backs of the charts into an even line. Lang had told her that he hated to interpret. She wondered if he had told anyone else.

"Lord." Bryce reached for his cup of coffee, cooling and skimmed with gray. Grimacing, he took a mouthful. "How's she doing?" he asked.

"You saw her this morning. Hard to say."

"You're the one on duty."

"I saw her more on the late shifts. On the day rotation, the nurses are too busy." Shirley held Hai Truong's chart out to him and began to file the others in the chart hanger. In the hall by the elevators, an emaciated man with his hair in a braid began to pace back and forth, his hands stretched down the crease between his buttocks. He was a diagnostic mystery too.

She turned to Bryce Adams. "The committee may forget all about it," she said. "If *you* had time, you could look in on her," she added quietly.

"Once a day is enough. And it's been a good many of those days."

It was risky to challenge even a young doctor, but Shirley kept on. "You could just say hello from the door."

Bryce Adams snorted.

Suddenly, Shirley was angry. Psychiatry was the least gender-oriented of all medical specialties, man and woman being subject to the same psychic twists. But Hai Truong had had three children drawn out of her body. And she was tiny. It was easier to ignore her than it would have been to ignore a man. If Shirley hadn't spoken to Dr. Smith-Fragon herself, Hai would still be getting twice the necessary sleep medication. She weighed only eighty-nine pounds. "Normal dosage" wasn't normal to her.

"Want to go out tonight?"

"What?"

"Hamburgers, hot dogs, shrimp creole. Rent a bike and pedal the seawall. Wallow in the sand. Enjoy ourselves." He must have known her answer before she spoke it, because he was already on his way to the elevator, white coat pushing out behind him. He inclined his head in her direction.

"Some other time, Dr. Adams. And don't you have a girlfriend already?"

"Irrelevant. Don't turn me down too often. I'm going to be an overwhelmingly rich and respected psychoanalyst."

"I'll take that into consideration." Suddenly it was hard to smile, "But I'll make my own choice," Shirley added, and in the next second Lang walked around the corner from the Pediatrics wing, his black hair shining under the overhead light.

"Buy American!" Bryce Adams's voice was cut off in the middle of the final syllable as the elevator door slid shut. The emaciated patient watched its closure with interest while Lang came up to Shirley.

"How are you?"

"I'm fine." She began to take the charts off their hanger again.

The patient leaned on the counter next to Lang. "Buddha," he said, with a faint smile. His hands floated loose from his body.

"Might it be better if you went to the patients' rec room for a little?" Shirley asked him. She knew his name was Roger Hillsrud, but he never answered to it. She bent her head in his direction.

[104]

Roger Hillsrud continued to gaze at Lang. Lang focused on the opposite wall.

"Dr. Nguyen," Shirley began, but Lang was already moving away, starting down the hall as if she weren't there. Was he embarrassed by their encounter after the police incident? Was he thinking about the young Vietnamese girl in the ocean? Was he sorry he had told her any of it?

"You have a good day, Miss Nelson." He could have been talking to any staff person at all.

"Thank you, Dr. Nguyen," she said, irony in her voice. He disappeared, and the hall was empty. Roger Hillsrud sank into a chair in front of the patients' TV. He had been abandoned too.

A moment passed. Then Shirley locked the top drawer of her desk and walked down the hall to the patients' rooms, smiling appropriately at the aide who was delivering the filled-out menus for the dietitian. It was time to check her patients. One in particular. One who never watched television or used last names. *Any* names.

The door to Hai Truong's room was shut. Shirley knocked, tapping with the tips of her fingers. The aide should have checked. Closed doors could be dangerous.

No answer.

With a push harder than necessary, her wrist tense, Shirley shoved the door open with one hand as her other hand turned the knob. Hai was lying on her bed. Both her hands were tucked under her cheek against the pillow, her knees drawn up almost to her chest. She was wearing the black pants so many Vietnamese women seemed to wear, if you looked at the pictures, and another Goodwill blouse. Her little shoes were lined up on the floor. Thank

God her thin chest was going in and out. Her eyes were shut.

"Hai?" For someone else she'd have said Mrs. Truong. Or was it Mrs. Nguyen, after her husband? Was it sexist to use his name for her? Was *every* Vietnamese named Nguyen?

There was no answer, but under her lids Hai's eyes were rolling back and forth. She'd had her meds, if she'd actually swallowed them, but Valium was more a muscle relaxant than a narcotic. It seemed unlikely she'd be sleeping.

Shirley stepped nearer the bed. Surely Hai knew who she was—even with a memory deficit from the ECT. *"Hai!"* she said, louder.

Nothing.

Should she touch her? Shirley flexed her shoulder muscles, giving her hand permission. But before she could extend her arm, she saw moisture under Hai's eyelids. For a moment, she thought it was a medical problem, like excess phlegm, like incontinence. Then she realized that the wetness was tears. Hai was crying.

Briefly, Shirley wondered what to say. Foolishness. Instead, she moved over, slid herself down gently onto the bed. Her hand hovered, then lowered itself to Hai's shoulder.

"Hai, what's wrong?"

Hai's eyes opened. The tears, as if generated by a completely separate system, cut glistening slices down her cheeks.

"Hai?"

Nothing.

Shirley looked at her watch. She had half an hour before the ward meeting. In the hall, she heard the aides talking—duty was being discharged without her. The doctors were being official somewhere else. Hai was crying.

Gently, Shirley reached out and took Hai's hand. It was tiny and hard, not calloused but simply firm all the way through, as if the skin, flesh and bone were all of the same consistency. Hai didn't pull back or resist, but her hand stayed passive, willing to be picked up or put down, whatever the holder decided.

"Hai, sweetheart, what is it?" The intimate word came out without thought.

No answer. Even without Hai's permission, Shirley eased her upright as if she were a large doll. Automatically, Hai's legs moved under her body until she was sitting in the yoga position, bare feet tucked into the tender spaces behind the knees. Her arms hung limp. The tears fell in splotches on the front of the Goodwill blouse. Shirley reached for the Kleenex box on the bedstand, then held back. There was nothing evil about tears.

"Hai, can I help you?" But of course Hai couldn't answer. One hand reached into the air and snatched at nothing. The fingers passed through a frond of her hair on the way down.

Suddenly Shirley knew. Hair was the key. She pulled her legs up under herself too, not as hard a task as one might think, for which she thanked a natural suppleness. She squatted next to Hai, a little behind, not touching her but not refusing the possibility. She felt like half of a clam shell. From the pocket of her jacket, she pulled her comb, a brown plastic one. "Shall I comb your hair, Hai?" she asked, and she began to move the comb through the long black tangle. She was very careful not to pull, not to force, and when she got to a snarl or the beginnings of a snarl, she eased the comb up against it and loosened the twisted

[107]

hairs a bit at a time. It wasn't fine hair, but it wasn't coarse either, and not as oily as it might seem.

Hai began to sway a little, back and forth, but there was no tension in the swaying, and even though she was still crying—if that was what it was when tears washed down your face without having to be choked back against pride, pain, resistance—her eyes were open and her hands clasped in her lap. Shirley combed and combed, working her way along the side of Hai's head, and when she put her hands against the temples and moved the skull slightly, Hai shifted her whole body, like a bird on a wire, so Shirley could move on and do the other side too.

It was a peaceful act, Sunday dinner around the family table on any side of the world, tying a three-year-old's shoes, watching the sunset over the rice paddies, sisters taking care of each other, a mother, a daughter. It required no language. Short-term memory loss was irrelevant.

My head hurts. Like before. My head hurts.

The doctor says Hihihi. I forget him. I forget when he comes in the room. He points at my head, and I forget him.

The Vietnamese doctor comes. He is not my husband. Not any husband. He talks to me. I forget him too.

What I remember is from before. I remember from before.

My mother came to the beach with us. I held her hand. I kissed her gold locket. I said, "Con kinh trong ma. I honor you, my mother, for all time."

She put her hands on little Linh's cheeks. She said she would light the joss sticks. She said we would have much money in America.

Then we went to the docks. It was black, the no-moon

time. I had the clothes for Linh, my sweater, the picture of my wedding to Phuong. It had cost us three million dong, that wedding. All my cousins from Te Mon came. My mother wore her black ao dai. Phuong was happy.

In the dark night, Linh slept in my arms. We went under the docks, in the mud and shells. On top, Phuong walked and laughed with the other fishermen, like on any night. They made it look like any night so the police would not know. They talked about New Year's, about Tet. They put the nets in their boat like always.

My head hurts.

Then the others came. They were very quiet. It was full under the docks, and I was tight among the men and women. Linh woke up, and I gave her my breast. My legs were like wood, and my teeth banged in the damp. One of the other women was crying for her mother. Her husband hit her two times. Then she prayed, but in a little voice.

When the right time came, we crawled out. Phuong and his friends made noise like they were drunk so no one could hear us. They yelled and stumbled, but not too much. We all crept into the boat. I saw my mother on the beach one last time. She was watching us. I held Linh up so they could see each other to remember.

When my mother dies, I will not be with her. I am her only daughter. My cousins will be the ones to wrap her in white. Perhaps she will die and I will never know.

Then we were going. All of us lay belowdeck, our faces in the dirty water. No one could see us. The boat was heavy. The engine was tired, pulling us out to sea. Linh was asleep. At first I thought she was dead, she was so quiet. But when I put my finger on her throat, I could feel it move.

The waves were her cradle. She slept in their rocking. Nothing hurt her.

Day came. And night. I couldn't tell. We could go up on deck, but there was no room to lie down there. The air smelled of diesel. Linh wanted to crawl back and forth, but I was afraid she would fall into the water. She screamed and pulled my hair. Then she was sick. She smelled so bad. I had no more milk for her. One of the women had brought some roots, but we had no good water to make tea for a baby. Linh cried and cried.

"Hay Can dam len!" said Phuong. "Be brave! We can do it." He watched the edge of the sky. Sometimes he held Linh with one arm and the wheel with the other. He gave me his water.

My head hurts. Did the American doctor come? I forget everything.

There were many days. I think the compass was broken. Then one morning we saw another boat. There were birds too, white ones, and they sailed above our boat like its soul. We were so happy because we were near land. I washed Linh's face with water from the sea. I thought of rice and oranges. I thought of my mother.

The other boat came closer. They shouted at us. We all stood and waved; we all hung on to the rails. They would help us. They would give us water and show us the way to America. I held Linh up high. "See your uncles!" I said. "They will give you what you need."

In a little while, the boat was next to us. Phuong threw a rope to them. But then we saw their faces up close, and they were not Vietnamese faces. The men had fat cheeks. Their bodies were too small. With fear we all looked at each other. They were the Thailand pirates, and they would kill us all.

I ran below with Linh. I hid under the engine. Hot grease ran down my back, but I made no sound. I put my dry breast in Linh's mouth so she couldn't cry, and I prayed with my whole being that my mother would save us. I prayed to my father's spirit too, because I had always been the one he loved most. Before he died, he gave me my earrings of gold and jade. I wore them always. I was wearing them now.

"Hay tha cho chung toi!" I heard Phuong say. "Spare us!" Then I heard him offer money. Then there was much noise. I made myself small. I held Linh to me. The other women cried, but I made no sound. I prayed for my husband and my child. I asked my ancestors to protect me. I held the hand of my mother.

My head hurts. I forget the rest. I shut my mind to it. I felt only when they ripped my ears for the gold, I put my head in another place. What they did was to wood. I was wood.

They made my husband watch.

When they left, they took Linh and threw her into the ocean. Phuong jumped in after her. The Thailand pirates laughed and shouted. When he came up with her, they hit him with the steering pole. They broke his shoulder, but he held Linh and did not sink. They left him and went to their own boat.

Two days more and we came to the camp in Malaysia. No one died.

15 Lang checked the address that he'd copied down when they'd called from Carver School about talking to the Vietnamese boy. The projects. Beach Terrace, Palm Terrace, Oleander Homes. One bleak set of brick buildings after another, built only to two stories so they'd look homelike. Little American villages. Grass trampled into pulp, then into clay and finally into dust that rose if you walked in it. Half his patients came from the projects. Sometimes when the patient was Vietnamese, he had to interpret, though he no longer liked to. They were all like Trang, peasants from peasant villages. They weren't polite. They said inappropriate words. When he interpreted, he had to clean things up a little. Although it angered him, he was responsible for them as countrymen.

Lang pulled his Renault to the curb by the west side of Beach Terrace and got out. Even here in the middle of the island, the air tasted of salt, moisture, filth. But it was a familiar taste, and it must seem so to this Xan Van boy as well. Did they call him "Dan" in school? Whoever had called him for assistance had had to spell the boy's name out. His own last name they called "New-gin," never

"Win." He had given up correcting them.

Lang walked across the trampled grass to the right door, where there were three pairs of thong sandals. Vietnamese house, all right. There was no doorbell, so he banged the mailbox cover set into the wall. A black girl with blue rubber bands around her many braids looked at him as she skipped past outside. "You want them Chinese?" she asked.

He didn't answer her. Did he not look Asian himself?

"You a doctor?" she asked, her hands on her hips. She grinned, her bright pink tongue floating between her teeth. "You look like them doctors," she said. "*Lots* of doctors in Galveston." She stretched out her arms. "Maybe I be a doctor when I grow up."

Embarrassed as to whether he should encourage the girl or not, Lang was grateful when the door slowly opened. At first it seemed as if no one was there, but then out of the darkness, with the eye of the television blinking, he saw a man and woman. She was pregnant, and probably no prenatal work-ups either. They looked at him with a combination of delight and puzzlement.

"Is Xan home?" Lang asked. They were beckoning him inside even as he spoke.

"You want my son?" The accent was northern, rough. Lang noticed that the little finger of the father's left hand was missing to the first knuckle. The Communists used to do that as punishment.

"Yes." Already the mother was hurrying upstairs, her heavy body swaying as she climbed.

"He is in his room. My wife will bring him." No question, no exploration of his purpose. "Come, have some beer."

Lang refused politely.

[113]

"Soda, then. Coke? Orange?" The father stood at a respectful distance, but he had still managed to edge Lang toward the sofa.

"No thank you."

"Tea then?" His tone was becoming desperate. The teapot, chipped along its edges, sat on the coffee table, the Chinese cups on the plastic tray next to it.

"All right." Lang lowered himself. At the edge of the room under the front window, a mouse raced across the floor. A second mouse followed it.

"Good!" The father poured a cupful and handed it to Lang. "I am happy you come to my house," he added. The foreshortened finger stuck out from his hand as he gestured, and Lang found he could not take his eyes from it.

"I want to talk to your son."

"Good! Talk to my son!" The father leaned closer. "What is your village?" he asked. His shoulders were heavy for a Vietnamese.

"I come from Can Tho."

"Ah!" The father smiled broadly. "When I have money, I go there every year at Tet to see my cousins."

Tet. The dragon parade. The altars. The new year. "My parents still live there," Lang said.

"Ah! When will you bring them to America?"

But they would be miserable here, Lang thought, as he held the cup in his two hands and looked at its brown-stained inner surface. "I don't know," he answered, feeling a surge of guilt.

The man rose. "I am sorry," he said. "I am Phuoc Van. My village is Ha Tien. Welcome to my house."

"Lang Nguyen."

"You work here?"

"I am a doctor," said Lang.

The man's eyes opened wide. "Ah!" he said again, and then, with a clatter on the stairway, a boy like the father in miniature arrived in the living room. His sneakers were untied and flapping. "My son," said Phuoc Van. "You help him, Doctor." Clearly the father had translated the entire issue into some mysterious medical problem, and his expectations were high. Except for the arrival of another Vietnamese, the contact the school must have made with him had communicated nothing.

"May I take him for a drive?" Suddenly Lang felt an overwhelming desire to leave, and he regretted only that the boy would have to go with him.

"Of course." Phuoc Van sprang to his feet and hurried to the door. He bowed as he pulled it open. "Goodbye," he said in English as he ushered the two of them outside.

The little boy who followed Lang out to the old Renault didn't say a word, even when Lang began his own careful speech in simple nonregional Vietnamese so there wouldn't be any dialect problem. In fact, the child hardly looked up. Deaf? Attention deficit problem? Who would know? He sat himself on the passenger side of the front seat and allowed the seat belt to be put on him without argument, his torso square and hard against the upholstery. Lang noticed the scabbed knuckles and also a reddened area on his cheek. Child abuse? The very words sounded foreign to him. Vietnamese parents always hit their children. He remembered his own father chasing him with a stick, making the air whir as he'd lashed at him. But afterward his mother had made shrimp pancakes for supper, his favorite.

The car slid through the light as it turned red, which Lang hadn't noticed. Guilty, he looked down at Xan, who flashed him just the edge of a grin, then dug his chin back into his collarbone.

Lang took the initiative. "Trouble in school?" he asked. He addressed Xan as "Little Brother," incorporating him into a family structure. It was the appropriate thing to do.

There was no response. Xan grabbed the seat belt as if he were going to undo it, but he didn't.

"Are you unhappy?" It was not a Vietnamese question, and it sounded strange in the language. No answer to that either.

Lang stopped talking and turned the car toward the seawall. Below him, not yet in sight, was the gulf. The street pointing ahead ended in air, a rickety restaurant on one side, the Tern Motel on the other.

"Do you know who I am, Little Brother?"

Xan rubbed his eyes with one hand.

"I am Vietnamese, just as you are. I am a doctor at the hospital here." Lang paused. "Where are you from?"

Nothing. But the rigid chin raised itself a little.

"I myself am from Can Tho. I have cousins who are fishermen like your father." Lang would not normally have spoken of them, little dark men who gambled away all they earned. "I used to visit them," he said, waiting.

From the tight mouth came four words. They were not what Lang had expected. "Is your father dead?" Xan asked.

The car had reached the curtain of sky and turned onto Seawall Boulevard. To their left was the ocean. Yesterday at night a storm had swept over the island, and the waves were brown now from the torn-up sand. Spume crashed along their peaks. Halfway out along the breakwater, a surfer emerged on his board, swept down, reappeared. His wet suit made him look like a sea creature. Lang yanked the car back from the parking lane into which it had drifted.

"No, my father is alive."

"How you know?"

"Because I write letters to him."

"I think they are all dead."

Lang pulled the car to the curb. Xan's fists were clenched in front of him on the dashboard. Then, suddenly, tears burst from his eyes.

"Xan!"

The boy was grabbing the door handle.

"Dung ngay! Stop it!"

Xan plunged out the door, landing on his knees on the sidewalk, then leaping to his feet, Lang grabbed for him and then jumped out onto the street side, narrowly missing a passing pickup, to race after the boy as he hightailed it down the sidewalk. Two middle-aged American women, rolls of fat at the waists of their sunsuits, were riding one of the double seawall tricycles toward him, but Xan seemed oblivious and charged by. Lang felt a wild rage at the inappropriateness of a doctor chasing a boy down the sidewalk in front of everyone. And a Vietnamese boy!

A stairway led down to the sand. Xan was on it. His foot missed the edge of a step, and as Lang tore after him, he landed headfirst in the sand amid a tangle of Styrofoam cups, pop bottles, and picnic debris. Full of anger at what seemed to be an unending rescue operation for small Vietnamese, Lang flung himself on top of the boy.

"What are you doing, fuck it!" There was no more Little Brother.

"I hate them! All! And now my father hit me!"

Lang held his shoulders down, squatted over the boy's

body. The impulse to violence shook him, but he twisted it back. He willed his energy into his arms, into his hands on the boy's upper arms. Xan crumpled.

"Tell me what the matter is." Lang's thumbs loosened, moved in circles on the shoulders of the boy's T-shirt.

"I hate them all! No food! My mother sends me away! My aunt hates me! I eat her garbage!" The boy's fists flexed as if they were going to punch, but he simply trailed the dirty sand with his knuckles.

"Your aunt?"

"Hong Kong."

It didn't make sense. "How old were you?" Lang asked. It was a foolish question. To Vietnamese children, age didn't matter. But Xan was an American boy now. Long ago, Lang had learned to volunteer his own age as if it defined him, Twenty-eight. The Americans liked it that way.

"I go on the boat. I was six. My mother sent me. My father was in America. My mother had money only for one."

"You came to America alone?" Lang shifted his weight. His right leg was cramping.

"No. Hong Kong. To my aunt. I worked for her."

"For how long?"

No answer. The boy's fingers clutched the sand.

"But your mother did come?"

"Yes. Later."

"And you came to your father in America."

"Yes."

Lang thought of what the lady from Carver School had told him over the phone. Xan was probably twelve. He'd come to America with his mother sometime in the last year, to Galveston sometime around Christmas. Before that they'd been in a camp in the Philippines. A year. The arithmetic was coming clear. At least five years alone with some aunt in Hong Kong. *Five years.*

"Are you happy to be here?" Lang asked, knowing the answer, knowing that there was no answer.

Underneath him, Xan was wiggling, pulling himself up to a sitting position among the beach discards, digging his hands into the sand like a baby as he crawled into the cave of Lang's arms and hung on to his shirt. Adjusting to the boy's presence, Lang patted the sturdy little back. He had forgotten his handkerchief, and of course Xan didn't have one.

When he was done crying, and it didn't take long, Xan straightened his shoulders, his neck, lifted his head. His shoulders went back. "You're a doctor," he said, not as a question.

"Yes. Dr. Lang Nguyen." No doubt about the pronunciation here.

"Vietnamese can be doctors in America." That wasn't a question either.

"Yes."

Xan put his hands straight down at his sides like a soldier and stood up. *"I* will be a doctor," he said. Then he jumped into the air sideways, kicking so hard that one flopping sneaker burst loose. "But *first* I kung fu all bad people," he shouted.

I don't know what they want. Teacherteacherteacher. All the time they say words, comegolunchstandup. I watch the others. I watch them all the time. I do what they do. But I too slow. The lady come to me. She smell like dead flowers. She make noises. My ear shut up. I see her mouth like a fish. I don't hear it.

The other children. They all colors. Dirty skin. First day, they just look. Then they not look anymore. Then they poke me, they laugh, they put fingers in mouth. They make bad sounds with their bottoms. They say dirtychink-dirtychink. My name is Xan! Nobody say my name right.

My legs very strong. I see kung fu on TV. On TV, the Vietnamese men do it. I fight with my feet. I kick out their teeth. I want to.

My father go away to America. He not want to live with us. My mother send me to Hong Kong. She tell me help my aunt. My aunt make me take care of her baby. I bad boy. I eat baby's food. I steal money, but only a little bit money. My aunt hit me with her fists.

Then my mother come. Her face always angry. We go on a boat to camp with many people. My friend teaches me fighting. I like it.

Now we live in Galveston. I am bad boy. My father hit me. When I see him, I afraid. He know I am bad boy. He whip me with stick. No food in icebox because it is broken. We eat only rice.

I talk to Vietnamese Linh. I talk to Vietnamese doctor. Maybe they like me, but I not sure. Maybe they pretend.

Please, Grandfather, teach me what I need. I don't know it. I kung fu too much.

I so hungry.

16

"You *big* Vietnamese girl."

"You shut up, Xan."

"I kung fu you."

"You don't kung fu people anymore."

Xan paused. "Not *all* people," he said. "Dr. Nguyen don't want it." He raised one leg tentatively, then pulled it back. "You like Carver School?" he asked.

"It's okay." Linh could tell he was trying to be good.

"You study hard."

"Yes."

"You live in Beach Terrace like me?"

"Xan, you know where I live."

"Your mother crazy."

"My mother is *sick.*" Linh paused. "But she is coming to live in our house again."

The two of them sat on the steps going down from the front door of the school. It was late on Friday. All the other children were walking home, were halfway there, maybe almost all the way. Linh had been helping her teacher straighten the writing tables because then she got to keep the broken crayons for Harry and Gary. Xan had stayed to work on the new spelling list and hang the rope in the gymnasium. They had come out the door together. It was easier to talk sitting down.

"How old are you?"

"I am ten years old. You know that."

"You too big girl for ten."

"My paper says ten years old."

"Your paper don't say true. When you born?"

"*Cop.* Year of the Tiger."

"Then you twelve."

Linh didn't say anything in response. Already her blouses were tight across the front, and Eric, the black boy who sat across the aisle from her, kept trying to touch her when they stood up for the Pledge of Allegiance. She was almost as big as Trang, and Trang was in high school already.

"Maybe I am ten on paper too. So I can go to school more years and learn good English. But I'm not ten." Xan grinned. "I'm an old smart man," he said.

He was sweating. Under his T-shirt, his shoulders stuck out like a football player's. His fingernails were dirty, but his hands looked pretty clean. Linh thought he must have washed them on purpose.

"My father is coming to school soon," Xan said.

"Why?"

"Give shrimp to my teacher."

"Why?" Linh checked her own fingernails, which were satisfactorily clean.

"Say thank you. Because Dr. Nguyen talk to me." A little smile started on Xan's face. "My *father* is crazy," he said.

Linh nodded.

"*I* not crazy." His face had a look of mild puzzlement.

"I smart," he said. Then, "When you grow up, you go to college?"

"College is expensive." Linh savored the big word.

"If you smart, they give you money."

"Who?"

"The American president."

"He doesn't know me."

"He writes you letter. You don't even say thank you."

"Who says?"

"My teacher Mrs. Fillmore. She says we work hard, we get money from the president." Xan slapped his big hands together.

Behind them, the door opened. The art teacher came out the door, her folder under her arm. "Aren't you two going home?" she asked, but she didn't wait for an answer. She walked down the sidewalk and over to the parking lot.

"Who you marry?" Xan was looking at the flagpole, his chin tilted up so high that Linh could see the lump go up and down when he swallowed.

"What?"

"Who you marry?"

"I am too young!"

"I know."

A ragged man pulling a wagon walked by the school, his free hand waving in the air. His wagon had so many garbage bags heaped on it that it looked as if he were pulling a fat person on wheels. The man kept glancing back to make sure the wagon was following him, and each time he did, he smiled a big smile that split his brown beard in two and wiggled toward his cheekbones.

"I will never marry," said Linh.

"Everybody marry."

"Not in America." She started to retie her sneakers, making the bows perfectly equal from one side to the other and tucking the plastic ends of the laces into what was left of the nearest holes that the laces went through. "That black lady in the office doesn't marry," she said.

"How you know?"

"She run her own life," said Linh, the words surprising her as they came out. The ragged man was turning the corner of the playground, edging the wagon around behind him. "I want to live by my own self," she finished.

"You won't have rice."

"I will buy my own rice."

"How you get the money?" Xan had been to school long enough to know that girls could get money just like men in America. Linh was so big, she might start getting it even sooner than he would.

As if a decision had been made, Linh rose too. "I will go to college," she said. "I can be nurse, doctor, artist. I buy my parents two houses. I buy red car for me."

"Maybe your mother dead by then." Xan's hands clung to the sides of his jeans.

Linh looked at him so hard he teetered on the steps. "I take care of my mother," she said.

17 "Why you crying?"

"I'm *not* crying." Trang turned toward the window so her cousin couldn't see her eyes.

"Okay." Tri took a big bite of the noodles in his bowl, the loose ends dangling off his chopsticks as he fed them into his mouth. "Where's your noodles?"

"I ate them."

"Such a little bit!"

"That's all I wanted."

Tri stuffed in some more noodles. A fleck of carrot appeared on his upper lip, and he licked it off. "Where'd Mama go?"

"She's not my mama."

"I *know.* I know you're just my cousin, not my sister, but we're all family, like in Vietnam."

"It's *not* like Vietnam."

Tri slurped up his last bunch of noodles, then lifted the bowl and finished off the brown sauce. He pushed back his chair and got up to put his empty bowl on the counter next to the sink where dirty dishes, discarded chopsticks and food leavings piled high. He shoved the bowl into the collection, then joined Trang at the window. They stood together.

"I'm almost as tall as you are."

"So what?"

"I always think you're bigger than I am."

"I stopped growing, Cousin Tri. You still grow. That's why you get bigger."

"If you ate more noodles, you'd grow too."

Trang glared at him, her eyes narrowed. "Your mother thinks I eat *too much*. She wants me to be little, little, little. She wants me to disappear!"

Tri was quiet. Down below on the street, the ice cream man was forlornly pedaling, dinging his little bell. It was still early for the ice cream man, even though the air hung moist and warm.

"Trang?"

"What?"

"You remember the camp."

She didn't reply.

"You remember how they gave us clothes?"

"Rags."

"They gave me a shirt with a horse on it."

"And you lost it."

"No I didn't! My father took it for the boat while I was sleeping. And we were already in America."

Trang remembered sleeping in the camp. They had strung a dirty blanket from rope salvaged in the wreck so the people passing by couldn't see in. It made their square of space dark and hot, and dusty too so that her hair had always been grayed with layers of grit. No one gave her a comb, not her uncle, not the people at the table who wrote down everything you said, so she had used her hands to smooth the long dark strands. At night when she curled on her mat in the corner, she turned her fingers into little tunneling mice that worked their way down through the surface and undid the mats underneath.

That was when her aunt was in the camp hospital. Since the shipwreck, she hadn't eaten. She lay curled up like her stomach hurt, but there was no food in her stomach. When they had taken her to the camp hospital, they carried her on a cot like a dead person.

"Trang?" Tri was talking, and she hadn't been listening.

"What?"

"My father says you cook good."

Trang shut her eyes.

"I think you cook good too. Shrimp pancakes. *Banh cuon.* Dumplings for Tet."

A little smile came out on Trang's face. She put her arm around Tri. He held an old toy truck in his hand, his favorite plaything, one that he'd brought all the way from the camp even though that had been years ago. The top of the cab had broken off, like the American jeeps. Suddenly she remembered the jeeps near her village. They hadn't needed tops because the soldiers in them wore roofs on their heads. Metal roofs that gleamed in the sun.

"Trang?"

"Yes?"

"I liked it at the beach with you. The day you saw the nun." Tri ran the truck along the table. "You go again?" he asked.

She hesitated. "I went one more time," she said.

"Did you go in the water?"

There was a long pause. "A little," she said.

Tri tilted his head back against her even though he was too big to be a child anymore. He held his truck up to the light from the window. She knew he was going to ask something more, maybe several things. She waited.

"Is Vietnam still there?"

"Of course."

"But we're not there."

"That doesn't matter. It stays where it is."

"How do you know?"

"I'm old. I know lots of things."

"Did they teach you those things in America or in Vietnam?"

"Both places."

Tri put his truck down and started to pick at the plastic cover on the table, digging at the edges of the hole that his father had burned with his cigarette. The edges were still charred, and the plastic opened back like a little mouth.

"Don't do that. Your mother won't like it."

Tri kept digging.

"Don't do that."

"Is my brother Tuan still there?"

Trang's voice stayed even. "Where?" she asked.

"Where we put him. In the sand. After the water killed him."

Trang felt the pulse in her forehead begin to beat. "He must be," she said.

"Will we go back and get him out?"

"He's not alive anymore."

"Can the doctor fix him?"

"No, nobody can fix him." She couldn't say the word that would mean he was truly gone.

"They can't fix him even in America?"

"No."

"I remember him. He used to give me sticky rice."

"Yes."

"He didn't have any clothes on when we put him in the hole in the sand."

"The waves took them."

"He had cuts."

Trang's voice was almost a whisper. "I know," she said.

Tri lifted his hand from the tablecloth and stood up. "Your mother is my mother's sister," he said.

"Yes."

"So my mother is your aunt."

"Yes, she is. You know that."

Gently, Tri moved his hand toward Trang's hair. It was bad luck to touch a girl's hair, so he didn't. Instead he held his fingers in the air like a little tree, slanted against the wind.

"Why isn't your hair black like mine?"

"Because my father was an American." She had never said it to Tri before.

"Can we go visit him?"

The ice cream man had finished the block and was coming back past their house. Down the street at Beach Terrace, two black boys were waiting for him. The black children in the project always got money from somewhere.

Trang rose. "I've got money too," she said. "I'll buy you ice cream."

"Where'd you get money?"

Trang buttoned Tri's shirt where it had come open and straightened his collar, even though Tri was big enough to do it for himself. "I am *bui doi*," she said. "I steal. I took it from under your father's pillow."

When I was a baby, I was the only baby in my family. No one talked about my American father. My grandfather came to my house and took me with him for all day because he loved me so much. When he was dying, he told my mother and her new husband not to bring me to him. He didn't want little Trang to be sad. When they put him in the graveyard, my mother wouldn't let me go with them. I cried and cried. I thought he had gone away without me.

Then I was ten years old. My mother was at the market. I was watching my little brother and sister. My mother's husband came to me. His face was dark. He said, "Tonight you go stay with your uncle and aunt."

I liked my uncle and aunt. They had two boys, Tri and Tuan. Tuan was the older. He always drew pictures in the sand for me. I said yes to my mother's husband and ran to my uncle's house in the next village. I went down a long road with trees on each side. The birds were singing. My mother's husband had given me pancakes with meat inside. He said to save them, but I ate three right away. Only one was left.

At my uncle's house, my aunt was crying. Tri and Tuan and I played in the yard. We did gambling, only we didn't have any money. I lost, and I had to give them my last pancake. Tuan shared his piece back with me.

Then it got dark. My aunt came out. She said, "We are going to sleep on the beach tonight."

That was a new thing! I helped her carry the blankets. The beach was not far. My mother's husband and my uncle were both fishermen, so they lived near where the fish were. When we got to the beach, I helped spread the blankets. Tri and Tuan made a big temple in the sand. Then Tri wanted Tuan to lie down so he could cover him up in the sand. Tuan was always nice to his little brother, but he didn't want to lie *down. Tri started to cry. I put my arm around him.*

After that, the moon came out over the water. I lay down on my blanket, but the others didn't. Some more people came. First there was a fire, but they put it out. They looked out at the ocean. I was so sleepy. But then my uncle picked me up. My aunt took Tri, and Tuan walked by himself. We walked into the waves! I was frightened. Then we saw a boat come. It was a fishing boat like my mother's husband's. It came near us. We went out to it, the big people walking and carrying the children. We climbed in. It smelled so bad of fish and diesel, and the engine was coughing. We crouched on the deck and held on to each other. I thought it was funny that the ladies were going fishing. It is not good luck for ladies to go on fishing boats. Thuy Tinh, the goddess of the sea, doesn't like it.

When we were all settled, the boat turned into the big waves. I was so sick. I threw up and threw up. Tuan held me so I wouldn't fall over. Tri was sick too. My uncle helped with the engine. My aunt cried. Then she lay down underneath the deck and curled up. She didn't cry anymore.

In the morning, the sun was like fire. The next morning was the same. On that day, the engine stopped working. My uncle took all its parts out. His fingers bled, and his nails wore off. I was sick again. I tried to fall into the water. Tuan held me back. He sang me the old song about white birds. His voice was funny, like sand. He sang and sang. I went to sleep.

We were in the boat for days and days. Sometimes the engine worked, sometimes it didn't. The rice was gone. The water was almost gone. We each had one drink of it in the morning. Tuan gave me part of his. He was the oldest son. He wanted to take care of all his family, and I was his cousin.

Then the skies got dark, darker than night. The wind came. We couldn't hear each other, just the wind. No one heard me cry. The engine broke again. We went up and down, up and down. It was like mountains falling. My uncle took a rope and tied it around my wrist, around Tuan's and Tri's wrists, around my aunt's wrist. The other people tied ropes too. If anyone fell into the water, we could pull him back. If the boat turned over in the water, we would all die together. Then we would not be lonely. Our spirits would live in one house.

The rope hurt my wrist. I cried. Tuan held me.

Then I saw the dolphins come. There were six for each side of the boat. When the dolphins die on the beach in Vietnam, we bury them like people. Everyone cries. Now they came to help us. They slid under the boat and moved it forward through the waves. They were black in the water. They took us far. They started the engine of the boat again. On the edge of the sky, we saw birds, then the dark line of the land. The storm was over. The dolphins were gone.

"America!" my aunt said. Her hair was wild on her head. "America!"

"No, Mama," Tuan said. He untied his wrist and touched her. "But land. America will come."

We got as near as we could. My uncle held the wheel. The engine was coughing again like a sick person. My uncle prayed. We could see the beach and the palm trees, but the boat wouldn't go in. The waves broke on it. We swung around sideways, and my uncle couldn't turn it. The engine stopped.

"In! In!" my uncle shouted. He held the boat straight. The people began to jump. Their black heads dotted the waves. My uncle held Tri. Then they were both gone. Tuan was gone. My aunt had big eyes. She jumped, but she hit the boat on the other side. Blood came. A wave covered her.

I stood on the deck. I was ten years old. I could not swim. The boat went up and down like a crazy thing. Someone was on the shore, waving. Did he see me? I couldn't stand up anymore. My head was dizzy. A big wave came. It ate me up. I was gone in it.

Then I was on the shore. My uncle was screaming. In his arms he was holding Tuan. Tuan's head was cut in half. "Who helped you?" he screamed at me. "Who helped you? Why didn't they help my son instead?"

"Nobody helped me," I said. Salt was in my mouth. All the people were crying. "Nobody helped me!" I screamed. I screamed and screamed. Nobody came to hold me. My aunt was on the sand. They put bandages on her. Tri sat like a little boy by her. All his clothes were wet.

My uncle walked on the sand holding Tuan's body. Then he fell down on his knees. He laid Tuan by him with his arms straight. He dug in the sand with his own hands. He dug too much. He dug. The men came to help him, but he said bad words. He chewed his own arm. His face was white like a ghost face. He dug a deep hole. Then he put Tuan in it. Tuan had no clothes on. The waves had eaten them. He had big cuts on his body. My uncle covered Tuan with sand.

18 "But who was it?" Lang rubbed his hand across his eyes. It was after midnight, and he had been working since hospital rounds at seven that morning.

"Jesus, Lang, I have no idea. Someone small. A girl. That's all I know. By the time I got into the hall, she was hell and gone around the corner."

"You didn't look out the window after? To see where she came out?"

Karl Mike put his hands in front of his eyes like binoculars. "Sure I looked out the window. Ran inside like a flash of lightning and looked. Took her large paper deposit with me. But whoever it was wasn't driving any car. Every metal machine was just sitting in place. Not a sign."

"She must go out through the lot."

"Not if she went down to the basement. Or through the emergency exit. I just hope no one's planning to do you in, Win-Win. Wouldn't be that hard in this apartment building. Wouldn't be easy to pick up any witnesses. Better watch your act and keep your nose clean."

Lang reached up and touched his nose. He always washed his hands before he left the hospital, but not always his face. Perhaps he should do that too. Americans cared about cleanliness in surprising ways.

"Jesus, not your *nose!*" Karl Mike shouted. "Not your nose as in 'n-o-s-e.' That's an idiom. It doesn't mean what it says."

"But my nose is clean?"

"Just forget it."

"What?"

"Just *forget* it, Lang. It's too late for even my famous interpreting skills. Put your energy on who the Bag Deliverer is. It looks like she has some special interest in you. Otherwise, why would she be leaving large soggy packages at your doorstep?"

Eyes half shut, Lang slid down into the lounge chair just inside the doorway. The package, a chunky grocery bag, stayed in his line of vision. Despite all his years at school in Galveston, despite his efforts to be polite to everyone, he really was not friends with many people. Karl Mike, who grew on him like a coconut. Bryce Adams, a little bit. Julian at the pharmacy, but they only went out to lunch together once every two months. And for a little while, Shirley.

"Are you thinking or sleeping?"

"I am thinking."

"Well, at least this time it wasn't a machine gun."

"No."

"Although next time it might be. The little yellow people will try anything."

Lang sprang to his feet. Exhaustion made him dizzy, and the florid hanging on the wall above the sofa waved in zigzag layers behind his eyes. "What you mean, 'little yellow people'?"

"What do *you* mean what do I mean? You *know* what I mean."

"I thought you say she American."

"I didn't say anything about what she was. It was a miracle of my alert body and quick mind that I even knew it was a *she*. But she was a smallish one, and the hair was dark. Maybe not black, but dark. I figure if anyone is delivering you mysterious parcels, it'd be one of your mysterious countrymen." Karl Mike yawned. "Jesus Christ, I've had it. Next thing, you'll haul me up for being prejudiced, and they'll put me away for the remainder of my medical school career."

"Take that in!"

"Take *what* in?"

"What you say," Lang swayed on his feet. He clenched his fist.

"I don't know what you're trying to say. Get back, Lang. I'm twice your size. Get *back!*"

Without logic, Lang sprang at him. Karl Mike held out the palms of his hands and deflected him in midair. Lang bounced back as if he were in a game. His knees started to buckle.

"Are you all right?" He was sitting down, and Karl Mike was bending over him.

Lang's mouth was stiff. He could hardly articulate. "Take it *back*," he finally managed to say.

Karl Mike slid to the floor beside Lang. "Okay, it's prepositions, isn't it?" he said. "Take it in, take it back. Take back what I said about the yellow people. Back. In. Not to speak of 'on' and 'by.' It's a wonder anyone who wasn't born to it ever learns this blessed language." Sighing, Karl Mike stretched his legs out. He was wearing sweat pants even in the heat.

"Why you wear them?"

"What?"

"Why you wear those hot pants?"

"I'm *not* wearing hot pants. What in hell are you talking about?"

"I give out," said Lang.

Suddenly they both began to laugh. In the humid apartment, their voices rose in hoots and chortles, drowning out the ticking of the Asian clock on Lang's desk, the one with the butterfly glued to the second hand, and the drip of water from the kitchen faucet that the building manager never fixed because they never remembered to tell him. Karl Mike rolled over next to the door and battered it with his fists. Lang squeezed himself with both arms to hold the laughter back. He got a cramp in his side, then in his belly. Finally he held his hand over his mouth until he could get control of himself.

"What is in the parcel?" It was lying just inside the door where Karl Mike had put it.

"Maybe a bomb, but I don't think so. For one thing, it's dripping on the carpet."

They rolled over and examined the mystery. SuperValu, folded shut at the top. The bottom half was soggy. When Lang reached to move it toward him, it began to rip.

"I think we should open it, Win-Win."

"Maybe baby inside," Lang started to giggle again.

Karl Mike swept his hand in a courtly gesture. "I give it to you, Dr. Lang Nguyen. One-two-three."

With both hands, Lang unrolled the top of the bag, leaned over, looked inside. He turned his head toward Karl Mike.

"What's the matter?"

"I think somebody crazy."

"Don't tell me it really *is* a bomb. I refuse to die before I get my M.D."

"No bomb."

"Give me the word, man."

"Ice cream."

"Ice cream!" Karl Mike bent over the bag and looked in. "My God," he said, "you're absolutely right. Fudgesicle. Mr. Moonbar. And my goodness, I think that damp lump in the middle might just be the remains of a SuperSloop. Someone loves you, Win-Win. Some sweet little person from your side of the world really loves you."

19 For the first time in almost a week, the spring morning came without mist. Not even the edges of Beach Terrace were blurred when Linh looked out the kitchen window. It was a good omen. The air was less sticky than it had been, and when she wiped the kitchen counter, her fingers at the edge of the rag stayed dry as they moved over the worn plastic.

She already had the library books laid out in a neat pile by the door. Harry and Gary had looked at theirs hundreds of times. *The Little Engine* was stained with orange pop where Gary had spilled his glass, but the cover was gold anyway, and she didn't think the librarian would notice.

Her own books were at the bottom of the pile because they were the thickest. *Women in Medicine* had the most pages, but she had read only part of it. It was too hard, the words too big, the names of things full of strange syllables. *First Aid* was better because it had so many pictures. If Harry or Gary ever broke his arm, she would know how to fix it, at least until the doctor came.

Already it was almost nine o'clock. The library opened at nine on Saturday mornings. By ten there would be a line of children and even grown-ups waiting to check out books. They were mostly white American children. Some black ones and some Mexicans, though she couldn't always be sure. She hadn't been sure with Xan. The guard always stood by the stairway in his special blue suit, his face angry all the time. When children went upstairs to the room with the ball of the world, he made them walk straight on their feet and go slow even if they were little. He didn't let them talk loud. The library must pay him a lot of money because he worked so hard to make things right.

"Sister!"

Linh turned toward the stairs. Harry and Gary, shoving each other, were coming down. They had combed their hair with water, and their T-shirts were wet across the shoulders. She had been thinking so hard that she hadn't heard them in the bathroom.

"Come eat." She pretended she had been making their breakfast and set their bowls on the table. This week they were eating Frosted Flakes. Since their mother had gone into the hospital, they hadn't ever wanted noodles for breakfast. If she argued with them, they wouldn't eat anything.

Both of them sat down and picked up their spoons. She knelt next to them, first Harry, then Gary, and tied the laces of their sneakers even though they had their legs wound around the underparts of their chairs. Harry knew how to tie his own shoes, but he wouldn't. Gary was still too young.

"How many books can we get?"

"Six each."

"I can carry sixty!"

Gary grinned at his brother and drank all the milk in

his bowl. "I can carry two," he said. "I want *Mother Gook.*"

"Mother Goose."

Still grinning, Gary got up and ran out the door before Linh could stop him. "I play!" he shouted. "I wait for *Mother Gook!*" He raced across the grass to where the project people had set up the metal swing frame. The swings were broken, but Gary climbed the poles anyway.

Harry was more polite. "Time to go," he said in the businesslike voice he used when he wanted something very much. Linh put her hand on his shoulder and fingered the dampness. He couldn't read yet, of course, but he knew his alphabet, and he was teaching it to Gary. Even without their mother.

"Linh-oi!" Her father was shouting from upstairs.

"Yes, Father."

He didn't answer, but the water was running. She had gained his permission only last night for them all to go to the library. He hadn't drunk much beer, so he would remember.

Harry heaved the pile of books up into his arms. "I am big," he said. Outside, Gary was perched on the iron pole across the top of the swing set, his feet hooked underneath. He was waving both arms.

The water turned off. Linh heard her father go to the bedroom and open the closet. "Linh-oi!" he called again, but before she could gather her voice for a response, she saw him at the head of the stairway, pulling up the jeans she had ironed and holding one of his good shirts. He was barefoot, and his thong sandals were outside by the door. He would put them on later.

"Where are you going?" He ran his hand through the shock of his hair.

[141]

"We are going to the library." She was afraid to remind him that he had given permission last night. Surely he would come to remember by himself. "Shall I cook soup?" she asked, knowing that he wouldn't be hungry.

"No." He opened his pants and tucked the tails of his shirt inside all the way around. His skin was as brown as leather, even on his stomach. Her mother had lighter skin, and now without the sun it would be like the white tissue paper in school. Already when Linh visited the hospital, she felt herself dark beside her own mother.

They waited. Sitting next to the pile of books on the floor, Harry had his eyes shut. He wasn't asleep, though. Outside, Gary was hanging upside down from the top of the swing set, his ankles crossed over the bar. His eyes were shut too.

"I will go with you."

"To the library?" Linh's voice started to tremble.

"Yes."

Linh's father had never been to the library. He never read books, or papers either. Not even the Vietnamese papers that they bought in Houston. He just looked at the pictures or the lottery numbers. Or maybe he did read them at night, after he let her go to sleep.

"It is open now." If her father was going, then they should be early. Many people might scare him. Or he might get angry because they were all in the same place that he was. He might say bad things in Vietnamese. The guard might shoot him.

"Then go." He didn't offer to take the books from Harry, who jumped up at his words. He didn't say anything about visiting the hospital, but perhaps they'd go later. Anyway, her mother was supposed to come home in three days even though she was still crazy. The nurse had told her, and later she'd explained to her father what it meant.

Before they had even gotten the door locked behind them, Gary thudded down from the top of the swing set. "I can carry," he said to Harry, staggering under the weight of the book pile.

"No."

"I help."

"*No!*"

Gary started to tug at the bottom book. The whole pile began to tilt as they stepped onto the sidewalk. "*Yes!*" he yelled. He tried to tangle his feet with Harry's.

"*Dung lai!* Her father slapped Gary hard on his bottom, then yanked the books out of Harry's arms. He didn't even hesitate as they reached the corner but marched right out into the street and up the curb on the other side. There were no cars, but it was still wrong not to look both ways. Linh paused on the curb, then put her arms around the boys and crossed behind them.

The library building was only four blocks away, and from the open curbside at Beach Terrace, anyone could see its roof sticking up over the two-story buildings. The roof was green, but not the old green that grew on statues. It was like green pottery. Tiles, they called it. You could imagine ghosts tiptoeing from one side to the other. The library was a rich building. It cost a lot of money to buy all the books inside it too. It even had a fountain by the stairway, with a little pool. A fountain inside! Everyone threw money into the pool, silver and brown. Linh thought they must clean it out at night and buy more books with the money. But even when she got to the library early in the morning, the bottom of the little pool was still sprinkled with coins. Maybe they only cleaned it out once a week.

Maybe people gave them the books so they wouldn't have to spend so much money on them.

She felt a tug on her hand. It was Harry. He pulled her ahead.

"Why is our father coming with us?" He usually said "papa." Now his face was serious.

"He wants to."

"Why does he want to?"

"I don't know," Linh said. "If he wants to, he can come with us anywhere."

"Mama never went to the library."

"You know Mama can't read." Linh heard the crack in her voice and cleared her throat.

Harry stopped talking. Anyway, they were coming up the sidewalk to the front doors of the library, heavy squares of iron set into the stone. Linh had gone through them so often that all their patterns were familiar to her eyes, but today there was a new white rectangle fastened to the right side and a second one to the left. Already Gary was running his fingers around the right one.

"What's this?"

Linh focused her eyes, "A sign," she said. "USE REVOLVING DOOR."

"What's 'revolving door'?"

"The one in the middle that goes around." They must be fixing the regular doors on the sides, because now she could see that each one had a chain across its handle. Linh had never used the revolving door because it seemed to be a kind of jail. But now she would be brave.

Behind her, Linh could hear her father breathing. The boys had their noses to the glass. Inside the library, she saw the librarians standing at the counter watching them. In the part by the fountain, the guard was watching them

[144]

too. Linh bent down so she could get a clear look at him through the glass, but he didn't seem to be wet anywhere. He must not have picked out the coins yet.

"Tai sao doi o do!" Then suddenly, before Linh could explain to him how the door worked, her father gave it a shove with his free hand, the books anchored against his chest. For a moment, she saw his shocked face as the door moved forward, but the door behind him also moved forward, trapping him. He was swept partway inside.

"Papa!" Harry and Gary shouted in unison.

Through the layers of glass, Linh could see her father halfway through the revolving door. He was standing still, caught. She gave the panel of glass a sturdy push and watched the movement transmit itself through the other panels. The glass inside slammed into her father's back, but he braced himself against it. The door quivered and halted.

Harry and Gary were jumping up and down. "I want to go in!" Gary shouted.

Their father stood unmoving, the pile of books in his arm. With a shuffling step, he separated his legs farther and anchored himself. Already the guard was staring.

"Di toi! Go forward!" Linh said, as loud as she could. She wasn't sure whether her father heard or not. Nothing happened.

Harry and Gary were both looking up at her now, sensing that something was wrong. "Sit down," she said. *"Ngoi xuong."* For once they obeyed her and dropped to the pavement. Freed from the responsibility for them, she moved into the path of the stubborn glass, inserting her slender body into the crack that was open. Then she moved forward until she was sandwiched against the body of her father, separated only by the long pane of glass. It seemed as if she could feel his heat coming through. She pressed herself against his outline.

"Father!" His legs were like trees. Even his toes in their thongs were tightly biting the ground.

"Father!" She made a small fist and knocked on the glass just below where his shirt ended and his jeans started. His muscles contracted, but his feet stayed firm. One book from the stack tilted toward the edge.

On the other side, the guard had begun to move in their direction, and her father must have caught a glimpse of that too because he jerked himself straighter. But his feet did not advance.

Leaning against the panel behind her, her arms at her sides, her shoulders clenched, Linh launched herself at her father. She felt her hands hit the glass, and she forced her body behind them. For a moment there was a movement, then a pause, and then a burst of pressure that slammed the door against her back so hard she fell forward into empty space. The moving door panel swept her along, and before she knew what had happened, she catapulted into the library, flung like a caught fish on top of her father and the scattered stack of library books.

"Child, you all right?" The voice was familiar.

She could barely croak out a "yes." Her father had leaped to his feet as if he were about to be shot.

"Wait just one minute." The large familiar figure from Carver School swept back through the spinning glass and beckoned to Harry and Gary. Guiding them in front of her, Azelita entered the door again, propelling it forward with her shoulder. They arrived inside.

"There." Azelita straightened up. "And don't pretend you don't know me, girl. I can even say your name right. We had one serious talk with each other not that long ago." Her lips firm but her eyes warm, she reached out her arm and wrapped it around Linh's shoulders.

Under the embrace, Linh stood silent. Harry and Gary were transfixed. Linh's father was carefully picking up the books, aligning them in his arms.

"Now. You goin' to the library. Good thing too. Your mama will be real proud of you all when she gets home." Azelita moved over to Linh's father. "You got one fine girl," she said. "You take good care of her. Good thing you bring her to the library. Lots of American parents don't even do that. Her mama will be proud."

The ladies at the checkout counter were staring. Even the children's librarian had risen from her little desk. The guard hovered as if waiting to be called into service.

"Linh, these are your brothers?"

"Yes." She managed to get that out.

"You all got library cards?"

"Yes." She stopped. "Not my father," she said, truth rising in her.

"Well, we'll fix that." Azelita took Phuong Nguyen's elbow, guiding him to the counter. "We want a card for this gentleman," she announced. "Time he joined with his children to be American like all of us."

"You are right," said one of the ladies. She pulled out an application form and opened a ballpoint pen.

"See, Mr. Nguyen," said Azelita. "*Am* I sayin' that right? Take this pen. See this line. Write your name here. Then your address here. You got to set a good example for that little lady of yours."

Phuong Nguyen took the pen clumsily in his fingers, aimed it for the line. Everyone watched. He tightened his back and began to print. Harry and Gary had started fishing for coins in the fountain while the guard had turned toward the counter. Linh realized she had moved closer to Azelita. Only Linh saw that her father's fingers were trembling.

20 "Is this discharge paper an indication of failure on the part of the medical profession?" Shirley put extra irony into her voice.

"You've got it."

"Is there going to be any follow-up? Are you just relaxing because the hospital's not going to be sued? You can't just abandon her."

"No, you can't, but we're going to." Dr. Bryce Adams leaned against the nursing station counter and held his pen above the sheaf of notes in the chart. "Your friend and mine, Dr. Smith-Fragon, the Bouncing Brit, has taken sufficient time from his racquetball to decide that the Vietnamese influence on the ward has passed its prime. Bless his heart, he actually *thought* about the good of the psychiatric establishment."

"Did someone interpret the decision for her?"

"I called the med tech. She's on vacation until next Wednesday."

Shirley bent her head over the heap of papers on her desk. "Did you speak to Dr. Nguyen?" she asked

"I thought he was rotating through Surgery."

"He finished last week."

"My, aren't you the smart little woman to keep track of his ins and outs."

"Be polite, Doctor."

Bryce Adams looked surprised. Shirley always kept her cool. She was programmed to put things in order, and like any good nurse, she knew her place. "You touchy on this Asian issue?" he asked, signing his name black and bold to the release form.

"I have some concern for my patients."

"Give me a break, Goldilocks! Nothing else we've done to her has made any difference. Pills don't work; shock either. She doesn't talk, she doesn't eat, she still grabs the air and squats on her bed."

"I know that."

"Then why are you so uptight?"

"Just some legitimate professional commitment to my patients." Shirley knew that there were very few doctors to whom she could talk this way.

Bryce Adams slammed the chart back down on the counter, but he had the start of a smile. "Moral mission, moral mission. If you care so much, *you* go extract Dr. Nguyen, our last hope at the interpreting table. Hai Truong is due to be discharged within the hour."

"He's in the cafeteria. He'll be here in fifteen minutes."

"You talked to him already?" Bryce Adams ran his hands through his hair and shook his head.

"I knew she'd be leaving. Dr. Smith-Fragon talked about it in conference on Friday." Tempted as she sometimes was, Shirley could never use any of Smith-Fragon's multitude of insulting nicknames.

Half laughing, Bryce said, "Well, since I've signed her out, I'd better make sure she's still alive. Hate to have her pass out into the wide world of Galveston if she wasn't breathing."

"She's breathing."

"You've been listening?"

"Yes."

"Nurses are real health care professionals."

"That's right."

"Who's going to pick her up?"

"Her husband."

"How'd you know *that?*"

"I phoned him."

Bryce moved away from the counter, his arms waving. "You talk Vietnamese?"

"Of course not. But their daughter has quite good English. You know that, Dr. Adams."

"Next thing you know, you'll be adopted into the family."

Shirley turned and went out into the hall, walked down through the patient lounge area. "There could be worse fates," she said. At the door of Hai Truong's room, she slipped out of her white loafers. It was a Vietnamese custom she'd read about, and it was a painless gesture. Then she tapped on the door.

No answer.

"Hai?"

No answer, but the rustle of bedding.

"Hai-oi?" Shirley didn't know what the extra syllable meant, but she'd heard Hai's husband address his daughter that way. It seemed to indicate intimacy of some sort, mild urgency, an affirmation of the person to whom the name was attached.

The door opened. Hai was standing there, her black hair in a bush around her head. She was so short that her gaze centered on the soft gap between the tendons of Shirley's neck, and Shirley felt it rest there. Half consciously, she raised her hand to the spot, exposing her gold ring. Hai reached out and touched it. *"Anh duoc vang,"* she said, barely a whisper. Then she moved her hand to her own neck and touched the small jade ornament hanging from its gold chain. When Shirley looked close, she saw that it was the tiny figure of a woman, robed, her head bent. Small as the miniature pendant was, it looked godlike. Hai patted it possessively.

"You're going home," Shirley said. She pointed to Hai's purse sitting on the bedstand, then gestured toward the door. "Home."

Hai seemed to understand. She walked back to her purse and opened it. At first Shirley thought she was looking for her house keys, but instead she drew out her wallet and unfolded it. Did she think she had to pay directly for her hospitalization? She was covered by Medicaid, as were all charity patients. But she surely understood nothing about that.

"Hinh cua toi," Hai said, opening an inner compartment of her wallet. She pulled out a pack of photographs, went to the bed and beckoned Shirley to join her. It was hard to think of this woman as a schizophrenic, a depressive, someone who had gone through a series of shock treatments and who had been a medication failure. It was hard to think of her as crazy. Whatever had possessed her before seemed today to be sleeping. Perhaps all the attributes of mental illness were different in Vietnam.

On the brown hospital bedspread between them, Hai laid out the photographs. All of them were worn soft at the edges. Several were formal studio portraits in a faded brown tint. Others were snapshots of palm trees, bright ocean, huts with thatched roofs. Hai pushed these to one side and picked up the first portrait. It was a woman, her hair pulled back so harshly that her cheeks stuck out. She was wearing a long black garment. *"Ma,"* Hai said.

"Mama?"

Hai inclined her chin. She pointed to the woman in the photo and then to herself. *"Ma cua toi,"* she said, and a little smile crossed her face. She spoke several words in Vietnamese, then she stopped smiling.

"You miss her?"

Hai pointed with both index fingers at the sides of her head. "Bang," she said. "Pow." She clacked her lips, and her eyes filled with tears.

Not sure what to do, Shirley looked at the next picture, cradling it in her hand. It showed three little girls, standing straight as three arrows, backed by what looked like the folds of a dark curtain.

"Who?" Shirley raised her eyebrows to make the question clearer.

Hai was quiet for what seemed a long time. Then she pointed to the one in the middle. *"Hao,"* she said. Slowly, she moved her finger to the one on the right. *"Thuan,"* she whispered.

"And this one?" Shirley's white finger was a startling contrast against the faded photograph. The girl she was touching looked as if she were squinting against the sun. One hand was cupped toward the camera in a questioning gesture.

Hai pointed to herself. Rising from the bed, she reached both hands in the air as if she were snatching something passing by over her head. "Hai," she said. "Hai, Hai, Hai."

Outside in the hall, Shirley heard footsteps. The elevator door slushed shut. "Dr. Nguyen?" she asked, rising and moving to the door. It didn't seem right to call him Lang when she was with a patient. He had arrived exactly on time.

Hai looked up.

"Miss Nelson?" He had started calling her Shirley, but perhaps he felt that was too informal now, just as she did.

Shirley stepped forward. Hai moved next to her. She tapped Shirley on the shoulder, a firm, intrusive knock with the ends of her fingers.

"Toi co cai nay cho anh," Hai said. She extended her other hand, then opened it. It was full of small white and red pills, some of them worn at the edges. There must have been at least a hundred of them.

"Toi co cai nay cho anh," Hai said again. Then, slowly and with a smile, "Med-sin." Taking Shirley's hand in hers, she carefully poured the little cache of unswallowed pills into it.

21 "Xan is doing much better." Azelita was directing her comment to the principal, poised between lunchroom and official business.

"I'm grateful for that. What happened?"

"I think we owe it to that Vietnamese doctor." Azelita ran her hand over the soft but organized fluff of her hair. Every strand shouted "compromise," but she'd gone to the beauty parlor on her own sturdy legs and paid with her own good money. Wilson Freeman was coming for dinner that night, and he liked hair that had attention paid to it.

"Yes, the Vietnamese doctor." Ms. Hopkins leaned toward the door of her office in a graceful slant. "They help their own people, don't they?"

Azelita touched her hair again. "Xan got the Student of the Week Award from Mrs. Fillmore last Friday," she said. "He's still got it pinned to his shirt." It was the same shirt too, an oily blue. Azelita didn't pass that information on.

The principal sighed. She was a woman for whom administration had been invented. Paper was her medium, paper and black marks on paper. When called upon to exert discipline, she wrote letters to the parents, even the

Hispanic ones who couldn't read English. Even the Vietnamese. Though she was white, an old Galvestonian, she had never seemed particularly interested in the proper means of communicating with anyone, even her own kind.

Azelita raised her head. The principal's door was shutting, edge sucking itself to frame. There was hardly a sound. In a school where various structures crashed into each other regularly, the silence seemed supernatural.

Thoughtful, Azelita leaned back in her desk chair. Wilson Freeman. Beauty parlor. No. Better think about lunch money, lunch tickets, free lunches. The ones who got free lunches used tickets instead of money. They had a separate list. She laid the two lists out on her cluttered desktop, checked to make sure none of the names had been duplicated. If the lists didn't come out properly, she'd never enter a beauty parlor again. Lord, Lord.

Because the air-conditioning unit was clanking and simmering, Azelita didn't notice the approach of a child. What she noticed was that the counter separating her desk from the hallway suddenly had grown a forehead. "Miguel, what is it?" she asked, setting the lists aside.

"Mizzuz Azelita, they's a *man* in the room."

Miguel was officially a fifth grader, but he was in the ungraded classroom because of his reading difficulties. His dad was black, his mother Mexican, his English crude. He did not contribute to anyone's sense of racial pride, especially when he had a finger in his nose, as he did now.

"What room?"

"My room. Me and my teacher's room. A man is standing *right there.*"

"Did your teacher send you to tell me?"

"She cain't move. I snuck mahself out."

Through the dimness of the chilled air, Azelita concentrated on what Miguel was saying. Strange people wandered into Carver School sometimes, through the cafeteria entrance, through the gym. Galveston had two thousand street people, someone had said. Carver was not in the best neighborhood. Most of the uninvited visitors were far more dangerous to themselves than to anyone else.

"Is he doing anything, Miguel? Miguel, stop picking your nose." Azelita handed him a Kleenex, but he let it lie on the counter.

"Nobody can't understand him, Mizzuz Azelita. He talk funny."

Miguel wasn't the best witness, but something must be going on. Azelita pulled herself upright and walked to the gate that separated her from Miguel or any other up-front visitors. His eyes were still peering at her over the smudged Formica of the counter. He hadn't even stopped at the principal's office. Miguel wasn't stupid, for all his reading difficulties. He knew who was in charge of what.

"All right, Miguel. Show me."

He hurried down the hall in front of her. From behind, she could read his T-shirt, obviously a hand-me-down. Or Salvation Army. Or Goodwill. KING OF THE ROAD, it said, brandished across the breast of an American eagle. She hadn't remembered seeing any design on the front. Miguel must have put the shirt on backward.

"Cho anh!" The sound shot through the opening of the classroom door.

Azelita stopped. One hand caught Miguel just to the side of the eagle's head on his skinny spine.

[157]

"That's him, Mizzuz Azelita."

"Who?"

"That crazy man."

Suddenly cautious, Azelita leaned back against the wall, Miguel glued to her knees. She sidled toward the entrance to the classroom. Mrs. Fillmore was saying something, but the sounds were muffled.

"Boi vi truong hoc giup Xan." A pause. Then, *"Cho anh!"* again.

Miguel twisted his head back. "He want Miz Fillmore do sompthin about that Chinee boy."

"What?"

"That Chinee boy!"

"Xan?"

"That one."

Visions of kidnapping went through Azelita's head but the classroom seemed too quiet for that. No gunshots. She edged farther along the wall.

"I kin go back in, Mizzuz Azelita."

"We'll both go in, Miguel." Without hesitating, in which case she might have thought twice, Azelita stepped to the door and into the room. The whole classroom turned toward them, except for Mrs. Fillmore plastered against the blackboard, her hands gripping the chalk tray. A small Vietnamese man wearing jeans and thong sandals was standing by her desk.

"What's he want?" whispered Miguel.

Azelita had no clue, but she had handled just about everything at one time or another: vomit, fist fights, a parental dispute that had ended with the mother fleeing down the hall and into the storage closet. No reason to stop now.

Mrs. Fillmore gestured desperately, and Azelita

[158]

strode forward. "What you want?" The more direct, the better.

The man turned. He was pretty small, even if square, about up to Azelita's chin. In one hand he had a large damp plastic bag, in the other a meat cleaver.

For a moment, Azelita hesitated, then she moved closer.

"What do you want, man?"

His upper and lower lips drew apart, then snapped shut as if by the force of words that couldn't be articulated. "I bring shrimp," he blurted out.

"What?"

"You help my boy, Xan. Bring Vietnamese doctor. I give teacher shrimp." With a thwack, he cut the cord around the top of the bag and there was a cascade of pink and gray shrimp onto the desk, their legs and antennae quivering. From his seat in the middle row, Xan looked on with horror and pride in equal measure.

Above the fishy swirl, the man smiled at Azelita, then at Mrs. Fillmore. He nodded his head, almost bowed. Then he started for the classroom door, the handle of the cleaver tucked neatly in the waist of his jeans.

Xan sprang to his feet. "Shrimp *good!*" he said, looking over at his father's departing back. Then he focused on Azelita. "For you too," he said, nodding quickly at Mrs. Fillmore as if to show that there would be enough for everyone. "*Lots* of shrimp!"

22 "Woman, I can tell you got somebody visiting tonight. You sound all *expecting.*"

Azelita sighed and readjusted the receiver. "Sisters know what's worth knowing, right?"

"Right and right again." Labella was clicking her pretty pink fingernails against the edge of the mouthpiece.

"Well."

"You cooking something tasty?"

"Shrimp."

"Man oh man. Must be the boss coming. Or Uncle Washington."

"You know Uncle Washington don't eat nothing that don't have a snout on one end and a little curly tail on the other."

"He just like our mama always was." The fingernails started clicking again.

"Who you go to for them nails now, Labella?"

"Why you asking me about my nails?"

" 'Cause I hear them like you was playing some drum set just to keep me from falling asleep."

"That's all I'm doing, just keeping you awake. What time he coming?"

"Who?"

"Whoever it is that's coming and ain't your boss or Uncle Washington."

"Soon."

"And you're cooking him them good Gulf shrimp? Where you buy them?"

"Got 'em as a present. In school."

"That's why they don't pay you no good money there. Got all them *extra* benefits."

"Like yellow pencils and hamburgers they make out of what's left when the cow says no more." Azelita put her shoulder against the wall by the little phone table in the hallway. The shadow from the cord swung back and forth along the cream-colored surface. "I am going, Labella," she said. "Cooking time."

"You cook *good,* Sister. You do a little more of that good cooking, and you might find yourself someone to eat it steady and keep you warm besides."

"Right. Easy catching when the pot's hot."

Labella snorted. "Mama always said that very same thing when she was making us a big dinner."

"Right." Azelita shifted her weight. "You be good, Labella," she said. "Give a good word to your man and the offspring too. Cook 'em a big dinner while you're at it."

She hung up. Her mama's clock clacked for six o'-clock. It had never chimed right, just let loose a little sound like wood blocks hitting together. Hard to know if there was something wrong in its innards or if that was just the voice of time passing the way Mama had liked to hear it. No time for bells and chimes, that woman. The hard tap of the world on the world was the music she liked best.

In the kitchen, the gumbo was simmering. Azelita had

[161]

canned tomatoes last summer, three bushels from the farmers' market at La Marque. Silliest thing ever, the kitchen steaming, her own sweat sloshing in the channel down the middle of her bra. But now the tomatoes simmered mightily in the black pot, along with the chunks of pepper, the onion slices, the generous sprinkles of cayenne and Tabasco. Bubbles rose and lolloped to the dark red surface, burst and slid back. On the counter, the heap of shrimp spilled over the top of the blue bowl. The heads were already snapped off, the shells in the garbage. Azelita didn't believe in all that business about the black stripe down the middle of the back. Whatever it was really made of, it tasted as good as the rest of those little bodies. Might even say that a touch of black made those shellfish *legitimate.*

Wilson's face colored itself on her mind. This was their third meeting since the dance. Once for a movie and a drink afterward. You'd've thought that loudmouthed black boy was still living with *his* mama, he was so polite. Second time they'd gone to dinner at Trentons, and he'd left the biggest tip on record. A little serious snuggling after that one. Tonight was the three-times-and-out night. Flowered sheets on the bed and a pot of gumbo on the stove. It'd been awhile, but Azelita had a good memory for *some* things.

And what would Mama be saying? Or thinking? She had had her own ideas about meeting and matching. Only now it was too late to make sure what they were.

When the knock came, Azelita had the big wooden stirring spoon in her hand. For a moment, she waved it like a weapon. The gumbo surged to the rim of the pot.

"Zeli!"

The crazy name he'd cut out of the middle of her right-ful one! She gave the gumbo a stir and waited.

"Zeli!"

"You know how to turn a knob," she shouted.

"Zeli!"

"Open that door, Wilson! My hands be in your din-ner."

Silence. Then the door. She heard him move through the living room, fancy shoes sliding on the carpet. As he got nearer, she could hear his arms rubbing against the sides of his shirt, and she moved her own elbows into the air for safety. Then his feet crunched across the bare boads of the hall floor, and he was standing in the kitchen doorway.

"My God, woman, that smell got me round the neck good as if you tied me with your little ribbon. What you making?"

"Gumbo." Azelita gave the wooden spoon in the kettle a solid swirl.

"Turn around now. You give me my answer. I want the rest of what I'm getting tonight."

"Such as what?"

"My, my. Can tell you work in a school. Got to have everything *specific.*" Wilson took two steps into the steam-ing kitchen and grabbed her from the back, digging his sharp chin down into the angle between her neck and shoulder. She shrieked and let the spoon fly.

"You leave me be!"

"This is just a little *appetizer,* woman." He nuzzled her neck, his arms roped around her.

"Wilson, you let me be like I said."

"What do I get if I do?"

"Gumbo." Azelita snatched up the spoon and pulled herself up against the stove, Wilson attached to her back like a snapper shell. From the shaking against her spine, she knew he was laughing.

"You are one fine woman."

Azelita stirred and nodded. Somehow she felt less a fine woman with both his arms so tight around her that she could hardly draw a necessary breath.

"I come here tonight a hungry man for *everything.*"

Azelita gave a tentative jerk. His arms tightened.

"You be so bad, I gonna make you *badder.*"

With a hard yank to one side, Azelita pulled herself free. She held her spoon in the air. "Don't you talk no more nigger to me, Wilson! I am at least as good as that little white lady who brought you your food in Trentons!"

"What you mean 'talk nigger'?"

Azelita grabbed the bowl of shrimp and dumped it into the pot. Smashing the bowl back on the counter, she pulled the cover off the container of rice at the back of the stove and gave it a furious stir. "I mean, talk like I am some stupid black mammy who's going to fill your belly and open her legs like they was one and the same thing."

"Who's talking nigger now, woman?"

The gumbo let loose a series of bubbles, propelling the shrimp up and around like little pink boats. "Take these dishes and set them on that dining-room table," Azelita said, pushing two plates and cups into Wilson Freeman's hands.

"I'm not talking dishes, Zeli."

"Just do it, Wilson. One curse on all black people in this country is that they got two languages, one for when they're with their own and one for when they're trotting round the block with whitey. When you don't own your own words, you don't own your own soul either. I see those Vietnamese kids at school, working their little tails off to learn how to do ABC in English, and wonder if they know who they are from one day to the next."

Wilson stepped back. "Why you messin' with them Viet kids?"

"What you mean why I messing with them? They go to Carver School. I sit in the office and *run* that school. If I got paid for half of what I did, the city would have to float a bond issue. Just today, I saved that Mrs. Fillmore from getting cleaved in two white pieces by a little Vietnamese father. Matter of fact, we're eating his shrimp right now. He brought a pile to school to thank us all for helping his boy, only none of us was smart enough to understand what he was saying."

"So that's his shrimp we eating?"

Azelita ladled the gumbo into two big white china bowls. "What difference that make to you?" she asked. "I don't notice you buying me no shrimp, Wilson."

"You ask me, I do it." His voice was cold.

A bowl in each hand, Azelita looked at him. "Why you sounding so serious, Wilson? I guarantee you there is no Vietnamese poison in this shrimp."

From the dining room, Wilson's voice came back slowly, "I got no fondness for what had a yellow hand stuck in it."

"What you mean? You got something against the other side of the world? I don't notice that our own country is all that fine, Wilson. I stuck in that school, for instance. No college gonna pay me to become a teacher, so I count lunch money instead. You done all right for yourself, but that's 'cause you worked one solid six years night and day to set up that car business. You *earned* that fancy machine you drive. I don't see this as a land anyone gotta bow down to."

"I got my reasons for how I feel."

"Wilson, come eat this gumbo."

He stood looking out at the porch, a tall black rectangle against the white curtains. Around his perimeters, Azelita could see the fringes of Beach Terrace, brown buildings and worn dusty lawns. At least she was a step up from that.

"Wilson, I like those little Viet kids. They got their own kind of slavery to grow out of."

"That be silly woman talk."

"I'm no silly woman, and you know that. I say what I say, and nobody change me. Now come eat this gumbo."

"I'm not feeling all that hungry."

"I do all this cooking for some crazy nigger ain't even gonna eat it?"

He spun around. "You cook for *me*, woman. You want you and me to turn into something, be more than just chatting friends, you shut that big mouth of yours and treat me with a little sugar. Any person got a right to ask for that, and I no different."

In a way, it made sense. But not Azelita's sense, not tonight. Like granite, she sat herself down and began spooning up the first hot sample of her gumbo. "You eatin' or not, Wilson?" she asked. "I listen to your speeches after we done justice to this dinner."

For a moment, he hesitated. The gumbo aroma rose from the table in rich waves. Then he wrenched himself away.

"Where you goin'?"

"Out."

"You go out, you never come in this house again."

"That be for me to decide."

As he stalked across the living room, Azelita noted his tight little bottom in his Halston pants, and a flicker of regret passed through her. The door to the porch opened. She waited for his steps on the porch floor, but there was nothing. Slowly, she turned her head in that direction, listened to check out what was happening. She heard voices.

"Who you?"

Silence.

"What you doing here?"

Silence.

"What you got there?"

This time a small voice came. Azelita couldn't hear what was being said. She pushed herself back from the table, then started across the carpet. Instead of the rage or disappointment she had expected to feel, she explored her innards and discovered only the good taste of gumbo, rich and hot all the way down. If Wilson Freeman was too much of a fool to share what she could give him, then that was *his* problem. And Mama would have voted with her all the way on that one.

In the living room, the door was open, spewing the air conditioning out into the vast hot sweeps of Galveston's spring evening. Beneath Wilson's arm, framed by the diamond of his elbow's angle, Azelita saw the small face of Linh Nguyen. Behind her stood Xan Van. Linh had her arm extended.

"Why you two visiting my house?" As soon as she had said it, Azelita regretted her hostile tone. After all, they lived practically across the street, and no doubt they knew exactly where she lived. Then she saw that Linh had a bag in her hand.

"What you want, child?"

"I bring you present." The girl looked back at Xan. He nodded.

"Well." Azelita held out her hand. "A present. It's not my birthday, though."

"That all right," Xan said.

"You two just doing this out of the goodness of your hearts?"

"My *father* did it," Linh said. "My mama too," she added.

Azelita reached again for the bag. Wilson had disappeared back into the dining room. "What you bringing me, you two?" she asked.

A smile flickered on Linh's smooth mouth, was reflected on Xan's, came back to Linh's. "More shrimp," she said.

"Didn't know if you was going to stay or not."

"Oh yes. Oh yes, oh yes."

"Wilson, I genuinely think this one part of me got smaller. Let me move around here."

"*Nobody* gets smaller."

"Well, it's been a time."

"And all that time you walking with your legs so tight together. Sad thing, woman."

"Got my own work in Carver School. Got no time for you men."

"But we got time for you. *I* got time. And that ain't all I got."

"Mmmmm. Maybe you got it right this time."

"Maybe I do. I like women I can find with my two hands. Not planning on grabbing a wrinkle in the sheet and thinking I got all there is."

"Then I am the woman for *you*. Keep right on."

"All you need is the world to appreciate you more."

"Right. That's right. That's *right.*"

" 'Cause I appreciate you already."

"I can tell."

"Now we going for real."

"I can tell."

"Now we swinging back and forth like that old Gulf."

"I can tell."

"You sure can tell most things, Woman."

"Uh-huh. Only next time you eating my gumbo down to the bottom. Yes, yes, yes."

23 Trang flung open the door of the house, which her aunt kept closed even when the still, hot air clung to them like a blanket. It was the time of day the Americans called suppertime, dinnertime, some strange sign that the clock never marked in any direct way. Even doctors finished work by now, Trang thought. With a shove of her arm, she slammed the door shut behind her, then waited to see if Tri would open it and follow her down the street. Sometimes he did, but this time he didn't.

Would he lie to her aunt for her? He might. She and Tri were tied together in the clammy city of Galveston as they had been on the clammy beach where the waves had dumped them like dead fish. Even though her father had been an American and she was not pure Vietnamese, she and Tri had a common bond. They held to each other because evil had sucked out their breaths and blown them back in.

A strand of hair waved across Trang's eyes, and she held it in front of her face as she hurried down the sidewalk and turned in front of the project houses. What if her father had been blond? Would she have been white-striped like a zebra on the TV? As it was, her hair was certainly dark, but when the light came through it, as it did now, it glowed brown on its surface. If she slept on it when it was wet, it crinkled. When she was little, she had thought that her father might have been a nigger. But she could make her hair stop curling if she brushed it hard. Nigger hair never stopped curling.

It was five thirty. He might be home already, but some doctors worked late.

Across the street, the last row of buildings of Beach Terrace split off from their companions. Two little boys were playing on the swings, but their hair wasn't curly. Linh Nguyen's brothers, they must be. Their mother was home now from the hospital. They were like her aunt's little children, too near being babies to care about anyone besides themselves.

Stolidly, Trang passed the projects, the library, the post office, the block with stores that sold auto parts. At Thirty-seventh Street, three men came out of a tavern and looked at her, their eyes sharp on her face and her front. *"Ha thap con mat cua anh,"* she said softly as she passed. "Lower your eyes!" Inside, she cursed their mothers. Her ears sharpened for footsteps following her, but there were none. It was still light. They couldn't sneak up on her in the light.

At Forty-fifth Street, she bought a hamburger at the McDonald's. Now she knew how to do it. It tasted like meat someone had already chewed up, and although they had put ketchup and mustard on it, she could not taste any sharpness. She held the sad meat in her mouth and let it wash down her throat. By Forty-eighth Street, it was gone. She had kept the top half of the bun in her hand, and she began to roll off little pellets of soft white bread, then toss them ahead of her on the sidewalk. As her foot came to each one, she put her sandal down on it hard. When the half of the bun was entirely gone, she was sorry.

At Fifty-second Street, behind the supermarket where the bins of discarded produce and boxes lined the curb, an old man was digging for his dinner. Although his skin was darker than hers, he wasn't a nigger. She hurried past.

It was later than the American suppertime when she finally got to Lang Nguyen's apartment. The lot was full of cars come home from work, with only a few spaces left. Trang stopped by the building she wanted and slid herself up against the entryway, a brick enclosure set around the door. She checked inside, then came out again. Attentively, she spat on her fingers and brushed her hair back from her forehead, rubbed her cheekbones to make them shine. She pulled the collar of her blouse back from her neck and used her fingers to line the *V* that the collar made. One at a time, she kicked off her sandals and cleaned the dirt out from between her toes, then put the sandals back on. She rubbed at her heels too, but since she couldn't see them all the way around, it was hard to know if she was changing their color or not. She had forgotten the lipstick that she had found outside her house. "How could I do that?" she said as her fingers dug hopelessly in her pocket for it. *"Me kiep!"*

"What are you saying?"

Surprised, Trang looked up, her shoulders back. A man her uncle's age was standing by his car door a little distance away. He held a car key in his hand.

"It's Vietnamese," she said back.

He smiled at her. "Boat lady, right?"

Trang stopped. "What you mean?" she asked.

"You sail off into the sunset and end up in America."

Trang glared at him. "Why you say that?" Her aunt

would have hit her for talking to him at all.

The man laughed. "Want a ride?" he asked, swinging the door of his car open and beckoning her inside.

Trang knew better than that. "Fuck off," she responded, the words with their sharp monosyllables sounding satisfactorily like Vietnamese. She turned away and stalked across the parking lot to the fire escape up the side of the building, not looking back once. Her heart wasn't even beating fast, and as she tiptoed up the steps, her toes in their sandals barely tasted the iron treads. No American could scare her, or tempt her, or make her do anything she didn't want to do. She already contained their blood. She was immune.

Lang Nguyen's apartment was on the third floor. She remembered from the time with the ice cream. And for that time she had remembered from what he had told her in the restaurant. His name was written in the apartment lobby. Somebody else lived with him, an American with three names like a Vietnamese. That meant Lang Nguyen wasn't afraid of living with Americans. That was a very good thing.

Within two minutes, Trang had climbed the fire escape to its third-floor exit. Next to the fire escape was one window only a short hop away. First, though, she took off her sandals and hooked them around her waist by their straps. With her bare feet, solid and broad and so calloused that the edges of brick were no harsher than sidewalks or tar, she stepped onto the sill and slid herself across it. The next window, her goal, was farther along, but the sills joined in an outcropping from the wall, so she walked easily along to it, bracing her back against the bricks. Half of the length of her feet stuck over the edge, but her heels held firmly. She had no fear of heights.

When she had stood on their little boat as the waves ate it and Tuan died, she had not been afraid. No matter what her uncle said, she was meant to survive by Thuy Tinh, the goddess of the sea. The goddess of the moon, Chi Hang, covered her with her strong hand.

Inside his apartment, Lang was vacuuming. With obsessive care, he angled the tube under the sofa, under the reclining chair, into the corners where the carpet was coming loose from the floor. He ran the vacuum nozzle up the wall by the door, dislodging a net of spider webs that had accumulated there. After he finished the carpet, he slid over it with his feet flat, pushing the nap in one direction so the color would be smooth.

Karl Mike was watching. "Is the photographer from *Good Housekeeping* coming, Win-Win? There can be no other answer."

"No photographer."

"And I'm spending the next five hours studying at the all-night medical library simply because I'm a student of such virtue?"

Lang was silent. He had gone out many times when Karl Mike had asked him to, still he felt guilt at having asked the same of Karl Mike. Yet it must be an appropriate custom in this country. This was how roommates were supposed to treat each other, even if they were not cousins.

"Is it someone I know?"

Without answering, Lang began to twist the cord of the vacuum around the handle.

"Some beautiful Asian maiden from the pharmacy? The X-ray lab? The phlebotomists' station?"

"No."

"I can't pry it out of you?"

[174]

Why not tell him? There was no need to make it a secret. But a block of silence came up in Lang's throat.

"Okay, okay." Karl Mike was wrestling his arms into his worn sports jacket, the tweed fraying on the cuffs. "You'll tell me when the moon is right. This place is turning into a psychic's dream orgy anyway." He shrugged his shoulders and let the tweed settle across them, then straightened the jacket evenly across the front. "I don't know if this is some sign of our mutual spiritual decadence or not, but for the last few minutes or so, I feel like somebody somewhere around here is watching us."

24 "So this is something you ate in your country?" Shirley eyed the bright yellow pancake, folded in a smooth crease over the medley of bean sprouts and pork. She edged a piece into her chopsticks, smiling across the table at Lang as she wiggled her fingers into the proper position. She pointed to the sauce bowl by her plate.

"What's that?"

"Sauce."

"What kind of sauce?"

"I don't know the name in English. It comes from fish soaked in water. I buy it in Houston at Vietnamese market, then I mix it with vinegar and soy. I cut carrots into it because that is important. My mother did it not quite the same when I was little, but I did not help in the kitchen. Now I do it from the pictures in my mind."

Shirley contemplated the sauce, the table, the fragment of pancake slipping between the tips of her chopsticks. "Lang, if I dip this into anything, I'm going to lose it."

"I get you a fork."

"But I want to try eating Vietnamese."

"Already you *try*." He placed the fork at the side of her plate. "You will learn. The fingers learn like the head learns."

"You sound like a psychiatrist." Shirley leaned the fork into the plate and detached a satisfactory chunk of pancake, then lifted it to her mouth. The taste was pleasant. On her tongue, the textures mixed, the bean sprouts crunching against her teeth. There was no hint of grease, even though the kitchen had been snapping and steaming with fumes just ten minutes ago.

"I never be a psychiatrist."

"Why not?"

Lang lowered his head in embarrassment. After all, Shirley nursed on the psychiatric ward. It would not be polite to challenge her choice.

"Why not? You won't hurt my feelings. Tell me."

Slowly, Lang opened his mouth to explain. The words twisted in his head. "I fix people," he finally said, knowing that was not the proper answer.

"But psychiatrists fix people too."

"I think not always."

Shirley nodded. "You're right," she said. "Not always. Sometimes they mess up big time. But pediatricians aren't perfect either. Or surgeons. No doctor is God."

"Not God."

"Lang, you'll have to explain it better than that." From the sauce bowl by her plate, she extracted a limp sliver of carrot and slid it onto her tongue. "God's the wrong word anyway. Doctors have limited knowledge, and psychiatrists are doctors. They made me mad the way they treated Hai Truong, but they weren't *trying* to hurt her. They weren't being vicious."

"Hai Truong was not crazy." Lang's voice was low.

[177]

"I don't really think she was crazy either."

"In our country, we say she had a ghost."

"Had a *ghost?* What does that mean?"

"It is very hard to explain."

"Does it mean that someone she knew had died?"

"It is very hard to explain," Lang said again. "A spirit has come to live in her."

"Like being possessed?"

"The spirit does not *own* her. He has found a place in her to give him a life. Because she contains another person, she does not act like always." He hesitated. "Sometimes she is unhappy."

"You believe this?" Shirley's voice had softened.

"In my village, I see it many times."

"And if you were treating an American who was mentally ill, would you use it as a diagnosis?"

It was a challenging question, but Lang did not even pause. "It would not work for an American," he said. "It is true only for a Vietnamese."

"But then there is a truth for every country?"

"Yes."

His answer surprised her. Through his eyes, she saw the world as a collection of fragments, separate but containing the possibility of linkage, like a puzzle. In the palm of her hand, she felt the memory of the small collection of Hai Truong's pills.

Shaking her head, Shirley said, "Do you have any pictures of your family in Vietnam?"

Lang raised his eyebrows. "You like to see them?"

"Very much."

His hand near her elbow but not quite touching it, Lang guided her to the sofa in the living room, its cushions puffed with such care that it looked as if they had been artificially inflated. On the table next to it was a brown photograph album, laid out as if for inspection. As Lang picked it up, Shirley sat down by the sofa's far arm. It was impossible to lean against the back of the sofa for fear of disappearing completely, so she kept her feet on the carpet and waited. Again, Hai Truong's face moved into her mind, the thick hair a shadow behind her head.

"This is my mother." Lang was sitting so far from her that, with his arm fully extended, the album still lay only halfway across the middle cushion next to her.

Shirley leaned over. "And this is my father," Lang said. The two people sat together, obviously in a studio, their faces stern. They could have been grandparents, great-grandparents. Or they could have been in their twenties. There was no way of knowing.

"They look like a good couple."

Lang turned the page. "This is my sister," he said. "This is myself with her." Again, he moved to the next page. "And this is my village. I walk under those trees to school." His finger moved to the lower corner, where several children sat on a bench. "My cousins," he said.

"Are these recent photographs?"

"No."

"How often do you hear from your family?"

"When they have the money to mail letters." He flipped several pages. "This is how my parents look in this year. They send it to me."

Shirley bent over to see more clearly. As if Lang's mother had undergone a transformation, her hair was white. His father looked the same except for the twist on one side of his mouth.

"Do you have a recent one of your sister?"

Lang felt a flicker of irritation. It was not for this

American woman to demand that his family reveal itself in any way not of their choosing. But then his eyes fell on Shirley's wrists, stretched along her lap. They were thin for an American woman. All women were curious about people. That was why they were good mothers. Shirley was no taller than he was, and she was kind. He knew she had spent extra time with Hai Truong in the hospital.

"Not recent. I think it costs too much money."

"To take a picture?"

"In Vietnam, sometimes the photographer will charge for each person. At a wedding, for example, where there are many people, the photographer will earn enough to eat for more than a month."

Shirley made some quick calculations in her head. In the earlier picture, the sister had looked like a little girl, and Lang had appeared to be a young teenager. She must be grown up now, perhaps married. Did Lang feel as if he were still a part of their lives? What would it be like to have the ocean cut you off from your family?

Carefully, Shirley leaned back, her golden curls against the back of the sofa. "Would you like to see *my* pictures?" she asked.

"You have pictures?"

"Just a few with me. In my purse. It's over by the dining-room table."

Lang sprang up, retrieved the purse and brought it back. When he sat down this time, he put himself halfway onto the center cushion. Shirley noticed his smell, a faint pungent odor. It must have been the decades of that fish sauce. Half surprised, she realized that it was not unpleasant.

"These are just a few snapshots," she said, opening her wallet. "I have more at home."

[180]

"You carry them with you?"

"Sure. Then I can show them to my friends." She pulled out the plastic enclosure. "Many Americans carry family pictures with them, you know," she said.

"I think so." Lang bent toward her. "This your parents?" he asked.

"Yes. They live in Oklahoma. Tulsa."

"But you are so far away."

"That's all right. We talk on the phone. And I can visit them sometimes."

"And this?"

"My brother, Jed. He works in Dallas in an office. He's an accountant."

"A Texan like you."

"I guess you could think of it that way." She flipped the plastic. "This is the front of my house in Galveston. I rent the bottom floor. Last year I planted that bush, and it grew like crazy. Next year I'll have to prune it."

Lang put his finger on the green blur. "We have bushes like this in my country," he said.

"No wonder the Vietnamese like Galveston." She smiled. "But the best picture is coming up, Lang. Look at this."

A small face appeared, freckles across the nose. The hair was the color of beach sand, hanging in curls like Shirley's, the eyes blue and American.

"Your little brother?"

"No." Shirley began to laugh. "I'm not young enough to have a brother *that* little. Didn't you know I had a son?"

Lang looked at her.

"His name is Jason. Sometimes I call him Jay. He's four years old and runs me ragged. But he's one smart little boy."

"Are you married?" Lang asked, his voice stiff.

"No, no, I'm not married."

"Your husband is dead?"

"No." Shirley paused, the wallet resting in her hand.

"Do you have divorce?" Lang seemed to have trouble getting out the alien words.

Shirley flipped the wallet shut. "I was never married," she said. "Doesn't that ever happen to people in Vietnam?"

By now it was night, the black air thick and warm. Across the seawall, down on the damp sand, the black ocean waved fringes of white as the waves crashed in and left their foam behind. All the way from the Sand Dollar Estates apartments to the Beach Terrace projects, the night tightened itself around Galveston. Even the wind could hardly move through it.

Trang ran along the seawall, the shorter and dangerous way home. If she had stayed at Lang's apartment window any longer, she would have fallen off the brick ledge. Her feet throbbed from having gripped the sill for so long. It was later than she had ever been awake, except for Tet, the night of New Year. She knew from the quiet of the streets that all the people with homes were sleeping. All the fishermen were sleeping too. She held the black cloth of the city on her own shoulders.

The two of them had eaten the *bann xeo* pancakes. The woman with the gold hair had held chopsticks in her hand, but she had been clumsy as an elephant. And then he had given her a fork. He had smiled at her as if he wanted to touch her before they had even stopped eating! And she was not even half Vietnamese!

[182]

Although Trang had pushed herself against the window edge as hard as she could, she was still not sure about the rest. The two of them in the apartment had gone around the corner into another part. In a little while, he had come back to get her purse. Was she buying him? Was that how they did it in America? Would he cost much money because he was a doctor? Would she have to buy him every time she came to his bed? How could anyone get so much money?

A car came up behind her, slowing down. Trang slid over the edge of the seawall and down the steep steps to the beach. She curled up next to a big rock that smelled of dead fish, but she tightened her throat and kept herself from coughing. The car went on.

Up above her in the sky, the clouds separated for a moment. Half a moon sailed between them, yellow like dirty water. In America, men went and walked on the moon with their boots. Chi Hang had had to find another home. But perhaps she had never lived on the American moon. Perhaps she wove the night only for the Vietnamese. And the Chinese. And maybe the dirty pig Laotians.

Suddenly Trang felt as if her body had poured itself out and soaked into the sand. There were no solid parts left for her to walk home with. The clouds closed.

She could cut herself in two pieces. She could burn her hair yellow. She could walk into the waves.

But no such things happened. A siren sounded on the lower part of Seawall Boulevard, and she got up. Her legs wobbled, so she ran to make them hold her erect. Her lungs hurt, so she ran faster. Inside her head, all the old pictures came up, so she opened her mouth to let the wind blow them away and the black air cover the ones that were

[183]

too heavy to blow. Past Wal-Mart, past the church with two doors, past the auto-repair stores. A man with a shopping cart shouted "Don't go so fast, girlie" at her, and she shouted "Fuck you" back. Before she had to fall over, she was at her house again, and Tri had left the kitchen window a little open. She climbed through. No one was awake. In her corner, she buried herself under the old blanket as if it were sand.

In the day, the animals stayed away, hidden between the walls or digging in close to the foundations of the old house. They knew they were not as big as the people. Inside their heads were empty bowls. Words never filled them.

But now at night, the animals were not afraid. From where Trang lay, wrapped in the tattered cotton blanket against the far wall of the kitchen, she watched the hard-backed creatures with many legs parade along the countertops. They were not friends with each other, but they were not enemies either. They ate everything without any sound. Sometimes an edge of a crisp body brushed against a bit of paper, and a whisper passed through the dark air to her ears.

The animals with fur were more friendly. Mice. The word in Vietnamese was *con chuot*, but they had the same fur. They came out from the corners and looked for the leftover chunks of food, and when they found them, they tasted them right away. In the dark, Trang could hear their little teeth. Then they ran back to their homes with what was left, when they had made sure it wasn't poison. They were good mothers and fathers even if they had no words in their heads. They did their business well.

These were the animals that lived on top. They were not worms. They did not eat bodies. Her cousin Tuan was safe from them. It was all right to like them.

Trang turned over and pulled the blanket up under her chin. She was already wet from the hot air that filled the kitchen, but it was better to be covered at night. During the day, she had so much to do, and she could not cover herself. When the time came that she passed her American father on the street for the first time, he had to see all of her or he would not know her. And he might not come the same way again.

Perhaps Dr. Lang Nguyen might like her with few clothes too. Her body was smoother and more brown than that yellow-haired American's! He was younger than her father would be. He must like sex. She could bring him more presents, things better than ice cream. No one had touched her inside yet. Lang Nguyen had lived in America a long time, so her American half would not be strange to him. And all women had the same parts.

Off in the bedroom of her aunt and uncle, the baby cried. He was dreaming of the boat. Even though he had not been there as a person, he had been there as an egg. They had taught her that in biology. So perhaps he could see the waves too. They would look very big to a baby.

The animals did their business. Trang put her hands between her legs where she could make sure no one would get in. Sleep was mixing up her mind, but she knew that someone, somewhere, could make her an entire person again.

25 "Wilson, I got all of fifty-five minutes. How you going to take this lady out for lunch and get her back in that little time?"

Wilson Freeman rested his hands on the front office counter in Carver School. I parked right in front, Zeli," he said. "We can be to Trentons in five minutes. They serve lunch specials, ten minutes after you order, guaranteed or you don't have to pay. Half an hour to eat, then back here. No problem."

"Sounds like you got a stopwatch." But Azelita was rising from behind her desk, smoothing down the skirt of her green suit with its embroidered designs on the jacket lapels.

"So you'll be coming along?"

"Only if nobody's taken that handsome vehicle of yours, Wilson. Just because you run a dealership don't mean you're immune from Galveston's criminal element."

"I locked the door."

"If we're lucky, that may have been sufficient." Azelita tried to look stern, but without complete success.

"I guarantee only so much security." Wilson winked at her. "That, however, I *do* guarantee."

"Smart man." Azelita bumped open the little office

[186]

gate with her hip. "Smart man. No wonder I waste my days with you."

"Smart lady. But we got no reason to doubt that."

Wilson ushered her down the steps to the car. There was no doubt in Azelita's mind that lunch at Trentons, even with a forty-minute maximum, was preferable to a macaroni hot dish in the Carver School cafeteria. As the car pulled away, Wilson flicking the power steering, she looked down at her firm abdomen. Taste and calories weren't necessarily linked, either. But little luxuries made a difference in this or any world. The plush upholstery smelled newborn, and every dial on the dashboard glittered. That man treated himself to what he wanted, yes he did.

"Zeli, I got something to ask you."

"I hope it ain't marriage, Wilson. I too old to be interested in nonsense like that."

"Zeli, I'm not talking nigger here." His back tensed. "You remember when I threw that at you, right?"

"You made me so mad that night, there'd be no way I'd forget it."

"Healthy to get mad." But she put her hand on his elbow and patted the crunchy shirt.

Ahead of them, the sky met the sea in a line of white light. Already they were pulling into Trentons' parking lot, and Azelita was happy to note that Wilson's fancy Buick fit right along with the doctors' Oldsmobiles and snappy foreign cars. The heat sent the air waving off shiny bumpers and hoods. As they parked next to something sleek and foreign, Azelita craned her neck to identify the make.

"Audi," Wilson said.

"Audi what?"

[187]

"Zeli, you looking so hard for the name on that machine that I come to rescue you. I got no problem giving you what you need."

"That's what I get for going out to lunch with a big car man."

"That's what you get indeed." Wilson leaned toward her and put one square hand under her breast, hoisting it up against the lapel of her suit.

"Wilson!"

"Remember that I seen them without that green wrapping."

"Wilson, put your hand back where it belongs."

"*This* is where it belong."

"That being the case . . ." He had his fancy Strauss pants on, the ones with the slim-cut front. Feinting at his anticipated response, Azelita dug down into his lap, where she could see the nicely sewn bulge. His head banged off the ceiling of the car.

"You bitch!"

"*Black* bitch, Wilson. No use denying our upbringings. Be true to your true self, I always say." She opened her door and stepped out, putting her suit jacket in order. She could be as fancy a lady as anyone.

"That what they teach you in that school?" Wilson's voice came clear as he swung himself outside the car. "You ain't worth me buying you a special lunch."

"Fine. I got my own money. But I got no respect for men who go back on their promises."

Shaking his head, Wilson started for the restaurant door, Azelita following. She altered her step only to avoid bumping into three young white men standing by the entryway. They were all smaller than she was, but that was no surprise. Even their voices were small, so when the

mouth of the palest one opened and the word "nigger" came out, she scarcely noticed it.

"What you mean, man?" Wilson stopped at the door.

"Hey-hey." The man smiled a pale smile.

"You don't think I got ears good enough to pick up honkey dirt? You think your mouth so fine it can open up and let anything out?"

"Wilson." Azelita took his elbow.

"Hey, man. Not talking to *you.*" The three young men began to back down the steps, edging across the parking lot.

"Wilson, there's no *point*," Azelita said, expecting him to go leaping after them and not at all sure she could hold him back.

But he took her elbow instead and led her inside. She could feel his muscles loosening. The hostess, lipsticked like a movie star, guided them to a booth overlooking the seawall without even being asked.

"Wilson, what's this question you got for me?" Azelita asked, closing the door on what had happened on the steps. Spilled milk, her mama would have said. She began to study the menu.

He looked up but didn't answer.

"Wilson, you said you had something to ask me. I want to know what it is."

Slowly, Wilson lowered his menu from in front of his face. "Now that I think of it, Zeli, it's not so much a question. I believe you might call it an offer."

"An offer?"

"Yes."

"Not to sweep me down the aisle?"

"All in its own good time."

Wilson reached out a long arm and signaled to the

[189]

waitress. Then he looked her right in the eye. "I want you to go back to school, Zeli."

She could hardly believe her ears.

"You got a big mouth, and you make fun of your own brains. But you are a smart lady, and we both know it. You got no business wasting your life picking up after those white teachers and getting pennies in your paycheck."

"How I earn my living is one big step up from scrubbing some white lady's floors!"

"Yes, it is, and I don't deny it. But you've rested long enough on that big step. Now it is time to *climb*. I figure you can start classes in September, enroll right here in Galveston College. Two years, and then you finish up at Clear Lake. Get a nice little car for the drive. Major in teaching." He waved at the waitress again.

"How many college degrees you got, Wilson?"

"You know I did it with dollars, not degrees."

"Who's going to pay Uncle Washington and fund my food bill while I walking around with books under my arm?"

"I am."

The waitress arrived. Wilson politely told her they were limited for time, pointing to the big watch on his big wrist. The waitress nodded. Her name tag said WISTERIA. Azelita could only hope it was a mistake.

"So, Zeli." Wilson reached across the table and captured her hand before she could plunge it into her lap.

"So?"

"You willing to think about it? You get in a classroom, they'll make you Teacher of the Year. You can educate those little Viet kids you got yourself so fond of."

Azelita looked at him hard. "It don't seem to me that *you're* all that fond of them, Wilson."

He looked back at her even harder. "Most of them I seen in Nam came with grenades under their shirts, and I was the one they was throwing them at. But I'm not giving *them* anything. This is for *you*. If there's some little spillover, I ain't so small-minded that I can't live with it."

26 The sun rising over Galveston Bay had only begun to light the plate of the sky from underneath, reflecting back a gleam that lay on the surface of the waves. The sky, layered with cloud strips near the horizon, appeared so translucent that someone watching might expect to see the small fishing boats reflected in it. Everything seemed to be replicated in everything else as if there were no isolated elements in nature.

Xan and Linh sat on the edge of the cement bulkhead where the fleet of Vietnamese fishing boats was docked. They dangled their bare feet in the oily water, wiggling their toes under the surface. Around their ankles, the brown ocean circled and clutched, and when they lifted their feet up, their legs were marked by a thin ring of iridescence.

"The water's dirty." Linh was still half asleep. She had been deep in dreams when Xan had tossed the handful of rice at her window. Somewhere in her night mind, someone had been unwrapping a long, long shawl that she had wound around herself. As he pulled, the shawl unwinding in his hands, he had moved farther and farther away. Then the rice had hit.

"I don't like dirty water." Linh wiped her feet with her hands. She looked out through the tangled rig of the nearest fishing boat into the edge of the sky, which was now as orange and fuzzy as a peach. Above her, the peach washed into a pale blue. Gulls swooped and called.

"Which boat is your father's?" Xan kept his feet underwater, kicking them forward, then pulling them back. Waves rolled out from his ankles and slapped against the bulkhead.

"There. With the black line around it."

"Why he paint a black line?"

"So the ghost couldn't come on deck."

"My father says ghost don't come to America," Xan said.

"American people have Halloween ghosts."

"Those are for babies." Xan waved his arms. "Hoo, hoo," he whistled.

"Vietnamese ghosts are not the same thing," Linh replied. She reached for the big paper bag at her side. "We should hurry."

"You afraid?" Xan expected that his father would beat him with a big stick when he got home. His mother would yell and hide in the bathroom, but she wouldn't *do* anything. Now that she had the baby in her belly, she had forgotten about Xan. She just thought about the new American baby that could grow up to be the First Vietnamese President.

"No, I'm not afraid."

"If your father knows you are not home, will he beat you?"

"My father won't beat me," Linh said.

"How you know?"

"He never beat me."

[193]

"Will he go look in your bed to find you?"

Linh got to her knees, then to her feet. "He doesn't want me to cry," she said, hoisting the paper bag. "Besides, my mother is home from the hospital. He won't think about me today."

"Your mother not crazy anymore?"

"I don't know. They send her home."

"The American doctor fix her?"

"I don't know."

"If she is home, you don't have to cook anymore."

A little smile came up on Linh's face. "I can cook just as good as she can," she said.

Xan wiggled his feet into his big sneakers, then jumped over the strip of brown water to the deck of the nearest boat, landing on the flat boards between a coil of rope and the shrimp boxes. "Come on," he said.

Linh jumped after him, the bag in her arms. The two of them ran to the front of the boat where the piles of green nets were coiled. One behind the other, they climbed up on them, then jumped down to the back of the next boat. Linh's father's boat was fourth in line, tucked in the corner of the bulkhead. In a moment, they stood together on its stern, their black hair glistening as the first real rays of sun spread across the water.

"Did you ever see your father make the offering?"

"No. But I heard him talk about it."

"It's not the right time of year."

"You are supposed to do it when the fishing season starts. But we're not asking for good fishing."

Xan hesitated. "Maybe Thuy Tinh will be mad if we do it now."

"We should try. She already knows not to let storms

come when the boat is out. She's very strong. She can do more than one thing."

Xan had squatted down by the twisted pile of heavy rope. "You got it all?" he asked.

"Yes."

"You buy it?"

Linh opened the bag. "I saved my money for the duck," she said. "I bought it in A & P with Harry and Gary. It was frozen like a rock."

"Maybe Harry and Gary will tell your father."

"No, they won't. I bought them Milky Ways. They promised."

"What about the whiskey?"

Linh shook her head. "I couldn't buy that. I'm too young." She smiled a little smile. "I took it from under our altar," she said. "My father has lots of bottles there."

As they spoke, the gulls were wheeling faster than ever, looping in spirals against the strengthening blue of the sky. On the bulkhead next to the Vietnamese fishing boats, a pair of white birds with gray stripes on their wings marched among the rusty metal and discarded rope ends. They looked like fat sentinels, and they bobbed their heads with medium-grade interest at Linh and Xan.

"Did you ever see *your* father do this thing?" Linh held a greasy package in one hand and tore at its wrappings with the other.

"No. In Vietnam I was too little."

"But you were here this year when the boats started going out."

Xan pulled the second package from the bag. "Yes, but my father was mad at me then. He went out with his friends. They did the boat blessing."

Holding their parcels, the two of them clambered over the rope heaps to the prow of Linh's father's boat. A little chop had come up, and the boat began to rock against it. The others, tied up together with their sides protected with strips of old tires, rubbed and rocked too. Like dancers, the entire landscape of boats lifted and fell.

At the front of the boat, Xan stopped. He kicked off his sneakers, then leaped up onto the little pointed wall at the prow.

"Take this." Linh held out the half-unwrapped parcel.

Xan grabbed it with one hand and shook it. The greasy paper crackled and opened. He shook it again until the paper caught the wind and fluttered down between the boats.

"Now?" He held the roasted duck out over the waves.

"Yes," Linh said.

Xan waved the duck out toward the water, holding his hand under its shiny brown body. *"Nghe chung toi,"* he said. "Hear us. Thuy Tinh, *nghe chung toi."* He looked up at the sky and waved the duck as high up as he could reach. *"Xin on tren che cho chung con mai ma. Chung toi hoi anh."* Carefully, he peeled a tiny strip of brown skin from the side of the bird and let the wind take it. The gulls circled.

"Did you tell her what we want to do?" Linh asked.

"You *heard* me. I said she should bless us."

"Did you ask her not to make any storms for us?"

"You *heard* me!"

"Do you think *she* heard you?"

"I tried to say it loud."

His answers weren't completely reassuring, but Linh accepted them. "Now this," she said, handing him the other package. He slid the duck back to her.

Overhead, the sun was riding like an egg yolk above the blanket of morning cloud. Far out in the bay, a shrimp boat floated past. Xan stood on tiptoe at the prow, paper bag at his feet, bottle in his hand. "Do it," Linh said.

"Should I make it up?"

Linh remembered third grade, Mrs. Evans, the words "Try, try with all your might" printed on the margin above the blackboard. "Do the best you can," Linh said. The juicy duck lay on the deck next to her like the body of a cooked baby.

Stretching upright, Xan held the open whiskey bottle over the ocean. "Thuy Tinh!" he demanded, slinging a brown line of liquid out of the bottle's mouth. *"Chung goi hoi anh! Xan chuoc ve Linh. Linh thuoc ve Xan."* He waved another line of liquid, then another. The sharp smell of liquor came back to Linh's nose.

Xan threw the final spurt, then looked back. "Okay?" he asked, suddenly become an American boy who had just sacrificed the meat and water of life to the Vietnamese goddess of the sea.

"Say it to her in English."

"What?"

"Say it to her in English."

"Say *English* to Thuy Tinh?" Xan was astonished.

Linh settled herself on the deck, ready for the picnic. She laid the duck out next to her and began to pull its legs loose. "Say it in English," she told him again. "Make *sure* she knows she should bless us. When we grow up and marry, we will marry here in Texas. Thuy Tinh will understand because she sends the ocean around all countries. Then you come down and we eat before I have to go home."

27 Lang held the letter for a long time before pulling out the kitchen drawer for a knife to slit it open. The tissue envelope was worn around the edges, held and pressed on its journey, rubbed by the fingers of postal intermediaries, felt by the sun as it lay with a heap of letters in an open bag on the docks of Can Tho, rained on, dried, caught by the edge of mold belowdecks as the ship tossed in the waves. He knew the letter had come by airplane, sent with an official air-mail stamp, but at the back of his mind where all his thoughts took root, he always saw the letters on a boat where the salt air softened their margins, delivered to the American shore after weeks—even months—afloat. It was not possible that a journey which had been so long for him, a journey still continuing, could be accomplished in the heavy overnight hum of a transport aircraft's motors, that the swift eating of distance could deny all the stretched lines of his own allegiances.

He shifted the letter to his other hand, his fingers edging up around it. Letters didn't usually come so near each other. The last one, the picture, had arrived only three months ago. Usually he heard twice a year. It was hard to get a letter written, hard to get money for the stamps, hard to take it to the post office in Can Tho and mail it. He understood that. In America, these things were so much easier. He himself wrote every month, sending whatever money he could afford. Ten dollars meant two weeks of rice and pork. Even five dollars meant the difference between comfort in the stomach and a fierce hunger that hurt like a blow.

He knew that too.

Outside his window, the parking lot glimmered in the evening sunlight. Tiny specks of mica were embedded in the tar, and when the lights hit them, they shone like jewels. Karl Mike called the mica fool's gold. "And we're the fools," he said, laughing. "The guys who laid that stuff get fifteen dollars an hour, and no medical school debts to pay back. No malpractice. No crazy crock patients. Face it, Winner, when the road forked, we got the big head and took the wrong turn."

Lang didn't know what half of that meant. Karl Mike always went on and on.

With a sharp paring knife, he slit the envelope across the top and pulled out the thin sheet inside, the Vietnamese words with their accent marks showing through the blank side of the paper. Only one sheet this time. He turned it over and unfolded it.

At first, the words seemed ordinary. His name was there, and it was the name he had always had. The writing was his father's, careful and stiff after the stroke. He was using a pen Lang had sent, and the smooth American lines of ink seemed to blur the short Vietnamese words. *Ma* came out, for "mother," and then "sick" and then "ceremony" and "family" and "March 27." *Ma* and *binh* and *le* and *gia dinh* and *Ngay 27 thang Ba*. There were other words and he could read them, but he had no place to put them in his head. The word *chet*, for "died," floated the furthest away. Even when he read the letter through again, there were spaces around words that colored them with so bright a light that the letters swayed and twisted.

He felt his thumbs and fingers gripping so tightly that the paper dampened with his perspiration. Gritting his teeth, he tried to hold his hands firm. They wrenched apart, the letter torn in two between them.

"Jesus Christ, Win-Win, what are you doing to that shelf? We only rent this place, you know." Karl Mike threw his armful of medical books on the sofa, then flung himself after them. Leaning against the cushions, he looked at the bookcase on the opposite wall, the two top shelves empty. Lang, balancing on the kitchen stool, was hammering what looked like side walls to the top shelf. Small waves of plaster dust filtered down.

Lang kept hammering. After the last nail had gripped the wood, he smoothed its edges with his fingers, then climbed down and went to his room. When he returned, he held a roll of bright yellow crepe paper and a small brass vase.

"Halloween?" Karl Mike asked.

No answer.

"Look, Win-Win, it's nigh on midnight. Old George upstairs will be calling Galveston's Finest to evict us."

Lang, back on the kitchen stool, draped the crepe paper around the second shelf and began to tack it into place, overlapping the edges with the top surface. When he had completed the drape, he stretched higher and began to hang another strip from the edge of the shelf above. As Karl Mike watched, a sheltered structure grew, a small and hidden house framed with bright trim.

"Wrong career? Changing to interior decoration? Professional opportunities I haven't heard about?"

Lang set the brass vase in the middle of the lower shelf, his hands gentling it into position. Then he climbed down again. He moved into the kitchen, and when he came back, he held a saucer, one with red flowers painted on it. In the other hand, he had four small oranges.

"Just how creative can you get?"

Lang didn't respond. Placing the saucer next to the vase, he arranged three oranges on it, then balanced the fourth delicately on the base of the first three. Then he went to his room again, returning with the picture of his parents and a pair of scissors. With one slice of the blades, he cut his mother's image away from his father's and turned back to what he had built. Once more climbing the stool, he leaned his mother's picture in the middle of the shelf and bowed his head.

Karl Mike stood up, his arms spread wide. "Boy, *my* mother would admire that little work of art," he said. "But what if we want orange juice for supper?"

"*Du ma may!* Fuck you!" Lang shouted, flinging himself at Karl Mike and toppling him to the carpet. Upstairs, someone banged hard on the floor. Then Lang wrenched himself away from Karl Mike and crawled back across the room next to the bookshelves. A small sound came from his mouth, and he began to cry.

"Lang!" Karl Mike struggled to his feet, unhurt. "What's going on?"

"I have no joss sticks to burn. I have none."

"What?"

"No fire for her." His voice choked.

"*What?*" Karl Mike was going to put his hand on Lang's shoulder, but the sharp white space around him was as solid as ice.

"I must light the joss sticks. I must pray to her spirit. I must ask that her spirit come to me and help me. I must honor my mother, who has died when I was not with her."

"Your mother's *dead?*"

Lang began to sway. "I never bought the joss sticks for her honor. I never built the altar. I never welcomed my ancestors at Tet. I never gave them what they had a right to demand. I put my feet on the face of my homeland. I forgot my own people."

"But you're American now."

"I am *not* American." Lang shook his head fiercely, "I must honor her with light and fire. She must forgive me."

"Jesus, Lang." Karl Mike's voice had a desperate edge to it. "You can't go running up to Little Saigon in Houston at this hour. How about a flashlight? I'll get mine." He turned toward his bedroom, then looked back. "Hey, Lang, your *mom*'s dead? Man, I am really sorry."

But Lang had risen to his feet and grabbed Karl Mike with both his arms. Though he was almost a foot shorter, the strength in his hands held Karl Mike still. "No flashlight!" he screamed. "No flashlight! No American thing! On the altar there must be *fire, fire, fire!*"

28 "Azelita, thank God you came in tonight. Can you draft one of the Magnolias to fill in the Forget-Me-Not chorus? Somebody's out sick and didn't call in."

Azelita nodded and moved off to the fourth-grade classroom. It was Spring Festival night at Carver School. Already parents were assembling on the folding chairs facing the makeshift stage in the gym. Already the fifth-grade orchestra was tuning up.

If she resigned and went off to college, she would miss it all. For those four years, anyway. But that was a decision still to be made. Wilson would just have to wait until she made up her mind.

Through the doorway into the auditorium, Azelita could see an immensely fat white woman pulling two small chairs together so she could sit on them. She wore a shapeless housedress with poppies on a purple background. Three white-blond children braceleted her legs, and she slapped one as she eased herself down. Thank God she's not black, thought Azelita. Let the whites mess up once in a while.

In the classroom, she recruited a Magnolia for the

Forget-Me-Not ranks. "I ain't gonna wear that blue hat," said Geoffrey, his eyes squinting.

"You wear it now, boy, and then when your song is over, you sneak back out and get your pink one."

"I ain't gonna," he mumbled, but with less defiance. "I didn't practice no blue song."

"You don't have to sing it. Just stand next to Felicia, hold her hand, and open your mouth."

"Felicia's got them sticky fingers. Yuck!"

Azelita took the leftover blue bonnet from the shelf, set it solidly on Geoffrey's head, and tied the ribbons underneath his chin. "Go ahead, boy," she said. "They lining up now. You look real cute."

Geoffrey squirmed but acquiesced. Outside in the auditorium, the fifth-grade orchestra was still tuning up on "Home on the Range." Their other song was "God Bless America." Azelita knew every scratch and whine of their struggle toward melody.

"Ready?" The fourth-grade teacher stuck her head in. "Thank God it's a short program."

"Yes. I'll keep an eye on things." Azelita watched the Forget-Me-Nots start their procession out. On the other side of the wall, the audience began to clap as the Forget-Me-Nots climbed the steps to the stage, a ragged thumping marking their progress. The orchestra encouraged them onward.

With a deep breath, Azelita sat down, shoving herself into the confines of an elementary-size chair. There was a *ssss* sound as she made contact. Puzzled, she listened. The sound came again, but from slightly to one side. Then, two seats over, she saw that a coat thrown across the back of a chair bulged slightly and was moving in and out. The sound occurred once more, and a hand emerged suddenly from the top of the coat. Then a head with black hair. A very small Vietnamese boy looked right at Azelita.

"I Harry," he said.

"What you doing here, boy?"

The boy's mouth widened into a huge grin, showing two rows of tiny teeth. Then, with the grin still splitting his face, tears began to flood from his eyes. *"I Harry,"* he said again, almost loud enough to be heard in the auditorium where the off-key violins were spreading both home and range as thick as butter.

Azelita reached out for Harry but he shrank inside the coat. She felt along the sides until she located what had to be his shoulders and worked her hands down into his armpits, hoisting him up. He was so rigid that it was like holding a small refrigerator.

"Harry, you all right?"

The refrigerator did not melt.

"You here with someone, my friend?" Somehow the boy seemed familiar.

"Fuck," said Harry.

Azelita raised one knee to help balance him against the chair, and with her freed arm unwrapped the coat. Harry had stopped crying by now. "Fuck," he said again.

In the auditorium, they were letting the deer and the antelope roam. A solitary cymbal clanged enthusiastically on the offbeat. Some parents had begun to clap prematurely.

"Harry, do you have a sister here? A brother?" This child looked more and more familiar to Azelita. Who were the Vietnamese children participating tonight? Only Linh. And she had brothers, yes she did.

Harry stuck out his tongue. There was an abraded red spot above his nose, centered between his eyebrows. It looked like a caste mark. He wore a Zorro T-shirt, much too big, but tucked in at the belt of his jeans. Like Xan, his big sneakers gaped loose.

In the auditorium, or rather the gymnasium, everyone was clapping. The program must be ending, Magnolias and Forget-Me-Nots open-throated in climax. The Rodriguez family, whose ninth one-a-year child was now in third grade, would be rising like a tide from their seats, waves of proud Spanish washing out of them. The principal would be shaking hands as everyone left.

"Fuck," said Harry. He took her hand. "I love you," he said.

Past the classroom door, which Azelita had quickly opened, the children began to parade. Harry watched them with great care, holding on to Azelita with confidence, standing on his chair with the big coat wadded behind him. When Linh appeared, he raised one hand straight above his head as if in salute. She came directly to him.

"Good boy?" she asked Azelita. There was no doubt who Harry belonged to.

"Did you bring him?"

"Father brought us." Linh began to slip Harry into the enormous coat. "He wants to go to school all the time."

"Why didn't your father watch the program?"

"My father has only a little bit English," Linh said, "and he holds Gary outside. Gary is too little to come in the school."

Azelita nodded. "Well, at least Harry is learning English."

"Little bit," Linh said, smiling. "I teach him."

Azelita wondered what treasures of the English language Harry would say next. "Will your father come in for you?" she asked, cutting off any further display of vocabulary.

"No," Linh said matter-of-factly. "He is scared. Like in the library. You remember." She took Harry's hand. "We go to him. You come with us."

"You want *me* to come?"

"Yes. To greet my father."

"Greet?" The word had a strange sound.

Linh looked concerned. "Not the right words?"

"No, no, girl. It's fine. But I'm not your teacher."

"That's all right," Linh said. "You are my *ban than.*"

"Could you say that in English?"

Linh stopped and thought. Like many nonnative children, she learned her new American language in independent chunks. To switch to a parallel line was not easy. Harry looked up at her from deep inside the oversized coat, then sat down on the floor. The stiff fabric rose around him like a teepee.

"It means my best friend," Linh said. "Come."

Outside, the playground, a parking lot for the evening, was filled with parents and children climbing into cars and heading home. The air smelled of salt and sewage, and haloes of yellow surrounded the playground lights. *"Nhieu trang,"* Harry said, raising his hands.

"What's he saying?"

"He says 'many moons.' "

"Is that what he thinks they are?"

"He is a little boy," said Linh, as if that explained everything.

The air seemed to thicken as the fog took on strength. Only a few minutes had passed, but it was as if the night had suddenly defined itself. Behind them, the doors of the school sucked shut as the principal came down the steps.

One of the lampposts animated itself and separated into two posts. One post advanced. It turned into a small Vietnamese man, wearing jeans and thong sandals, holding a very small boy. Azelita recognized the man from the library fiasco.

Linh stepped forward. "Father," she said.

The man smiled.

"Father," Linh said again. *"Anh nho co ay.* You remember her. She is my friend."

Clearly, the man understood the word "friend." He reached out and took Azelita's hand, shaking it briefly. "Phuong Nguyen," he said. His palm was rock hard. In the library, surrounded by books he couldn't read, he had seemed almost frail.

"We will go home now," said Linh. Only two cars remained on the playground, one a tiny immaculate Ford Fiesta and the other a huge rusted ancient Chrysler with tail fins. Not hard to tell which one had a Vietnamese name on its registration.

The little family moved off, turning away from Azelita so slowly that they seemed a part of the advancing night. Linh moved closer to her brothers.

"Bye-bye," said Phuong Nguyen, turning halfway. He raised one hand, but he didn't wave.

Harry had begun to circle his father, skipping. "Fuck," he shouted. "I love you."

29

"I got a bite!"

"It is just the waves."

"No!" Xan gave his pole a big wrench. The end of his line spun out of the water, a small silver body attached to it, then dropped back. "See! Now I'll bring it in! You can have it for supper!" He began reeling frantically, tilted against the pull of the surf.

Lang Nguyen stepped behind Xan so the boy wouldn't crack his skull if he plunged backward. Lang's own line dangled untouched in the waves. Beginner's luck. This was Xan's first fishing trip in America, and Lang was an old hand at it.

"See!" Xan was pulling in so fast that the spinning reel whined. The line approached the edge of the cement fishing pier, where the waves broke with less force, and he gave it a final flap up onto rocks that supported the structure. A round-sided mullet lay at his feet. Xan wrenched the hook from its mouth.

"Look at this!" He held the dripping fish up, inches from Lang's face. Lang kept himself from wincing at its odor. Mullet tasted like mud. There was nothing you could do to purify their flesh.

"Where's the stringer?"

"Here."

"Good. Now I'll catch you another one." Xan began to rebait his hook. He was using pork rind, each piece more fatty and repulsive than the last.

"I think your fish should go home with you to your parents," Lang said.

Xan stood up, his baited hook waving dangerously. "No! My fish are for you! You help me in school, and I give you a present. My turn!" He reached out and patted Lang companionably on the shoulder. "Besides, we are Vietnamese men. We help each other." He cast his line with a wild surge. "If *you* catch lots of fish, you can share them with me and my family."

Lang looked at his own smoothly riding line. It seemed to represent everything his life did not: control, self-sufficiency, lack of desire. He could not imagine that a fish would rise to take it. He did not *want* a fish to take it.

Xan began to stalk back and forth at the edge of the fishing pier, his sneakers slapping the cement. An elderly fisherman with a bushy beard surveyed him from the other side, mouth turned down. Xan didn't notice. He swerved close to the old man, then swung back.

Lang knew that Vietnamese boys were not favorites of Galveston natives. "You better stand still, Xan," he said.

"But I want the fish to think my bait is *alive.*"

"The waves do that."

Xan stood still for a moment. "You know a lot about fishing," he said, turning away from his line. "Is that because you're a doctor?"

"I don't think so."

"Doctors fix people all the time," Xan went on. "They know a lot about everything, especially American doctors." He paused. "If your mother was here with you in America, could you have fixed her so she didn't die?"

Lang was stunned. Nobody in Vietnam would ever say something like that. "I don't think so," he said again.

"That's all right. You know a lot anyway."

"Not so much."

Xan stuck his pole into a crack and came up to Lang, his hands on his hips. Lang braced himself.

"Do you have a girlfriend?"

"What?"

"A girlfriend. Men have girlfriends."

Lang felt caught, as definitively as the mullet.

"Because *I* have a girlfriend," Xan went on. "Linh Nguyen. We sacrifice to Thuy Tinh to bless us so we can marry when we grow up. But we must wait a long time. You can get married now if you want."

"I don't think so," Lang choked out, feeling ridiculous as he said the words for a third time.

"You like Vietnamese girls or American girls?"

Lang was speechless.

"Because I think it's this way," Xan went on. "Vietnamese girls, they know how your life is. They help you. If there was a hurricane, a Vietnamese girl could help me with my boat. That's why I will marry Linh when I grow up." Xan twanged his tight line where it hung between the attachments on his fishing rod. "But it's not the same for you," he said. "You are old. So you could *teach* an American girl about your life. As long as she was short like you, you could teach her anything."

Lang began to reel in his line. At least his hands still functioned.

"And then your children could have yellow hair," Xan went on. "Like the sun!"

[211]

30 "It isn't *brown*, Trang."

"It *is* brown." Trang held strands of her hair out on both sides of her head as if they were wings. "When the sun shines on it, it is *very* brown. More brown than black. Not black at all." She pulled her hair so hard that her head shook. "If my hair *was* black and my father was Vietnamese, your mother would never be angry with me."

Tri was stunned. This was nothing Trang ever talked about. Tri's mother never mentioned it either. He had believed that his mother hit Trang because she didn't like big girls. Or because she was still angry that Tuan had been killed on the beach and Trang was still alive.

Trang had stopped pulling her hair now and was beginning to climb out the window. She sat on the sill, her feet dangling inside, then pulled the window down until it hit against her knees.

"Trang, don't do that! You'll get hurt!"

But Trang wiggled her toes and leaned back, her fingers against the frame of the window. "Get me some paint," she ordered.

"Paint?"

"P-a-i-n-t. *Son mau vang*. Yellow paint." She pointed.

[212]

"In your desk. The school box. Left over from the project for science."

"Why you want paint?"

"Get it! Get it, or I will fly down and you will never see me again."

Tri hurried to his desk. At first, he couldn't remember where he'd stored the school box, but it was wedged in the back of the bottom drawer under all his old papers from his study of fish.

"The yellow's almost gone," he said.

"Just give it to me!"

Tri slid the jar under the window frame. Trang reached down to take it, then handed it back. "Open it," she said. "If I let go, I'll be dead."

Quickly, Tri unscrewed the top and returned the jar to her. "Do you want a brush?" he asked. Did she want to paint a picture on the window? Paint the peeling frame? He always obeyed Trang's orders except when it meant that his mother would beat him later. This time, the risk was entirely her own.

"No!"

"Okay!" He stepped back and watched for what would happen next.

Nothing did seem to happen next. Trang examined the paint, tilting the jar to make sure it would flow. She held it up to the light. Her eyes narrowed, and even through the smeared window glass, Tri could tell that she had a serious plan. It was all too crazy for him to be afraid.

Then, before his very eyes, Tri saw her hold the jar over her head, tilted down. The yellow ran into her hair like a golden shower. She rubbed it in. Her eyes narrowed to tiny smiles as she moved toward her own image. Her lips kissed the glass window.

[213]

Tri could hear his mother calling. She beat on the kitchen ceiling with a broom handle. Tri turned and tore out of the room, not daring to look back.

In the meantime, Trang continued to stare into the dim glass while her strange transplanted image stared back. The yellow in her hair looked like a careless cap, half covering the dark underneath. There was not enough to change her into an American yellow-head, and even if there had been, nothing had really changed. She had just made another foolish mess.

Trang flung the empty jar to the pavement. Glass shattered, but she hardly heard it because she was already inside. She bent over Tri's desk, yellow dribbles staining her blouse, and ransacked the drawers one by one. In the second drawer to the right, under the lined tablets, she found the scissors. Tears mixing with the streaks of yellow paint, she held out the stained wall of her hair and began to chop it off so close to her head that her scalp cringed against the sharp steel. Bending her head, she chopped harder.

"Trang, you must stop this," Lang said. "It is not appropriate for either a Vietnamese or an American."

Trang said nothing.

"I do not like to go out to my car in the morning and find notes on the windshield. It is not safe for you to be out at night in Galveston. You are a young woman." Lang's voice tightened. "It is not appropriate," he said.

Trang said nothing. She looked carefully around their part of the Clam Shell Restaurant, doing it all without moving her head. She wanted him to see exactly how he looked by the expression on her face. She wanted to be a burnished mirror for him. She needed to make sure no American waitress was coming to distract him. If one was, she would send a silent curse.

"The ice cream was not appropriate either but I thought you meant it well. Ice cream melts very rapidly here." There was something strange about Trang's head, Lang realized. It appeared to sit a great distance from her shoulders. Had she changed her hairstyle? Her forehead seemed to have enlarged. Under the tight tan skin, he could imagine nothing except intensified conspiracy.

"Do you understand?"

Trang tilted her chin upward. "Will you marry that yellow-haired American?" she asked, first in Vietnamese and then in English, so he could not possibly misunderstand. Her face was intent but not enraged.

"What?"

Trang waited. She knew that there were many yellow-haired American women in Galveston, but she was sure Lang Nguyen knew only one.

"I do not plan to marry anyone for a long time." Moisture filled the trough behind Lang's lower lip. He swallowed.

Trang didn't believe him. Clearly he did not know his own mind. That was not unusual for Vietnamese in America, who stood between two cultures. As a *bui doi,* she knew her own mind much better.

"But you must not bring me presents," Lang went on. "You must not come to my apartment. You must not be so forward. It is not appropriate. It is not *phu hop.*" He lifted his iced tea to his lips, but the lemon slice slid around to the front of the glass and prevented him from drinking. Trang held her fingers still, knowing it would take only a moment to remove the lemon and allow his lips access to the glass. She would do it when he was not looking.

"You are only a friend, Trang. I am like your Vietnamese uncle." Why did her face look so small, her head so fragile as it drifted above the straight line of her shoulders? Why did she appear to be waiting for something to sweep her away?

Trang reached into her lap. She pulled up a parcel and handed it across the table to him.

"What is this? Not more ice cream?" It was a bad joke. He could see that she would give it no more attention than it deserved.

"Not ice cream." Her hand ran along the tissue fold on the top of the package. It was not sealed. "This is from me. Open it."

Lang's hands stayed around the iced-tea glass. He felt as if the package contained something that would rise up and dissolve his life.

"*I* open it for you?" She was asking in English.

He inclined his head.

As if this had been her intention, Trang reached across the Formica table with both hands. She touched the paper first, assessing its strength. Satisfied, she placed her thumbs in the middle fold, then pulled the paper apart. When she looked up, her face had an expression of having moved silence to meaning without the intervention of words.

Lang looked down at the contents of the package. On the double sheet of tissue, snarled and stained with irregular spots of yellow, lay the twisted lengths of Trang's hair.

31 The social worker was built like a hockey goalie, with a low center of gravity anchored in his swivel chair. He seemed to be looking for a small hard object that would assault him from a direction he had not anticipated. "Who filled out this SSI form for you, Mr. Truong?" he asked.

"I no Truong."

The social worker looked at the name at the top of the page. "But your wife . . ." he started, his eyes checking the form.

"I Nguyen. Like this." Phuong Nguyen leaned over the desk, took a pen from the china mug that said GLORIFY GALVESTON, and printed his name on the top of the pad below the red line.

"Noo-gen?"

"Vietnamese say 'win.' "

"W-i-n?"

"Write N-g-u-y-e-n."

"You're not married then, the two of you. In that case, someone else will have to . . ."

"We marry. Hue Province. Vietnam. 1975."

"But her name?"

"She have name of father." Phuong Nguyen placed his hands carefully, as if they were breakable, on his jeans just above his kneecaps.

Outside the office, a child cried. Another young voice hushed it. A third voice, older and female, let loose a string of Vietnamese words.

"All right now." The social worker spoke slowly. "This is the report I got." He pushed a packet of paper across the desk, but not so far that he couldn't keep a finger on it. "It says that your wife has been diagnosed as being depressed. She has received shock treatments for depression." He studied one of the lengthy paragraphs. "An early diagnosis was schizophrenia." He glanced up. "Are these details accurate?"

Phuong Nguyen looked at him politely. From the lobby, there was a loud thump.

"Are they accurate?"

"I sorry."

"Do you understand?"

Phuong Nguyen nodded, smiling doubtfully. "I sign?" he asked.

"What?"

"You want name on paper?"

"What name?"

"Phuong Nguyen. N-g-u-y-e-n . . ." He nodded. "Win," he added.

"Stop." The social worker felt his center of gravity shifting. "I'll look these over later. You've been referred by the hospital. Your wife is sick." He tried to choose the simplest words he could, and he said each one as if it were a tiny stone being projected from his mouth. "The government in this country gives special Social Security benefits to . . ." He realized that his words were not registering, although Phuong Nguyen's eyes were on his and a faint smile encircled his lips. There was a scream from the lobby, then a burst of Vietnamese. Phuong Nguyen lifted a hand as if waving good-bye and then dropped it again to his leg.

"In America," said the social worker, "we give money. Sometimes. When someone has been incapacit . . ." He stopped. "When lady sick," he went on. Phuong Nguyen leaned forward. "Because she can't work."

"How much?"

"How much what?"

"How much you give lady no work?"

"The maximum amount is approximately five hundred dollars per month. However, in your case, *if* your wife is eligible, it would be less because she has built up no work record. Possibly three hundred dollars." The social worker felt all the instructions for his position collapse. Specific amounts were never to be mentioned. It was up to the client to prove eligibility, after all.

"Three hundred dollar too much," said Phuong Nguyen. He clasped his hands on the desk.

"*Too* much?"

"Very too much."

The social worker shook his head as if to replace it properly on his shoulders. "Just how incap . . . ill is your wife?" he asked.

"She Hai Truong."

"I know. Even though your name is Win. Spelled N-g-u-y-e-n. But that's not what I'm asking. How sick is she now? She's been home from the hospital for two weeks, is that correct?"

"She sick."

"Yes, I know. Can she work?"

"She cook. My girl help."

"Did she cook in a restaurant?"

Silence.

"Do you mean cook in a restaurant?"

A polite smile. "She cook rice," Phuong Nguyen said. "Now she cook rice like before. But she see man at night. He say 'Go Vietnam.' She say 'No, no' and run away. She go outside. My little boys cry. I go find her. She say I not husband." He smiled a wider, embarrassed smile. "She hit me," he went on. "Then she sleep little bit." He rubbed his stiff hair. "I no go boat. I no get money. Very hard." He laughed cheerfully. "American doctors very good," he said, with no edge of irony.

From the lobby, a burst of laughter disintegrated into loud sobbing. A child screamed. "Please," said Phuong Nguyen, rising to his feet, then moving toward the door in a glide. To the social worker, it looked as if he were on wheels. *"Im di!"* he shouted, and a girl's voice answered. The words had a fierce staccato sound.

"It's all right to bring them in," said the social worker, as if he were explaining a minor rule of a difficult game. But Phuong Nguyen had already opened the door and was lifting up two small boys. An older girl stood in the doorway, her hair loose around her face. She bowed her head to the social worker. "My mama is crazy," she explained, her English shaped in a perfect Beach Terrace slum child accent with Asian overtones. She pulled her shoulders back and walked in to stand next to her father.

"Where is your mother?"

The girl and her father nodded to each other. "You want?" Phuong Nguyen asked.

"It would be ideal if I could interview her briefly." They were the wrong words, too big, too official. The so-

[220]

cial worker started to rephrase the sentence, but the girl had understood him. "I get her," she said, and moved back into the lobby. The two boys clung to their father, who eased himself into the chair, one boy on each arm. "Harry," he said to the social worker, pushing the slightly larger one forward. "Gary," he said, reversing his motion. The boys had identical faces, but one had a small mole on his cheek. They were wearing Grateful Dead T-shirts and unlaced sneakers.

"Your sons?" A silly question.

"Boys."

"I know." Harry leaned forward and grabbed for the social worker's writing pad. The father moved him back with great gentleness.

The girl stepped into the office again and spoke briefly with her father in Vietnamese. He responded and gestured toward the lobby. *"Co ay dang den,"* he said, with what might have been anger or hopelessness or even enthusiasm. "She is coming."

And then a Vietnamese woman walked through the door. Her blouse hung on her thin body, and her feet were bare. Blankly, she rotated her head toward each person, but without focus. She placed her hand over her eyes.

"Mama," said Harry and Gary.

The woman hesitated, then bent down and began to crawl around the room, close against the wall as if the open space in the middle were impenetrable. She scuttled along the right wall, under the typewriter table with a movement so adept that its wheels never moved. At the corner of the room, she turned and continued until she neared the bookcase, at which point she moved out and then inside to the wall again. When she reached the far corner, behind the desk but not so far behind that the social worker couldn't see her, she squatted upright, her back against the corner of the wall, her arms tight across her breasts, her knees up to her chin. Her feet, pressed together, seemed a single appendage. *"Toi se o lai day,"* she said.

"She says she stay here," the girl interpreted.

"But we close in half an hour."

"She means she wants to stay with the ghost husband."

"Ghost husband? Him?" The social worker gestured to Phuong Nguyen.

"No." The girl pushed at her hair. "The husband in Vietnam."

"Is that why her name is Truong?"

"Truong is the name of my grandfather," said the girl. "She means she do not want to stay with my father, Harry, Gary, me."

"Why?"

"When we die, she will be sad." The girl's face showed no expression.

The social worker shook his head. "But you won't die," he said as if stating both a fact and a new discovery.

Now Hai Truong unfolded her arms. She held them in front of her face and began to move them back and forth in a motion that was eerily familiar to the social worker, yet seemed out of place. It was hard to pin down what she thought she was doing.

Then the social worker recognized the motion. She was swimming. "Is she all right?" he asked. But of course she wasn't all right. She could swim around his room until the clock struck midnight and she wouldn't reach shore, wouldn't be saved, wouldn't be all right.

"She still little bit sick," said Phuong Nguyen. "But

this my girl, Linh," he added. "She help work. I have same two wives." He beamed proudly. "Very good."

His voice desperate, the social worker broke into hurried speech. "I'll just finish up these papers and send them in," he said. "She's certainly entitled to the supplemental payments for disability. I mean, anyone can see ..." His voice trailed off. "I'll add a special recommendation to implement and prioritize the case," he finished, recovering himself.

Hai Truong had now raised herself to a standing position as far away as she could get from the chair and desk. She was whispering in Vietnamese, touching her earlobes. Then she lowered her hands and stared straight ahead. But when Gary pressed himself against her side, she touched his shoulder with the tips of her fingers.

"You'll be hearing within a month. Perhaps two weeks. If I don't hear anything in two weeks, I'll phone them personally. There's no doubt that she's incapacitated. With the payments, you can hire someone to watch ..." The social worker realized that all of them were staring at him benignly and intently. Hai Truong even flickered a smile.

The social worker stood up. "Go home," he said. "Please. It's okay. Money come."

The family rose too. Hai Truong slid through the door to the lobby first. "Thank you you welcome," said Phuong Nguyen, holding out his hand, small and bony but hard. The social worker took it. "Now she get well," Phuong Nguyen said.

"What?"

"Money come, she not sick."

"I don't understand."

"We give money. He fix."

"Who fix?"

"The man in Alabama," said the girl named Linh.

"He Vietnamese," said Phuong Nguyen. "When trouble in head, he fix. He talk *bao mong.*" He looked at his daughter for assistance.

"He talk spirit talk," she said. "To ghosts. All ghosts. When he talks, they go away."

Meanwhile, Hai Truong had reached the middle of the lobby. The family seemed in no hurry to join her. Instead, it was as if they were taking leave after a pleasant social call. The girl wiped Harry's and Gary's noses, straightened their Grateful Dead T-shirts. She hoisted Gary onto her hip while her father balanced Harry on his. He looked around the office. "Very good," he said. "You work here. Very good."

"Yes, it is very good." The social worker felt a strenuous pulling inside his skull. *"Very good,"* he said, so loudly that his voice seemed to bounce back from the diplomas on the wall.

"America," said Phuong Nguyen. "Very good." He smiled. "Lotsa money," he said as he walked out the door with his daughter and the boys to where his wife was sitting cross-legged on the floor of the lobby. "America fix," he said as he bent down to her.

32 "I haven't seen you up here for a while. Is everything all right?"

Lang's English, as always, began to drift into strange crannies when he felt nervous. "I busy," he said to Shirley. He tried to force himself not to be tense, realizing even as he did so that the whole idea of relaxation was contradictory to the concept of trying. "I am very busy," he continued, holding his hands in the air as if he were forcing out the correct sentence.

"Have you been doing any cooking lately?" Shirley didn't seem embarrassed or uncomfortable.

"I cook when I am home."

"So do I, you know." She smiled at Lang, as if she were about to go on. "Jason wants *real* food. He's not just a McDonald's kid."

How could she talk so openly? Where was her shame? Lang put his hands in the pockets of his white coat and stood silent.

"It's nice to see him grow," Shirley added. "I'm glad I can provide for him. As long as the money comes in, I can handle even our friend Smith-Fragon."

[225]

Why did she talk so much? Lang felt trapped in the ocean of her words. And she was just a nurse while he was a doctor. It had been a mistake to invite her to his apartment. Her skin was the wrong color, her hair more wrong yet. It had been a terrible mistake.

Behind him, the elevator door opened. A night orderly stepped out, and then, with a crunch of rubber tires over plastic molding, came the book cart with the black lady pushing it. She wore a green sundress with an unbuttoned white volunteer coat over it, and the brown plateau of her breasts was as solid as chocolate. In a replay of that night in February, the cart slid forward on the tile, her hands on the handles.

"I haven't seen you in a long time, Ms. Simpson," Shirley said.

"I only come twice a month these days," Azelita explained. "Got a little more action in my life, you might say."

"Busy?" Lang heard Shirley say the word, and he hated it as much as he did when he himself said it. All this American busyness was invented, an excuse for setting other people aside. If you were busy, you were no longer obliged to be polite, to be appropriate, to be bonded as family. No one in Vietnam was ever busy when someone needed him.

"I guess you could say I'm busy, all right," Azelita said cheerily.

"But you work in Carver School, don't you? And isn't school out for the summer?"

"One more week. They running late this year because they gave time off for Mardi Gras." Azelita shaped the books on her cart into a solid row, not a bound corner protruding. "The weather's been so hot I been thinking summer for weeks already."

"Summer seems to be Galveston's only season."

They were chatting like two old friends, Lang thought, as he rammed his hands deeper into his pockets. He should go check on the lab cultures. He had no business on this floor, no need to be here at all. He had made his resolution. If he never found the right woman from his own country, he would not marry. And after his encounters with Trang, finding the right Vietnamese woman seemed most unlikely.

"You're never too old," Shirley was saying. "I went back to college when I was pregnant with my little boy."

"Woman, I don't have *that* motivation. I just never had anybody offer me a free ride before. I wonder which one of us is crazy."

"Nobody's crazy. You're giving *him* something too. Did you know there's still a two-year nursing program at the community college? You might like nursing."

"I got no intentions of being some doctor's little bought lady." Azelita paused, looking around at Lang. "Whoops," she said, the cart rattling. "You can put me away for *that* one."

"Don't worry." Shirley's voice sounded lighter, and Lang, head down, was saying nothing. "I earn a decent living. If any doctor gives me trouble, he'll learn pretty quick that I don't belong to anyone but myself."

Azelita had come up closer to Shirley and was whispering to her. Lang felt embarrassed. He hardly knew why he was still standing on the rim of their conversation.

"It doesn't *matter* what color." But Shirley's voice was edged with laughter.

The book cart started off down the hall. Shirley turned toward the desk. Lifting his hands from his pockets as if they might contain whatever it was he wanted to say, Lang moved toward her.

"Lang, this is crazy. You don't have to talk to me at all if you don't want to. When you act like this, I'm *afraid* of you. I don't understand what you want."

Lang hadn't said anything since he'd brought Shirley down to the beach, and almost nothing before, except the invitation. All his words, in whatever language, had dissolved. His mind was melting into the waves.

"Are you sick? Do you need help? *Tell* me."

She was smaller and whiter than ever, but she sounded as if he had been born from between her legs. If he told her what he needed, she would call the police, run up the steps to Seawall Boulevard, and have him arrested.

"I know it's hard to be Vietnamese in America but you have done it so well. I'm *not* being condescending, damn it. Is that what the trouble is? Can't you tell me?"

Everything Shirley was saying was true, but only the sound came into his ears. Before his mind could hear it, sort it out, respond to it, the damp warm wind swept it away. There must be an early hurricane blowing in from somewhere farther south, somewhere in those small islands in the Atlantic. He'd have to ask Karl Mike, who watched TV. He'd have to watch TV himself. He'd have to pay more attention to what was going on around him. He'd have to find a way to make words serve him.

"Lang?"

He couldn't answer.

"Lang?" she asked again. She did not get the vowel

sound quite right. Her arms were bare from the shoulders down, where her sleeveless blouse ended in a cascade of lacy fringe.

Lang could feel himself being filled and blown away by the Gulf wind. "I want to show you something," he said.

"Oh, I'm glad," she said, her voice happy now.

He waited, silent. The waves rolled onto the beach like the cloth behind the paper ships in the Chinese opera on Duc Trinh Street. The watery moon sat dimly on a plate of cloud. No one else was on the beach so far as he could see. The police cars on the seawall were not flashing their lights. He had removed everyone so that the place could be private for the two of them. He had served up the moon as food.

"Lang, what do you want to show me?"

He touched her hair, expecting her to pull back. Instead, she moved toward him. The yellow curls swallowed his fingers. "Look," he said.

"What?"

"Look," he said again, and shoved back the cuffs of his shirtsleeves. In the strange misty light, his skin was as pale as hers.

"I don't see anything."

"Feel," he said, and brought her finger down across the scars knotted on his wrists.

"What happened?" Carefully, she touched each scar from one end to the other, as any good nurse would. She walked her finger along his wrists and then took both his hands in hers. Amazing how powerful her hands were for an American woman who did not plant rice or chop the fish for *nuoc mam!*

"I did it to myself."

"You must have had a hard time."

"I was selfish."

"No one who hurts himself is selfish. He is suffering."

"You work too long on Psychiatry." For the first time in a long time, he felt a tiny spark of humor. She recognized it and smiled.

"Some things I knew were true before I became a psychiatric nurse."

"You are wise."

"No, I'm not wise, but life isn't easy. Not for any of us. And we shouldn't blame ourselves for what we can't help."

"Vietnamese have many responsibilities. To their ancestors. To their families. To their land. We cannot set them aside."

Shirley let his hands go but took his arm instead. Like a formal pair, they started down the beach at the edge of the waves. Far offshore, the oil rigs sparked their eternal Christmas lights.

"Sometimes I wish they'd grown there naturally," Shirley said.

"You say what?"

"I wish they weren't just oil platforms. I wish they'd *grown.* I wish the lights were messages from the natural world, not just Texaco making the big dollar. Then I could enjoy them more. They really are lovely."

Lang looked out at the rigs too. The lines on his wrists no longer seemed so important. No one had ever noticed them, after all. And now he had his own altar at home, as was appropriate. With oranges and apples and joss sticks to burn in honor of his mother. Shirley was a kind woman, even if she wasn't Vietnamese.

"I think we're going to be getting a corner of that hurricane in a few days." Shirley touched the foam at the end of the wave track with her toe. "I hope only a corner. This one's named Alicia. I don't think it's fair to give them the names of people."

None of her words made much sense to Lang. In the crook of his arm, he felt the pressure of her hand.

"Are you all right?"

"What?"

"Are you all right? I'm glad you could show me, you know." She tightened her fingers on his elbow, a strange but not painful feeling. "I told you about Jason, after all. We all have secrets."

I grew up in Vung Tao village. At first, I told people in America its name. They didn't know where it was. Now I say "near Saigon." They have all heard of Saigon.

In Vung Tao, by my house, was the house of my friend Thanh. We called each other "Little Cousin." His mother and my mother were friends too. Our fathers worked together. My little sister Thuy said she would marry him when she grew up. Long ago, we had had the same grandfather. He is in the graveyard now. When we were little, I and my friend Thanh went to visit him every year on his death day. We did it many times. Because we were little boys, we played in the grass by his grave. We sang songs. One time we ate the oranges that Thanh's mother had put out for the grandfather. Phew, that was bad! Nobody knew we ate them. We laughed and walked in the dust, licking our orange fingers.

When my mother found out, she hit me a hundred times. All the mothers hit their children, but my mother had never hit me or my sister. When she hit me for eating the or-

anges, I felt so much shame. I had brought dishonor to our family.

In school, Thanh and I liked the same girl. Her name was Muon. She was very smart, but quiet. One night I slept at Thanh's house. We talked in the night, together in his bed. His mother and father were asleep. I said, "Thanh, what girl do you like?" He said, "What girl do you like?" We asked and laughed and asked more times. At the end, I said, "I like Muon." Thanh said, "I like Muon too. But she can be your girl because you are my brother."

At that time, the war was in our country. I didn't understand about the war, but my mother told me. She wrote prayers for our safety in her Buddha book. She said to be polite to all the soldiers. She said that in the night all things are black. She held me on her lap even though I was too big to sit on her lap. She said I should save my growing until the war was over. She hid my books when I was not reading them. She dressed me in the clothes of a little boy. When I told her I didn't like it, she looked at me with eyes that ate my face.

Thanh grew up faster than I did. He was big for his age. One day the soldiers came and took him away. My father was in the fields. My mother hid me in the small tunnel in the pigpen, but the soldiers only wanted Thanh. I could not believe that he was gone. When my mother came to get me after the soldiers had left, she held me for a very long time. My legs dangled from her lap into the dirt. Her breasts punched my back. I was too old to feel my mother's breasts!

Three months later, I got a letter from Thanh. He said that the war would end soon because the VC would kill everyone. He told me to stay out of the army. He told me to take care of my mother. His parents had already left to go where it was safer, so I did not have to take care of them. He told me to take care of my father and my sister because I was the only son. His voice on paper sounded as if he were planning his own death with the death of our country.

As the weeks passed, the war got worse. Everyone talked about it. All the Americans were leaving, and the Vietnamese Army from the South was running away. Our life was ending. My mother wrote her prayers every day in the Buddha book. The weeds grew on my grandfather's grave. There were no more oranges.

Finally we sat together and talked about our plans. We knew that the Americans were taking people with them. The big helicopters were leaving full of Vietnamese who had worked for the Americans. The American ships were standing in Saigon Harbor, and they would take Vietnamese who could get out to them. My father said we must try. We must try to save ourselves. It was especially important for me to save myself, he said. My mother ate me with her eyes. I was her only son. If she gave me up, she would die. I have known this all my life.

We decided I would go to Saigon first. I would find out how to get on the ships. My parents and my sister would come two days later. We would meet at the herbal medicine store on Bien Tri Street near the harbor. They would pack what they needed. We would leave our country together.

But when I get to Saigon, it is like a nightmare city. Everywhere people are screaming and crying. There is no food to buy. The last Americans ride through the streets in their big cars, and all the people must get out of the way. At night, the guns sound like thunder, closer and closer, and the fire from the VC rockets slashes the sky. I am sixteen years old but when I walk in the streets, the people trample me as if I were a child. I cannot rent a boat. I cannot bribe

[233]

anyone. They laugh at my money. Their eyes are wild. They will not let me save my family.

After two days, with my eyes sore from crying, I go to the herb store. I wait all day. Thousands of Vietnamese walk by, but none of them are my parents. I feel as if I have swallowed a board. If I had a knife, I would kill myself.

Finally, an old man comes. He speaks with the accent of a village near mine. In his hand he has a small book. It is the book where my mother writes her prayers to Buddha. He asks my name and gives the book to me. I hold it in both hands so I will not drop it, but my wrists are shaking so hard that the book falls on the floor. I want to cut off my hands and lay them on it so it will be safe.

Inside the book is a letter. My mother has written it in her poor Vietnamese. She calls me "Beloved Son" as if I were old enough to protect her. She says that they cannot join me because my sister is too young. They will stay in Vung Tao and try to do the best they can. She wants me to go to America and be safe. She wants me to be strong in honor of our family.

I run through the streets with the book in my hands. I run to the harbor. When the crowds hold me back, I climb over their shoulders. I walk on their necks. Sometimes I crawl between their legs. I hold my mother's Buddha book in my mouth, in my pocket, in my waistband. I press it to me in all my safest places.

At the harbor, it has become night. Rockets are everywhere. There are more people than I have ever seen. In the thick air, their cries rise as if they were dying. They moan and scream. My mouth is open and dry, but I do not think I am making any sound. If I am quiet, I can keep my words for my mother.

At the edge of the shore, I find a plastic bag. The

Americans have plastic for everything. I wrap the Buddha book in it and tie it to my chest with my shirt. Then I leap in the water and swim as if I were a fish. I swim more than I have ever swum in my life. There is garbage in the water, and grease and oil. All the little boats bang in the waves, but no one will pick me up. I see a mother throw her baby to people in a little boat. They reach out their hands, but the baby falls into the water. Then I see the mother jump into the water too. They do not come up.

I look away from my country. I look to the big ships. They shine like cities in the night. The Americans watch my country die.

All around is noise. The night eats it. I think about Thanh, who has been gone for so long. I do not think that he will ever be able to marry Thuy. I think about my father and my sister, who cannot come with me. I think about my mother.

It seems like I swim for days. The ships are so far out. But finally the people in a little boat let me hang on to it. I am too tired even to make my fingers work, but I put one hand on top of the other and pray. I am afraid my legs will hit the dead baby in the water. I am afraid my mother will never find oranges to put on the graves.

When we reach the ship, the big Americans put down a ladder for us. We all climb up. When we get near the top, they pull us into a hole in the ship's side. I cannot make my hands let go of the ladder when the American pulls me. He says, "Let go, you motherfucking gook." Now I know what those words mean. Then I only knew that he was angry.

Because he could not move me by my arms, he grabbed me by the shirt I had wound around my chest. It broke, and my mother's Buddha book fell into the waves. The man behind me held me up until they could pull me into the ship.

[235]

*The next day, I found a knife in the kitchen on the ship.
I cut my wrists, but I did not go deep enough. I had not
studied medicine yet.*

33 It was the hundredth day after the death day. Of course, they weren't sure, because the letter from Vietnam had been late, very late, and the news of her grandmother's death had come word of mouth from the village to the cousin who had hired someone to write the letter. So it was hard to know if they were right about the timing, and Linh knew that the timing was important. The spirit needed to be given the food before it truly hungered, and it needed to promise to rest quietly after it had eaten. If the days were wrong, the promise might be broken.

Linh spread the red-and-white tablecloth across the linoleum of her living-room floor. She matched each corner to the corners of the room so all the edges would be straight. In the kitchen, her mother was crying, but in between her cries she was stirring the sticky rice so it wouldn't burn. She was making egg rolls with shrimp inside and a kettle of *pho* soup. Her mother cooked every day now, and her father was getting fat. Perhaps mothers cooked better than daughters after all.

On her hands and knees, making the tablecloth perfect, Linh heard the voices from the kitchen. Trang Luu's aunt was with her mother. In Vietnam, they had come from Hong Dieu and Luc Diem, two villages next to each other on the shore. Their husbands' grandfathers had been cousins. Trang's aunt was helping with the cooking for the celebration of honor. They would eat good things they usually had only at Tet.

On the altar was her grandmother's picture. It was an old one. Her mouth was tied together like a little purse. Were there teeth in it? Linh didn't think so.

Linh got to her feet and went into the kitchen. Harry and Gary were playing with their trucks under the table so no one would fall over them. "Where's Trang?" Linh asked. "Is she coming?" She knew it was not polite to ask her elders a direct question, but she had heard about Trang's new short hair and wanted to ask her how it felt. Did it make Trang look more like an American? Linh knew that she did not have the courage to cut her own hair, but if she thought about it over the summer, maybe she would get the courage. Then she could ask her father's permission.

"She went to the store."

"Will she come after she is done at the store?"

Trang's aunt glared at her with sharp eyes. "Look out the door," she said. "If you want that worthless Trang so much, your eyes will make her come."

Humiliated, Linh went to the door. Nobody stopped her, so she stepped onto the worn grass of Beach Terrace. Harry raced out the door behind her, and she turned him around with her hands on his shoulders before he could run away. "Fuck you," he said, but softly, so only she would hear it. Now he knew what the English words meant.

"Go back. When the people come, you will have good things to eat. Grandmother's spirit will leave enough for you."

Harry hesitated, then ran inside. Linh hesitated too, but instead of following her brother, she turned and looked toward the street. Black children were playing all around her, but they didn't count. The only black person she really knew was Miss Simpson, the lady at school. Her house glowed across the street as if a spotlight had been turned on it. She had been nice the night Linh and Xan had brought the shrimp. She wasn't dirty or on welfare. Maybe she came from a different country. Or maybe one of her grandparents had been Vietnamese.

"Hi, Linh Nguyen."

"Trang Luu!" Linh stepped forward and dug her toes into the sand spread around the swing set. "I was watching for you."

"I know that." Trang tossed her head. Her short hair hung crookedly just under her ears. Now that Linh saw it up close, she didn't think it was a very good cut, even though it was like an American one. When she had her own hair cut, she would go to the beauty parlor in Houston.

"Why you looking at me? My aunt tell you how bad I am?"

It was true that Linh had heard many stories about Trang. In Vietnam, the *bui doi* children lived on the streets, stole things, and then sold them. The girls used their bodies in bad ways. Linh closed her mind like a door on that picture. Sometimes girls had no choice about their bodies, especially if someone was stronger. "You're not bad," she said. "I know that."

Trang looked her up and down with her strange wide eyes. "Are you a child or a woman?" she asked. Linh didn't know what to answer and lowered her head.

"Do you need to go back inside?"

Linh looked back at the door. Soon the other people would come. The children didn't eat until later. There would be so many people that no one would notice she was not there. If they did, they would think she was playing somewhere. They would tease Harry and Gary instead.

"No, not yet."

"Come with me then."

"Where?"

"To my house."

"But your house is right over there."

"Not *that* house."

Linh didn't know what she should do. Then Trang put her hand on Linh's shoulder. They were not that much different in size, something that Linh still found astounding. "Come with me," Trang said. "It isn't far. Down by the docks on Twenty-fifth Street."

"That's *far.*"

With a little grin, Trang gave her a tug. "Not if you drive," she said.

"What?"

"Not if you drive."

"But you don't have a car."

"Just wait."

"Trang!" But they were already circling behind the last Beach Terrace building and crunching through the dry grass of the boulevard to a blue Renault parked so far from the curb that it was almost in the line of traffic.

"I drive *this.*" Trang's voice was proud. She opened the door and ushered Linh to the stunningly neat interior.

Linh sat down as if she were about to depart for the moon, with no guarantee of return. "Did you buy it?" she asked.

"I took it."

"You *took* it?"

"Yes, I did." Trang's voice was filled with something that was not quite pride. She started the motor and gunned the car out into the quiet street. Linh saw that she was pushing the pedals with her very toes.

"Why don't you move the seat forward?"

"Because then he'd know someone took it."

That made no sense. "Who?" Linh asked, sliding down so she wouldn't be seen. They passed the abandoned warehouse, looming elephant-gray on the corner of Thirtieth and Sealy. Whenever Linh walked by it with Harry and Gary, they always wanted to hide inside, and she never let them.

"My friend who owns this car."

"What friend?" No Vietnamese fisherman would own a car like this. They liked big old cars with room for all their families.

"My friend Dr. Lang Nguyen."

"You mean the one who takes Xan fishing?"

"Maybe he does that too."

"He lends you his *car?*"

Trang turned down Twenty-seventh, swerving a little over the yellow line. "He doesn't know I have it," she said.

"But he'll call the *police!*"

"He doesn't know it's gone."

Linh couldn't think what to say next. "Won't he be angry?" she asked finally, thinking how her father would be if someone had gone off with *his* car. The day the Mexicans had broken his windshield, he had stormed around the house like a hurricane.

"Not if I get it back before he is done at the hospital."

Trang brought the car to a stop at the place where the Vietnamese fishing boats were docked, and turned off the ignition.

"But isn't this stealing?"

"No," Trang said. "I bring it back. He leaves the keys under the rubber pad he puts his foot on." She was already out of the car, walking with her head in the air and her hands at her side. "He does it at his apartment and at the hospital too," she said. "I think he trusts people too much." When she got to the line of boats, she stood on the edge of the bulkhead where they were anchored, her feet steady. Then she leaped on board the nearest one, reached back, and grabbed Linh's hand. "Come on," she said.

Together the two of them hopped from deck to deck. Linh passed over the bridge of her father's boat, remembering the duck and the whiskey and the prayers to Thuy Tinh. She didn't know who owned all those boats, though they looked and smelled Vietnamese. Probably she didn't know all the Vietnamese in Galveston yet. There might be more of them than she had realized. Trang must know everyone.

"Where are we going?"

Trang looked back and smiled. "To my secret place," she said.

Linh had no idea what she meant. Besides, she was beginning to worry. It was time for the ceremony to be starting. Her mother might want her to look after Harry and Gary. Dr. Lang Nguyen might want his car. He might leave the hospital early. Trang might get in big trouble. "It's late," she said, the most noncommittal critical statement she could think of. She was a little afraid of what Trang might do if she got angry.

But Trang didn't get angry. "We're almost there," she said, and she jumped off the last boat right into the mud by the shore. Beyond the line of boats was a small space, then a twisted tree, then an old wreck of a boat that had sunk halfway under the water of the bay. Trang clambered up the side as if she had done it a million times, and Linh followed her. "Here it is," she said, ducking inside. "At my aunt's house, I sleep in the kitchen. I need my own room."

In the little deckhouse of the old wreck, leaning at a steep angle toward its final resting place at the bottom of the bay, Trang had made herself a tiny home. The walls were hung with blankets. On the floor was an old mattress, folded up under the window because it was too big to spread out. There was a neat pile of dishes and an old frying pan. On the wall next to the front window was a poster of a Vietnamese movie star. Next to her was a poster of an American movie star. Linh didn't know the names of either one, but they were certainly famous. The edges of their lipstick were perfect.

"This is really yours?"

Trang looked around proudly. "Yes," she said.

"Did it cost a lot of money?"

"No. I stole everything."

"Didn't anybody see you?"

"I came at night."

First the car, now the boat. Trang didn't seem to act like a regular Vietnamese girl. Maybe the *bui doi were* evil, like everyone said. Maybe they had devils in them.

Carefully, Trang wiped a speck of dirt from the window. "Do you like it?" she asked.

Even though it was a lie, Linh said yes. But then she stopped. "What's it for?" she asked, because one house was really enough, and the old boat was so low in the water that the next hurricane might put it on the bottom.

"It's for *me*. So I can have my own safe place."

Linh didn't understand. "This place is safe?" she asked, looking past Trang to the Vietnamese movie star.

"Because I need to belong."

"What?" Linh felt really stupid. She wanted to go back home. The police might put Trang in jail for driving Dr. Lang Nguyen's car.

Trang must have read her thoughts, because already she was stooping to get out on deck. "My safe place," she said again. *"Be* safe." She said it louder, as if more volume would bring more meaning. "Nobody helped me."

"Where were you?"

"Outside."

"What you do outside?"

"I play with Trang."

"Trang is too big to play with you."

Linh's father stood in the middle of the tablecloth on the living-room floor, his feet straddling the remains of the death banquet. Egg rolls, sticky rice, noodles with green onions, *pho* soup with pepper sprinkled across its greasy top all sat around him like witnesses. He held his thumbs hooked in the belt of his jeans. "Trang and I play talking games," Linh said finally, her eyes on the floor.

"Look at me." His voice was heavy.

Linh raised her head. "Yes," she said. She waited for the whisper to come into her voice, for the quiver that her father always put into her throat. It didn't come.

"Your mother is asleep."

Linh knew that wasn't true. Her mother was never

[244]

asleep. She stayed awake all night, silent on her pillow, her eyes glowing black in the blackness. Even now that she cooked sticky rice and washed Gary's face, she had not begun to sleep. She saw everything, as if she were hung in the sky over Beach Terrace. But because the ghost lived in her, she could not talk about it.

"Next week we take her to Alabama. Now that the money is coming. The man there will make her sleep all the time." Her father swayed back and forth over the piles of food. If he had had too much beer, he might fall into the *pho* soup. He would look silly with noodles squeezing between his fingers like tiny fish.

"Why you smiling?"

"I don't smile." But of course she was. She just needed to keep it farther inside.

"You want your mother to stay sick?"

No answer would be right to that. She gave none.

Her father pushed his face at her. "I think maybe your mother die," he said.

But that was not true! Her mother and Trang's aunt had cooked the whole death dinner themselves. Her mother might not get all well, might never learn to speak even the little English that her father could speak, might squat against the wall in the kitchen and snatch at the air, but her body was strong and her black hair firm around her head. And now she was getting all that money from the president of the United States because she was crazy. She would probably live a very long time!

Linh put all these thoughts together in her head. What came out on top of them was another thought altogether. She waited.

"It is late," her father said.

Linh kept waiting.

He moved his feet on the tablecloth. It was Linh's job to clean things up, and she knew it. He knew it too.

"Come to bed," he said. "Tomorrow your mother will clean."

"No." The word was not a whisper, and Linh's voice had no quiver in it.

"Come to bed," her father said again.

Head up, Linh took a step forward. Forward was better than back. She had to be close enough. She was the one who would decide how close. "I stay down here," she said. *"Toi se o lan day."*

Questioningly, her father raised his hands and turned to one side. He seemed to be looking at her grandmother's picture on the altar. Her grandmother seemed to be looking right back.

"Why?" he asked. Fathers in Vietnam did not ask their daughters why. He must have really heard her. He must be waiting for her to say the next thing.

Trang's voice came to her ear, tough and warm. "I need to be safe," Linh said, in Vietnamese. "I need my own room." Then she said it again in English. It sounded just fine in both languages.

For a moment after she had spoken, Linh thought her father might be angry. After all, he fed her and owned her body. But she was not a package! Her father could make her do some things, but some things she had a right to say no to. And now she was not afraid to do it.

But her father did not seem angry. His face got small. "I will go to your mother," he said, as if he knew that was what he should do. "Clean up like you are supposed to." He moved toward the stairway through the remnants of the death dinner and started up. Linh saw a bean sprout clinging to the heel of his sandal. If her heart had not been beating so hard, she would have laughed.

Hai Truong turned in her bed. Linh had gone. Where?

Harry and Gary were gone. Where? No, outside. They played outside. Or they were sleeping. That was good. Boys played outside and then they slept. That was as it should be.

Downstairs she heard voices. Her husband was talking, and her daughter was talking too. Her husband worked on the ocean with his boat. He caught fish and shrimp and squid and gave them away for money. When he brought them home, she cooked them. When she had been sick, Linh had cooked them. Linh had learned to cook like a woman. Linh herself was almost a woman, but she could not cook as well as her mother could. Phuong Nguyen liked to eat what Hai Truong cooked.

That morning, she had stood in the kitchen. On the table was an envelope with a window in it. Inside the window was money. It did not look like money. It looked like paper instead, but it was money. When it had come last month, her husband had taken it to the CHECKS CASHED, and then he had bought lots of beer. He had bought a new clock with butterflies on the hands. And he had bought her purple slacks and a blouse with purple flowers down the front. She had not worn them yet because she was too thin. But perhaps she would not always be thin. Her ghost husband had wanted her to be thin, but he did not give her money in envelopes with windows. He was far away in Vietnam. He could not understand American money.

Her head hurt. She could not sleep. The bed was hot

and wrinkled. Downstairs she heard the voices again. But she was not in the hospital anymore. Her mother had died in the old world, and she had still cooked her death dinner as she should. The window money had paid for it. She had burned the joss sticks and she had said the prayers. Her mother's spirit was far away, but it was not homeless. It had oranges to eat. It was not angry at her.

Under her pillow, there were many pills. She had saved them. They had sent them home from the hospital in little bottles, and they had put the little bottles in little paper bags. She was supposed to swallow the pills, but she could not read the words. She had never learned to read any words.

The air was thick and hot. It felt like a storm. Perhaps she should reach under the pillow and eat the pills. She could swallow them all. She could eat them like rice. Then the Americans would not be angry with her. Her husband would come to bed with her as he should. The storm would stay away.

But not all Americans wanted her to swallow the pills. One American had hair like the sun. She had not been angry. She had been kind. When she had seen that the old pills were still there, had never been swallowed, she had smiled. A little smile. A little smile that floated on the wave of her face surrounded by a sky of gold.

34 It was the last day at Carver School. And a good thing too, because the weather was so heavy and moist that even the most polite children were nagging and scrambling as they waited for their final report cards. It was too early for hurricanes, Azelita thought, even though June was the official start of their season. Hurricane Alicia was stalled off the Bahamas, a steamy spiral that had sent all the tourists heading for the airports and the natives running for the frail protection of their huts. Azelita and Wilson had watched the weather channel for a straight two hours on his wide-screen TV last night.

"Hi, Mizz Simper." Miguel. He placed a square box with a limp pink bow on the counter.

"Is that for me, Mr. Miguel?"

"Yesss, Mizz Simper." He tore down the hall while Azelita placed his gift in the bottom drawer of her desk. Miguel was brown enough himself to assume that he had a dark-skinned mama, so maybe the dusting powder would be more appropriate than the usual blush pinks she received. Or maybe not.

In a flurry of ramie and cotton, printed with irises, the principal scurried by to her office. Azelita swung a pile of perfect attendance certificates into her hand as she passed, waiting for her signature. Usually Azelita forged them, but today she didn't feel like doing that. Let the Lady Queen move her own ballpoint across the rectangles. "You owns what you signs," her mama had always said. That meaning was clear enough. Sign your own certificates. Feed your own brain. Teach your own class.

Azelita stopped short in shock at the idea. The phone rang. "Carver School," she said, then, "last day at Carver School" just in case the caller needed to be brought up-to-date on the calendar.

"Sister, I knew that better than you did."

"Labella, what you call me here for? You got me at my *job.*"

"Woman, I know what number is what number. Mama said we both have the same smarts. You got no TV in that office, right?"

A little Thai boy named Lapekek Susophorone stood in the office doorway looking at Azelita. In his hand was a fancily wrapped box, which he deposited on the counter.

"No, I got no TV. This is a *school.* We *read* here."

"Don't you do that I-read-more-books-than-you-read business with me, Azelita. I mean, you got no TV to watch the *weather* with."

"I watch the weather for two hours last night. I had enough weather to weather me right into retirement."

"Can't remember when you watch TV for two hours at your house. You getting old?"

"I wasn't at . . ." Azelita stopped.

"So where was you?"

Silence.

"You got yourself a good man this time? Or you supporting some Galveston tramp?"

"I ain't supporting *nobody.*"

Labella chuckled. "Couldn't be that he's supporting *you?* My Lord, Sister. He buy you any sparklers yet? Any permanent investments, Mama might say?"

"Labella, I supposed to be working here, not gossiping with you." Azelita looked at the counter, where a second box had joined Lapekek's. Bath salts? At least it wasn't shrimp.

"*I* know, but I been watching that weather channel. Hurricane Alicia is moving again, offshore. Gaining strength. Big storm coming. Mama would have the doors locked already."

"Like hurricanes stop to knock first."

Labella giggled. "Well, Mama had her good sense in other areas," she said. "Only thing she messed up on was getting you inside enough schools. Couldn't make my big sister into an educated woman, try as she might."

"She didn't do so bad."

"What you mean, woman?"

"What I say. She didn't do so bad. No need to give up hope, Labella." Azelita left a pause so Labella would have time to figure things out.

"You going back?"

"Thinking on it."

"I can't believe it."

"Not a matter of belief. Matter of the dollar."

"You win something big?"

"I win something *very* big."

"That mystery man of yours win the lottery?"

Through Azelita's mind flashed a picture of a little girl with pigtails all over her head and a garden of plastic barrettes holding them together. Smart little girl, Labella. "He did it all on his own," she answered.

"My-*my!*"

"Going to let a little of it flow my way come fall." Azelita couldn't figure out why all this information was running out of her mouth as if she had already made her decision. Still, here she was babbling away to Labella.

"Woo-*wee!*"

"Gonna go back and be Miss School Girl again."

"Woo-wee-wee!" Labella must be dancing around the kitchen from the sound of it.

With the phone cradled in the sturdy flesh of her neck, Azelita could see Xan in the doorway of the office, Linh next to him. They held their report cards out like little trays. They were both smiling.

"That's all, Sister. Gotta work."

"Call me tonight."

"Maybe."

With a snort, Azelita hung up. She looked at the children. "What you want, Mr. and Mrs. Saigon?" she said, not thinking this might be an insult. They knew she liked them and could remember their real names. "You bringing me a pile of presents? Or do I just get to admire all the good words your teachers wrote about you?"

"I not baby no more," Xan said. "I go fourth grade."

"My teacher say that I am number two in class." Linh spoke right out. Her usual shyness was gone.

"Why you not number one?"

"You shut up, Xan Thuan My Van. *Next* year I am number one."

Other children surged down the hall, banged against the door, spun out into the blinding June sunlight. For at this moment the sun had broken through, although the air was still heavy, heavier almost than before. Like butterflies, the children spilled out into their summer freedom.

"These good reports are like presents for me, young ones." Azelita touched the edge of each card with her forefinger.

"We got another present."

"What's that?"

Linh stepped forward as if about to recite a poem. "We come to your house and cook supper," she said.

"When you planning to do *that?*"

"Tonight." Linh looked at Xan. He nodded. "We bring food," she said. "You eat."

"What your mama think of that?"

"She don't know," Xan said. "My mama. Linh's mama don't know too. It's okay. We tell fathers. They say okay. Plenty of food!"

Linh hesitated, a slip back into her old self. "We bring friend?" she asked, a statement with a questioning lift at the end.

"Who you bringing?"

"My friend Trang Luu."

Azelita looked up at the clock on the wall. Wilson figured he'd gotten his word in for supper. Well, he had. He'd just have to join the crowd.

"All right. You all come. You're *cooking?*"

"Yes."

"What if I got somebody extra too?"

Linh started to nod her polite permission. It was Xan who jumped to attention. "You *got* somebody?" he asked.

"A friend. You saw him at the door one time already."

Xan nodded knowingly. "You big lady," he said. "You need somebody *big.* We bring *lots* shrimp!"

■   ■   ■

[253]

"Can't I come too?"

"No, you can't. They just invited me." Trang leaned forward in the driver's seat of Lang's car.

Tri wiggled in the seat next to her. "But they wouldn't be angry," he said.

"They just invited *me,* Tri. Linh just invited *me.* And Xan."

"What house is it?"

"You know. The one across from where Linh lives. The one with the yellow all over it. And the porch."

"The *nigger* house?"

Trang jabbed Tri in the shoulder with her fist. "Why you talking?" she shouted. "Americans call you little gook shit. Black people came here by boat too. Just like us."

"Is that why they talk funny?"

"No," Trang said. "They talk funny because they have to keep their mouths shut for so long. Otherwise they get killed by the people who own them."

"Nobody own me!"

"That's right. But their boats came a long time ago. People *bought* them. Then they had to work for the people who bought them."

"Couldn't they earn money getting shrimp with their boats?"

"No! They didn't *own* their boats. They just sat in them."

Trang's face had its dark look, which it always got when she was about to lose patience. Tri pushed down on the handle and released the latch. "Why does that doctor let you use his car?" he asked.

"Because he knows I need a car."

"But before you always walked."

Trang made a gesture with her hand as if to sweep Tri

out onto the curb. "But tonight it's going to rain," she said. "He doesn't want me to get wet."

Tri got out and shut the door behind him. Trang turned the key in the ignition. With a squawk, the motor started up, grinding against itself. But she was getting better at it.

"You go in, Tri." Trang settled herself in the seat. "Leave the window open. Don't worry about me. When you're grown up, you can drive a car too."

"But *you're* not grown up either!"

"Yes, I am," said Trang. The wet air was dancing against her eyes, and she rubbed them. *"Yes, I am."*

3 5 Shirley's apartment was different from what Lang had expected, although now he could no longer remember exactly what image he had carried in his mind. Something modern, with chrome and leather, and white tile floors. A little like the hospital. Cool and bare, with empty counters and a refrigerator that made no sound.

Instead, Shirley's apartment, the bottom floor of an old house, was a clutter of pillows, fabrics, and rugs that humped in the middle whenever you stepped on them. Her sofa was puffy and lopsided. The kitchen was awash with spatulas, paper towels, bowls, colored bottles. The dishwasher groaned with their supper dishes, the refrigerator struggled to turn on, then clanked alive. The air conditioner in the window, whining through its vents, fought against the prestorm air outside. Lang's shirt was glued to his chest. He was as hot as when he had walked over from the hospital after work, since Shirley lived only three blocks away. When he gave in to the sofa and leaned back, it rubbed against his skin as if someone were sitting on him.

Someone was. Jason was a solid little boy, built square

from his shoulders down to his hips. Even his feet were like boxes. He didn't look like Shirley, except for the hair, and she kept that trimmed close, as it should be, Lang thought.

"Dr. Win," Jason said. "Dr. Win-Win-Win." He laughed.

"Jason, that isn't polite." Shirley was in the kitchen.

"It's all right." Jason shifted his weight, and Lang's damp shirt loosened.

"He knows you won't be angry at him."

"How can he know that?"

"He can tell." Shirley came in, wiping her hands on a towel. "Come on, Jay," she said. "Bedtime. You've had a week's play in one evening."

"I want Dr. Win-Win-Win to put me to bed."

"Get off it, Jay. He's been much nicer to you than you deserve." Shirley pointed to Lang. "Say good night to our guest. You're worn to a frazzle."

"It's too hot to sleep." Jason moved off Lang's lap and sank into the sofa cushion.

"That's true enough, but I'll put the fan on, okay? Come on."

Jason turned to Lang. "Why you got funny eyes?" he asked.

"Jason!"

"Why you got funny eyes?"

Lang put his fingers at the outer corners of his eyes and pulled. Jason shrieked with laughter and pulled his own eyes until they stretched along his smooth cheeks. Then, with Shirley following behind, he galloped into the bedroom.

Outside, the air was completely still, as if the city were between breaths. Lang went to the window and

pushed the heavy curtain aside. With a plop, it came
loose from its rod and flooded his shoulders. He fought his
way up through the dusty velvet folds, coughing. When he
reached air, he folded the curtain into a respectable
packet and placed it on the side cushion of the sofa.

"What happened?" Shirley was beside him.

"It fell." He indicated the folded curtain, the bare
window.

"I've needed new ones for years."

"Yes." The wind was beginning now, a small whine
like a vehicle moving down the street.

"*Now* maybe I'll get them."

"Yes."

Shirley pushed her hair back and held it at the nape of
her neck. "Jason likes you," she said.

"He is a good boy. I think he like everyone."

"I'll have to admit that he isn't shy."

"Shy is not good."

"We use that word so carelessly in America," Shirley
said. "Sometimes people are just quiet or thinking about
things. Or considerate."

"Am *I* shy?"

"Lang!" She smiled at him. "Are you teasing?"

"Maybe I teasing."

"Are you *flirting?*"

"What is flirting?"

"It's hard to explain," Shirley said, blushing a little.

"I think I understand."

"What?"

"When woman likes man, she flirts." The words just
came out, overflow from some long-ago English lesson.
"It's all right." He stepped toward her. "When man likes
woman, he flirt too."

[258]

Shirley giggled. Lang loosened his arms from his sides. He was not sure how this worked, but, after all, Jason had liked him. Shirley had fed him horrible American pot roast, and he had eaten it without even minding. There was a next thing to do, and he would figure it out.

But he did not have to think about the proper action for long. Shirley put her hands on his shoulders, then around his neck. He felt them cross on his backbone, holding him into himself. She bent her head to one side like a Thai dancer. Then her lips touched his cheek. "I'm glad you're here," she said. Her lips moved across his face. He should have shaved again before he came, even though his beard was never rough like American men's.

"Let me," she said. Her mouth touched his, then moved on. He was afraid to open his lips for fear he would swallow her accidentally. Somewhere a shutter was slamming against the siding. Somewhere the waves were beating on the shore.

Then he felt her hands on his. "Like this," she said, but not as if she were teaching him anything, not as if she knew more than he did. Because he was a doctor! She lifted his hands and placed them on her body, one around her waist with his wrist against the soft fabric of her blouse, the other under her armpit where the edge of her breast swelled against it. "Like this," she said again, and her lips touched his once more, stayed, explored. He had only to respond.

A little later, he stood at the door. "You're going?" she asked.

"Yes."

"What for?"

So she was ready to do the whole thing! But he had

known that already. And why *was* he going? He would not be violating her, because she had not been a virgin for a long time. But that did not matter anyway. That was the old way of seeing things.

"I must."

"Lang, I'd like you to stay here with me."

So she could say it! How easy it was for American women!

"I care about you." She smiled a teasing smile. "You don't even smell of rice."

"What?"

"Don't Asians always think Americans smell of milk?"

How did she know that? There were no secrets! He looked down at his hand and saw that it rested in hers.

"I will come back."

"Tonight?"

"Yes." He tried to think of an explanation for going at all. All he felt was a need to be outside, to think about what was happening. It was not fear. He wanted to put everything in the proper place in his mind. Once he had done that, he could come back. He could enter her bed. He could let her teach him the American way of doing things.

"All right."

The whine of the wind caught them as soon as they walked out the door. He thought she would stop and go back, but she didn't. The wind polished their faces, and with it came an edge of rain. He would make it a quick trip. He would get his toothbrush. It was important to have good breath. Americans thought a great deal about good breath.

Her hand still in his, the rain beginning to beat on the

pavement, they rounded the corner where he had parked his car in front of the house with the iron fence. Speeding up a little, he moved toward it. Then he stopped.

"Not right."

"What?"

His car was there, all right, but the bush behind which he had parked it had moved, and now its sharp branches brushed his headlight. He would never have left his car where a bush might scratch it.

"What's wrong?" The wind threw her words past him.

"My car is not the same."

Shirley peered into the dark. "It looks the same to me."

"But it is not in the same place."

"Maybe you forgot where you parked it."

He didn't think so, but he didn't argue. He went around and opened the door on the driver's side.

Shirley stood next to him, leaning against the wind. "In Galveston, you ought to lock your car doors," she said, her voice raised.

"No." How could he tell her that he did not feel the car was truly his? Were he to lock it, it would be a selfish statement to the gods who had protected him, who had kept him alive even when he had wanted to die.

"Do you have your keys?"

"Here." He bent over the floor mat. They were there, in the usual place.

"Anyone could steal your car."

"Then my car was meant for them."

"What?"

"If that is what happens."

It seemed she might argue with him, but she didn't. "Go on," she said, and she put one finger on the sleeve of

[261]

his shirt. It left a damp line. "But come back," she said also. "Be careful. Broadway floods when it rains a lot. Don't get stuck."

Lang could hear the crash of the waves along the beach past the seawall. The storm was picking up in intensity. He could hear the beat of the pulse in his own chest, and it had the rhythm of the waves. In the wind, it was hard to tell them apart.

Then he remembered a gesture from the television. He placed his fingers to his mouth. Did you touch them with your tongue? Or teeth? Or were the lips enough? He was not sure, so he simply ran his fingers across his lips and held them up for her. What did the Americans call this? Throwing a kiss? As if a kiss were a ball that one could pitch across the brightness of the space between two people. As if two worlds could be bridged by such a very small thing.

36 "We could open some Chinee restaurant without looking nowhere for help." Wilson leaned back in the big chair, his cigar pointed at Mama's chandelier. "We got enough help in that kitchen to bring in the Seawall Boulevard crowd."

"Wilson." Azelita reached over and tapped him on the shoulder just like a teacher would. "They are Vietnamese. Get your names straight. Anybody rich as you are can at least put the right labels on things."

"You talk smart-ass, woman."

"Well, then, why you so set on educating me if you don't want no woman that talks smart-ass?"

Wilson swung around in the chair and took the cigar out of his mouth. "Listen to that wind, woman. Should blow some sense into you. Once you got that big degree framed up there next to your mama's picture, then you talk all the smart-ass you want and I buy it from the bottom up."

"Nice to know."

"You bet. I let you know what you need to know. No secrets, Zeli. I didn't bring in all them dollars by whispering down no drainpipe."

From the kitchen, the voices rose higher. Something was sizzling. "Take it off," said Linh, and then the big girl, Trang, said, "Let me." She didn't look like Linh or Xan although they had told Azelita that she was a relative. Her eyes were wider, and her short hair was not a pure black.

Xan stuck his head out the kitchen door. "You hungry?" he asked.

Azelita looked at Wilson. He probably expected to be poisoned. Or at least made sick. He waved his cigar at Xan. "Sure, man," he said. "I wait any longer, I be dead meat. Need me to pick up a pizza? I'm a big man. I gotta have *enough*."

Xan danced with joy. "I *know* you big man," he said. "We cook *big*. My father give me *this much* shrimp!" Xan held his hands wide apart. "We cook it all. Eat in one minute."

"Ain't you going to set the table? Zeli, don't the Chinee set tables?"

"You stop talking that Chinee business, Wilson. They're *Vietnamese*. And *I* set my table." As she started toward the dining room, Wilson patted her behind.

"You stop that now! They are *watching*, Wilson."

"All them Chinee sleep in one room. No surprise to them."

Azelita laid the napkins on the table with emphasis. "You behave yourself in this house."

With an exaggerated sigh, Wilson stood up and peered into the kitchen. "Who that big girl, Zeli?"

"Her name is Trang. She's a friend of Linh's. I know Linh and Xan from school. They got a friend, I got no objection to that friend."

"Sam? That's his name?"

"More like 'Tzan,' " Azelita said, her lips pursed. "Even after this year, *I* don't get it said just right. I don't think his teacher got it right either."

"You going to break some records once *you* get in front of a classroom, woman."

Azelita settled herself back on the sofa. "No promises yet, Wilson."

"Registration is in August, you know."

"I know."

"I sit here ready to open you your own school account."

"Wilson, I got my *own* account now."

"For Uncle Washington, yes. For the power and light. For the garbage, when Galveston remembers to collect this near the projects. For a few groceries, when the Vietcong ain't supplying you." Wilson put down his cigar, which, Azelita noted, he had never lit, and pulled out his chair from the table. "I ready to eat, Zeli. It don't smell so bad. I need some nourishment to stand against that wind out there when I head home. And if it happens I spend the night, I need my strength for that too."

Outside, the wind was exercising its own strength. The door to Azelita's porch was shut tight, but still the plaid curtains moved back and forth as if the wind could go through wood, even glass, even Mama's inviolate fabric. When Azelita looked out at the street, a heavy mist, almost like rain, was sweeping past the streetlight. They weren't going to be hit directly, the TV had said, and the weather channel had said it loudest. It was Bolivar that was getting it, but even the fringes of the storm felt bad enough.

Linh, with Xan at her shoulder, put a plate of egg rolls in front of Wilson. Trang stood a little to one side, holding

[265]

a dish of liquid with carrot strips floating on top. She extended it.

"What's that, babe?"

"Sauce."

"What's in that sauce, Miss Saigon?"

Trang looked him in the eye. *"Nuoc mam,"* she said.

"And just what is that *nuck*mam?"

"Dead fish." Trang's eyes were alight. "It tastes very good. Try it."

Azelita dipped her own egg roll into the carrot-crowned bowl and bit off the damp part. Sharp and good. In the gumbo category. She took another bite.

"Lord," said Wilson and dunked his entire egg roll, bending it in the middle so it could soak from end to end. He opened his mouth to his very tonsils and dropped the egg roll in.

"All right!"

Trang smiled a satisfied smile. She took a bowl of rice and one of shrimp from Linh, then placed them in front of Wilson. Azelita realized that Trang was paying *her* no attention whatsoever. Xan and Linh were the ones to keep her fueled.

"Aren't you two eating? You three," she corrected herself.

"We eat later," Linh said.

Meanwhile, Trang had eyes only for Wilson. She moved his sauce bowl closer to his plate, bending over him. Her blouse brushed his shoulder, but she did not pull back.

Azelita tried the rice, each grain separate from the next in outline but cohesive in structure. Over the white mound, she ladled the shrimp, chopped into pink pieces and interspersed with strange greenery. The taste was fragrant. Under Trang's eyes, Wilson seemed to be enjoying it too.

"This is very good food," Azelita said.

Linh and Xan nudged each other.

"You can cook fine food, you two."

They nudged each other again, grinning.

"Are you *sure* your parents know about this?"

This time Linh took charge. "I told my father our teacher invited us," she said. "I told him we bring the food for a present. I told him our teacher angry if we don't come."

Azelita felt her face getting hot. "I'm not your teacher," she said.

"But you help us in Carver School," they said, almost simultaneously.

"Yes, I know." Azelita swallowed a giant shrimp chunk, felt it edge down her gullet, leaving its delicious trail behind.

"And you teach us many things!"

"I suppose." She snuck a glance at Wilson. Trang stood tight to his side, her hands delicately moving one dish and then another nearer his plate. She could have been Madame Butterfly.

"Well, maybe I will be a real teacher one of these days." She thought Wilson might have heard her, and why not?

"I want to be a teacher too," Linh said.

"And what do you want to be, Trang?" She was so quiet, this young woman with the strange eyes. It was all too easy to leave her out.

"I will marry."

"But you need to study first. Go to college."

"Or I go back to Vietnam."

[267]

"Not much of a place, sugar." Wilson put his hand on hers. "I been there too, you know."

Trang stared at him.

"Dirt and heat and bugs and lots of ordnance. You be a lucky little lady you got out."

"Wilson was in the war, Trang," Azelita explained. "That's how most of us got to know about Vietnam. Not much of a way, for sure."

Outside, the rain had begun, banging at the side of the house. Good thing the project area didn't flood much. Maybe the only good thing about it.

No one spoke. Apparently, Wilson had said all he intended to about the war. Azelita didn't know what more to say either. They weren't in Vietnam now, none of them. Now the new land had to do the soaking up.

Then, suddenly, Trang fell on her knees next to Wilson. He pulled back, almost upsetting his chair, while Azelita grabbed the tablecloth to steady it. "Lord, child!" she said.

"Are you American?" Trang's voice was beseeching.

Wilson looked down at her. "Sure am, sugar. As American as you can get. We all came with boats to this country except for them Indians. My boat got here *way* back."

Trang tilted her head, eyes glowing, and bent to kiss Wilson's hand, laying it against her cheek. Then she rose, and just as suddenly she moved to the door, through it, and outside.

"Jesus Christ!" Wilson said.

"What you do to her, Wilson? She go off like she scared to death!"

"You saw me, Zeli. I didn't say one bad thing to her. She seen too much, that one. She got something in her that she ain't swallowed. That not *me* troubling her."

Linh moved closer to Azelita. "I know where she go," she said.

"What you mean, child?"

"I know where she go. To her place. To her *safe* place."

"She can't be out on a night like this!"

"She not afraid."

"That sure is not the point, Linh." Azelita was already in the front hall, extracting her slicker from the packed closet. "That girl is no grown-up lady. And not even no grown-up lady should be out on the streets here once it gets dark. *This* is no safe place."

"I kung fu bad people!" Xan leaped up as if he could perch on air. "I go save her!"

"Look." Wilson stood up too. "Look, you ladies. You too, kung fu man. We all go and bring her back. You, Lilly, you show us where she is."

"My name is *Linh*.L-i-n-h."

Wilson bent down to her. "L-i-n-h," he said. "Okay, L-i-n-h. Come on. Be my point lady. Show me where to go."

Like a lighthouse crew, they threw on coats and jackets. "Jesus," Wilson said as he opened the door. It might be only the lame edge of the hurricane, but the wind was ferocious. Water cut down in layers from the sky, then bounded back from the pavement. Wilson spread his arms wide and herded his charges down the walk to his car. "Wow!" Xan said, running his hand along the glistening wet fender. "You *rich* American!"

"You work hard, you get rich too." Wilson was stuffing them all inside with a speed to rival the rain.

"I get *two* cars! I work like crazy man!" As Wilson

[269]

started up, Xan buried his nose in the leather upholstery. "Smells like *cow!*" he said.

The car surged down the street toward the corner. "Okay, so what way?" Wilson asked.

"Down there."

"I got no idea what 'there' you talking about."

Linh leaned her head nearer his shoulder in the front seat. "Where the boats are."

"She means where the Vietnamese keep their fishing boats, Wilson." Azelita put her hand on the arm of his suede jacket, already spotted by the rain.

"This is no good neighborhood."

Xan kung fued the window. Linh peered out his side through the deluge. "Turn here," she said.

Wilson jammed on the brakes and spun the car to the left. "How come that little lady can beat us all?" he asked. "She didn't get no head start to speak of."

"She move very fast." Xan nodded his head. "She can run all the time. She get where she go."

"You got a smart mouth, kung fu boy. Now where?"

"Straight." Linh leaned forward so she could see out the windshield. The fat tires hit a big puddle, almost a lake, and as they surged forward, the car sent waves on each side.

"Boat!" Xan shouted. "We boat people!"

"Right on, Mr. Kung Fu." Wilson gunned the car next to the wharf. The string of little boats rose and fell, banging against each other. Water gaped between their sides and the bulkhead, closed with a crunch, gaped again.

"Lord, those boats will never make it through *this* storm," Wilson said, reaching for the door handle. "Don't look like there's no safe place here."

But Linh had already opened her door and slid out

into the rain. "She *make* a place!" she shouted back. "Down there!"

The rest of them climbed out. It was impossible to see very far, but Linh's finger held firm toward where the boats dwindled off into darkness. Xan started a kung fu kick, then held it back.

Azelita had her arm tucked in Wilson's. "Well, Wilson, you got your task cut out for you," she said.

"Down *there!*" Linh shouted. "On the old boat."

"How we going to get to it, sweetheart?" Wilson asked.

"We walk." Linh started doing just that. "It is easy," she said as she stepped onto the nearest deck with the delicacy of a ballet dancer. Xan leaped behind her.

Wilson took Azelita's hand. "The Chinee got fire-works before we did," he said. "And gunpowder. Which, after six months at Quang Tri, I can believe. Must be they was meant to be first in just about everything." He pulled Azelita up closer to him. They stepped unsteadily onto the bridge of boats, and, with Xan bouncing ahead of them, followed Linh to the end.

"She is over there."

"Where you mean, girl?"

"In there." Linh pointed again. Ahead of them, separated by several feet of mucky water, the tilted outline of a wrecked boat danced and plunged.

"Okay, LeeAnn." Wilson bent down and took off his shoes, then his soggy socks. "I gotta have some grip," he said. "Step back, all of you. If she is there, I get her out. Time we get half hour more of this rain, she be dead as they come."

Wilson braced himself, then leaped. The wreck plunged sideways, but he kept his footing, then slid down toward the deckhouse. "Jesus," Azelita heard him say.

But he did not have to go in. A slender figure, so wet that she had become a part of the rain, emerged and flung herself into his arms. "I know you come!" she shouted. And then, pressed so tightly against Wilson that she almost disappeared into his ruined suede jacket, she sent out a whispered surge of sound that Azelita couldn't understand. The final words, though, she heard.

"Are you my father?"

"Oh, baby, I ain't *anybody*'s father," Wilson said.

"But you were in my country! You were soldier. You are an American!"

"Sugar, wait a minute!" Wilson braced their bodies against the angle of the deck. "So that's why you got them big eyes. But if *I* were your daddy, you'd be black all over, like me." He patted her back with both hands. "It don't matter who's your daddy, sugar. What matters is who *you* are. Anybody cooks like you is pretty special, believe me. We boat people, we all special. Rain or shine. Night or day. We worked so hard and hurt so much, we gonna get every single thing we got coming to us."

37 "What are you *doing*, Winner?"

Lang laid his razor neatly inside his toilet bag, neatly laid his toothbrush and Crest next to it, and zipped the bag shut. The air-conditioning unit groaned outside and shook the wall of their living room. They were asking a lot of it tonight.

"Where are you *going?*"

"Out."

Karl Mike flung his internal medicine text from the sofa, then dropped his psychiatry text next to it. "Since when is this apartment not good enough for you? Should I clean more? Scrub more? Do you want fish sauce on your ice cream? Spare me!"

"I always spare you." Lang deliberated between his blue and his green pajamas, neither of which he ever wore. But he knew from the pictures in the magazines that American men wore them all the time. In this country, it was appropriate to wear pajamas. It meant you were covering the needs of the body in a dignified manner. He would not want Shirley to think he was not dignified, even if their bodies were together.

Karl Mike began to stalk around the living room. "I'm

losing it, Win-Win," he declared. "The big storm has started already. It will pick me up and send me away on a tidal wave."

Lang took the blue pajamas and placed them in his overnight bag along with his toilet case. He had never gone anywhere overnight, but Americans were supposed to have overnight bags. That was in the magazines too.

"Where *are* you going, Lang?"

"Out." He pushed past Karl Mike, leaning in the bedroom doorway. "To a friend's," he said, taking a small mercy on him.

"To *what* friend's?"

Lang stood in front of the hall mirror and brushed his hand over his hair. It was so black and straight. But when he pushed it back from his forehead, the skin did not climb up onto his scalp. The hair had good roots. It hung tight in his flesh.

In the mirror, Karl Mike's face appeared behind him. "Rose Red and Snow White," he said.

"What?"

"You wouldn't know. No Vietnamese princesses. Straight and honorable caucasians."

"Karl Mike, you make no sense." Lang's hand was already on the doorknob.

"Remember, American ladies have advanced ideas, Lang," Karl Mike said. "Don't be shy."

"I am *not* shy. I am . . ."—he thought for a moment— "I am considerate," he said. "I do not thump on things like you."

"Touché."

"Too-shay?"

"Sounds like a Vietnamese storekeeper, doesn't it?"

Lang looked up at Karl Mike, his bristly chin, his

freckled nose, his wide blue eyes framed with lashes like hairbrushes. "You wait a minute," he said, and put down his bag. He walked back into the living room and picked up a chair. "One more thing," he said, and set the chair down in front of the altar. "Karl Mike, just watch." Lang climbed on the chair and took a match from the packet in the corner of the altar shelf. He struck it and lit a joss stick. Then he bowed his head, waiting for Karl Mike's laughter. It did not come.

"Why you don't laugh?"

"Because it isn't funny." Karl Mike's voice was quiet, especially for him.

Lang climbed down and picked up his bag. "Good reason," he said. "When you graduate next week, maybe you smart enough to be doctor for real."

"It's raining so hard." Shirley's voice was a whisper.

"Yes."

"It's a wild night out there."

Lang propped himself up on his pillow. In the dark, the blur of Shirley's face and soft hair was the only thing he could see in the room. Then she placed her hand on his arm, and he could see that too.

"You're not afraid?"

"No, I not afraid."

"I *am* not afraid."

Lang smiled, even though she couldn't see it. "You make me forget English," he said.

"In the hospital, I never knew you had a sense of humor."

"Doctors very serious."

"That's one of their problems."

"When I first go to medical school, I think medicine very serious too."

"Well, parts of it are."

"Yes. But *doctors* not serious all the time."

"I have my doubts about Smith-Fragon."

"He people too."

"Your verbs are disappearing."

"Yes."

"Oh well. I'd better check on Jason." The white circle of her face moved across the room, then through the door. Lang turned on his side in the big bed. Why did Shirley need such a big bed just for herself? But perhaps Jason slept with her sometimes. In Vietnam, children slept with their parents all the time. Maybe Americans were not so different.

Then Shirley slid into bed next to him. "He's fine," she said. "He sleeps through anything."

"He is lucky."

"The verbs are back." Her hand touched his cheek. "He is young," she said.

Outside, the wind broke its rhythm and roared with a fierce gust. The rain pelted against the window. They were too far from the ocean to hear it, but even so, the night held the sound of waves.

"You are a fine woman."

"Lang, that's sweet."

"I do not know much about women in America."

"That's all right."

"But I learn."

"That's all right too." Her hand slid down to his shoulder and lifted the edge of his collar. He could feel her fingers gently rubbing the fabric.

"What you do?"

"Touching."

"Why you do that?" He would have touched her collar back, since he knew that it was appropriate to return gestures. But she was wearing nothing.

Her lips were on his. They were softer than clouds or water, or even the waves that ebbed and flowed between their lands. "I like your pajamas," she said.